Redemption

2017 tales from the
Writers Anthology Group
Of Moreton Bay Region
And other areas of Australia.
Illustrated by
Chelsea Lomandra

Copyright © 2017 the Authors and Bent Banana Books

Redemption

All rights reserved. No part of this book may be reproduced, stored in a retrieval system, or transmitted, in any form or by any means without the prior written permission of the publisher, nor be otherwise circulated in any form of binding or cover other than that in which it is published and without a similar condition being imposed on the subsequent purchaser.

First published in 2017 by Bent Banana Books in association with the Writers' Anthology Group.

24 Lorraine Court Lawnton, Australia, 4501. 617 3889 2118
Email bentbananabooks@gmail.com

Sponsored by Peter Campbell Realty
Phone 617 3264 2311 Email matt@petercampbellrealty.com
Web www.petercampbellrealty.com

A CiP catalogue record for this book is available from the Australian National Library. ISBN 978-0-9953947-3-5 (paperback)

Cover graphic and design by Ken Armstrong

More Contemporary Short Stories

Previous volumes in the Writers Anthology Group Arts Alliance Pine Rivers collection of short stories Published in conjunction with Bent Banana Books

Can You Believe It . . .
Sweet and Sour
Serendipity
Alpha and Omega
Inspired By . . .

Titles are available as eBooks from major on-line books stores

For a FREE sample of one of our short stories
Email bentbananabooks@gmail.com

Table of Contents

FOREWORD BY BERNIE DOWLING — P. 6

Akers Windmill Motel Raelene Purtill — P. 8
JUST A COINCIDENCE, poem, Margaret Dakin — P. 18
Pro Publico Bono Courtney Smith — P. 20
Five Words that Echo through Time Pauline Davies — P. 32
Finding Alisha Jenny Woolsey — P. 39
CITY IN THE MIST, poem, William A. Thomas — P. 54
The Deliverance Max Miller — P 55
WAR GRAVES, poem, Vera Murray — P. 61
Wartime Memories Vera Murray — P. 62
1945 THE WAR IS OVER, poem, Vera Murray — P. 68
Scarred Maddison Lanham — P. 70
Withered Seeds Jeanette O'Hagan — P. 77
Larkspur Tyleigha Collins — P. 93
A Young Elf's Atonement Kasper Beaumont — P. 100
MY GRANDMOTHERS ROOM, poem, Margaret Dakin — P. 110
Lifetime Regrets Roz Glazebrook — P. 111
THE BOARDROOM, poem, Anne Olsson — P. 118
The Potty Curse Bernie Dowling — P. 120
A LIFE GIVEN, poem, Pat Cannard — P.138
Lesson Learnt Lucy Pilgrim — P.140
First Impressions Are Deceptive David MacLaughlin — P.144

DEATH IS AN ESCAPE, poem, Bakthi Ross	P. 154
Running Margaret Taylor	P. 156
A Mouse in the House Pat Cannard	P. 167
Mothers-in-Law Margaret Dakin	P. 176
On Top of the World Jeremy Leung	P. 182
LIFE ON EARTH, poem, William A. Thomas	P. 190
My Obsession Ronald Holt	P. 191
We Stick Together Jessica Freiberg	P. 199
The Theatre of Life Anne Olsson	P. 208
DARKNESS, poem, David Bell	P. 222
Pay-Back, James Barrance	P. 224
A Loud Room Aaron Bowen	P. 232
The Wandering Jew Virginia Miranda	P. 237
COCA-COLA AD, poem, Mocco Wollert	P. 246
The Lost Wonders of the World, Giang Nguyen	P. 247
A TROPICAL REVERIE poem, David Bell	P. 255
Cleanliness is Next to Godliness Bakthi Ross	P. 256
THE HAT, poem, Mocco Wollert	P 262
The Twilight and the Dawn Nicholas Thomas	P. 263
FAMILY TOGETHERNESS, poem, Raymond W. Penshorn	P. 274
It's a Sin to Tell a Lie Raymond W. Penshorn	P. 276
Alabama 1954 Tylah Jackowski	P. 287
I Am Gunna Play Sun Sydney Bernie Dowling	P. 295
Unpinned Courtney Smith	P. 305
THE AUTHORS and ARTISTS	P. 317

FOREWORD BY BERNIE DOWLING

ON behalf of the Writers Anthology Group, based in Pine Rivers, Australia, I present our 2017 anthology, *Redemption*. This is the seventh anthology in the series begun by the Arts Alliance Pine Rivers.

We have short stories illustrated by artist Chelsea Lomandra who grew up in Samford, part of Pine Rivers district of Moreton Bay Region.

We also have poetry.

Some writers, our cover artist, Ken Armstrong, and editors have been with us from volume one; others are newbies; we thank all for their contributions. Authors range from people who earn or have earned a living from writing to those being published for the first time.

We include a lucky-thirteen stories from winners in the Peter Campbell Memorial / WAG Literary Awards for local high school students. Valued anthology sponsor Peter Campbell passed away in 2014, not long after he presented prizes at the inaugural awards.

Readers can have fun guessing from the style or topics which are the youthful entries. Biographies at the back of the book might give clues, and in some cases, the game away.

Redemption brings together a diversity of short stories and poetry. It is always fascinating to see how each writer interprets the anthology title as we editors give little guidance in that area. Within these pages you will find spices of humour, drama, fantasy, science-fiction, mystery, history, social commentary, and adventure.

It is always interesting to see different themes emerge from year to year. This year, familial or racial interchange features in many stories. On a lighter note, writers independently came up with the words 'Tis and 'Twas this year. We figured 'twas a way to see what the editors would do with the apostrophe. The bane of every editor, wrongly used ellipsis (. . .) was sent to try us again. It means words are left out. Do not use ellipsis for any other purpose.

We acknowledge the work of our editorial panel: Bernie Dowling, Anne Olsson, Ronald Holt, Raelene Purtill, David MacLaughlin, Vera Murray and Jenny Woolsey. You will notice each editor is a contributor as well. Especially welcome is Vera Murray's memento of life in Brisbane during World War II.

The WAG committee are all volunteers and we are always looking for new members, especially lovers of literature under 40 years of age. If you live in or near the Pine Rivers district and wish to be involved email bentbananabooks@gmail.com.

As I mentioned earlier our cover designer/ illustrator Ken Armstrong has created the previous six volumes as well as Redemption. Ken was founding president of the Arts Alliance and we are grateful for his continuing involvement with WAG anthologies after the alliance concluded its valuable contribution to assisting local artists, writers, and performers.

We warmly thank our sponsors, the Campbell family of Peter Campbell Realty, based at Albany Creek, and Bent Banana Books of Lawnton. Peter Campbell Realty sponsors both our anthology and our student awards. Our thanks go to Matt and the Campbell family. Bent Banana Books assists in editing, design, and layout.

Now, let the redemption begin.

– Bernie Dowling, WAG editorial committee

Akers Windmill Motel
Raelene Purtill

ELISE tucks a stray hair behind her ear. 'There's no need to speed, Sam.'

'I want to be there before dark.'

She turns her blonde head away from me. Beyond her, the paddocks skim by and the trees cast long shadows across the vanishing road. Her profile has turned amber in the light of the departing sun. When she moves a hand up and across her face, I detect tears and I turn my attention to the road against them, increasing the pressure of my right foot.

At the turn-off to our destination, a boy is playing on the sign post. He swings around and around, one arm held out. Another boy inspects the painted rock where he sits. Elise waves and the boy on the pole stops spinning. The other slides from the rock and stands to attention as we crunch up the gravel road.

A large blue arrow marked 'Office' in solid letters points us around an extensive veranda. Behind the counter is a girl with dyed hair and pierced nostrils with her name embroidered at her left breast pocket. She passes me a shabby leather tag with '6' burned into it. Attached is a single key.

'There you are Mr. Jameson. Your room is just here.' She points behind her. 'Dinner's at seven.'

Elise says, 'Thank you, Karen.'

The dining room is decorated with a variety of memorabilia. In one corner, an early Singer sewing machine hosts a vase of wild flowers. On the shelf above sit Arnott's biscuit tins, original Vegemite jars and a Bushells tea container. One wall is crafted in corrugated iron.

At our table, one of the boys is standing at Elise's elbow.

'Hello. Hello,' he repeats as he rocks back and forth to his internal soundtrack.

Karen arrives with her tray of home-cooked offerings and I breathe in deep the aroma of steak, gravy and fresh vegetables.

'Go away now. Go on,' she says to the boy. He departs reciting in a lilting echolalia, 'Go away. Go now. Go away.'

I watch him head toward the veranda where an older woman is standing with her arms out. She gathers him and ushers him away. Her breast pocket reads 'Janine.' She leads him down the veranda and out of sight.

Karen serves us. 'My brother, Mickey. Don't mind him. He always says hello to new folk.'

'We saw him at the turn off,' says Elise, placing her napkin to her knee.

'That's his favourite place to be.'

'Who was the other boy?' I ask.

Karen frowns. 'Just Mickey,' she replies, completing our plates and moving on.

The night comes in hot, without relief from the day. We are lying together watching the blur of the fan above us and listening to the distant rumble of the highway when we hear a scream followed by a thud.

Elise says, 'Don't get involved.'

But I am already pulling on a tee shirt, and soon out the door.

In a room behind the office, Karen sits on the floor crooning as she strokes Mickey's forehead. Around them is the debris from their altercation, forgotten now as his head lies across her lap.

Janine stands behind them. 'Sing to him, Karen. That's right. He likes that.'

Mickey is pulling at his ears and emitting a low groan. Karen moves to hold his hands in her own, away from his head, without interrupting her song. When the tension leaves his body and he is breathing evenly, she slides from beneath him and sees me.

'Oh, Mr. Jameson, I am sorry to disturb you. He'll sleep now.'

'You are very good with him.'

'Thank you.' She smiles and ducks her head. 'It's nothing I can't handle. Really Mr. Jameson, you should go back to your room.'

I retreat but the night invites me to linger outside and it is then I see the other boy peering in the office window.

'Hey.' I call to him but he dashes away into the darkness of the paddock. When I enter our room, Elise is lying awake, watching me with a disapproving frown.

'Come to bed, Sam. It's late.'

She turns over and is asleep instantly. I envy her. I stand at the window looking into the motel carpark for a long while before sleep sends me to bed.

During breakfast we are trying to ignore the raised voices coming from the kitchen. I cannot bear it and rise to investigate, Elise's protests following me to the source of the disturbance.

'Karen?'

'Mickey didn't want his Weetbix this morning,' she informs me. The rejected cereal is splattered up the wall and trails across the floor to an overturned bowl, confirming her statement.

The boy stands shaking his head. 'Bad boy. Bad boy,' he repeats.

From the sink, Karen takes a wet rag and leads Mickey to the wall. 'You must clean it up.'

She guides his hand until the motion is transferred, then she uprights the chair to the table. Janine stands beside him and watches with a compassionate smile on her face.

'That's right, Mickey. You are a good boy.'

'I am a good boy,' he repeats.

Karen turns with a frown. 'Just clean it up, Mickey.'

'We saw two boys at the junction. Who's the other?' I ask, watching Mickey, his face close to the wall where he is cleaning a particular spot. He ignores the rest of the soggy mess up the wall. Janine remains supervising.

'No other kids around here for miles.' Karen shrugs in such an offhanded way that I am rejected and turn to leave. From the corner of my eye, I see movement across the window. A chill travels through me.

Our sightseeing is welcome. For a brief, sunny afternoon, that which is unspoken between us is displaced and retreats, allowing us to glimpse hope. We return to the motel with the radio thumping and us singing along with it. Even the threat from the horizon does not alarm us. Those dark clouds bring the promise of a cooler evening. I am looking heavenward, indulging in the towering formations, when Elise screams. 'Look out!'

Mickey is standing in the middle of the road, the other boy calling him from the edge. I swerve, sideswiping the sign and spinning in the gravel before bringing the car under control. Elise is out and running to the junction.

'Where did he go?' She turns to me arms wide. 'I can't see him.'

She brings her arms in close then, hugging herself. 'Oh no.'

She collapses into my arms.

The first large drops of rain begin to darken the grey gravel as we cling together in our grief. The rhythm of her sobs ends and she takes in a sharp breath sucking the tears back inside her. I pull away. The other boy is standing close beside us and the hairs on my neck rise.

Mickey paces up and down the road. His arms are flailing in small circles and his fingers jitter. Elise watches his rain dance for a moment then goes to him.

'Mickey, you must not stand in the road like this. You could be really hurt.'

She places her hands on his shoulders looking into his face. His rocking ceases and he yowls, pushes Elise to the ground, and bolts up the driveway. As I gather Elise back into the car, there he is again. The other boy is watching us from the front of the car. The rain trickles down my back, cold fingers reaching for my bones.

Later, Elise and I sit dry and comfortable in our room. Our time together has connected us and our moment at the turn-off has sealed us. We are united against the elements of grief threatening to destroy us.

'Where do you suppose Mr. Akers is?' I ask.

'Men don't stay around when there's kids like Mickey. I suspect he's long gone.'

The boy's screaming can be heard now above the steady rain. There is a crash that is not of the storm, followed by the sound of breaking glass. I am at the residence in the seconds between lightning and thunder.

'Mickey, you must stay in your room.' Karen is standing at the doorway and before she closes the door I can see Mickey sitting on the floor. 'And stop that rocking,' she says as she shuts the door on the turmoil.

Janine slips out as the door is closed. 'He is safe. Get yourself cleaned up.'

Karen is holding her bleeding hand as she follows Janine to the nearby bathroom.

And then he is standing in the hall. I move toward him, my palm extended. 'I'm Sam Jameson.'

'My name's William,' he replies, but he makes no move toward our greeting, just stands, eyes cold.

'Did you come from in here?' I ask, but the room is locked. My hand is cold and I cling to the door for support as my knees release from under me. Then Karen is there. 'No. Mr. Jameson. You mustn't.'

She takes my hand from the door, her warmth melting the icicles possessing my fingers.

The boy too has drifted away.

The new day arrives fresh and clean following the storm. I am infused with new beginnings and keen to be on the road. I stow our luggage, stepping back and forth through the puddles dotting the carpark. On the surface of each is a liquid rainbow. It is a sign: the river of our sadness runs together with the oil of healing to form this spectrum for us.

Voices from behind the house are calling and yelling. I follow them to see Mickey climbing the windmill.

William is above, bidding him up. 'Come on Mickey. Come see the view from up here.'

Karen is calling him down, Janine beside her. 'Karen, get him down. How did he get this far?'

Mickey's laughter is high above us as I join Elise.

'Oh Sam. Help him.'

Karen echoes Elise's pleading and I am compelled. I climb the wooden frame. Mickey has almost reached the platform where William is perched beneath the sails, still calling him. I am engaged by open paddocks dotted with cattle and sheep. A distant line of green trees marks the path of the river and I can see the highway coming to life. Another time I would have appreciated the view, but now I am concerned for Mickey's safety. There is a memory of another time, another child whose safety I could not secure. I remember the football field in the suburbs, a runaway ball and a speeding car, and Joshua.

Today I have the power to rescue. I climb further with new determination.

'Stop, Mickey.'

He is laughing now and William is pointing. 'From up here you can almost see the city. Look, Mickey.'

'What are you doing?' I call.

'We're climbing the windmill tower.'

'And you think Mickey will understand the experience? It's so dangerous for him.'

The boy's eyes darkened. 'He's done it before. You remember the last time we were up here, don't you, Mickey?'

Mickey sits on the small platform, still and quiet, as if this spot is where he understands the world and he is in his right mind. I cling to my own position below them. 'It is time to come down now. Come back to Karen and your Mum.'

Now it is William who disturbs me with his unhealthy laugh. The shiver running through me threatens to remove me from the tower.

'Mickey, follow me back down, okay?' I say.

Mickey looks down. 'Karen'. He waves in his uncoordinated way and then he slips. I catch him and when I hold him it is our son I am holding and I have saved him. The red Ford does not collide with him. 'It's okay. It's okay.'

I glance up to see if William is following but he remains in his unmoving petulance.

On the ground, Karen confronts Mickey. 'Why did you do that?'

I look at her. 'William. He died.'

'That's right, yes.'

Elise gasps beside me. When I squeeze her hand, I am passing on the closure I experienced. 'I saved him. It was Josh I was saving.'

We hug.

Karen ushers Mickey inside the house.

'I should be there,' says Janine, watching them leave.

'William?' I go to the boy who has descended and is standing before Janine looking up at her.

'She still doesn't see me. She never looks at me.'

'Janine, why do you not acknowledge William?' I ask.

'William fell from this windmill two years ago. He's dead, Mr. Jameson. My son is dead.'

'Why can't you see me? Why don't you look at me?' William is searching her face for answers.

Then he says, 'Come on,' and we follow him across the paddock.

Under the wide branches of a large tree there are graves. One marker bears William's name.

'See.' William points to the second grave and I am paralysed: 'Janine Akers'.

Janine stands with her back to the stones watching the house. 'How will they survive without me? I am the only one who can manage Mickey.'

'You don't have to anymore, Janine. William needs you now.' Elise's empathy and compassion break through Janine's denial.

'William? Where is he?'

'I'm right here, Mum. I've been here all the time. Do you see me now?'

Behind us, the dead look after the dead as we remove ourselves from their reunion.

Elise takes the car keys. 'I'm driving.'

The sun is high and hot and the highway ahead of us is clear.

JUST A COINCIDENCE
Margaret Dakin

Was it just a coincidence that when I met you
The world expanded around me?
You brushed a crumb from the corner of my mouth
And picked a flower – a zinnia for friendship.
As I pressed it into my book of sonnets,
For the first time I understood the words.

Was it a coincidence that looking on our sleeping babe,
The world was contained in that room?
Three years, you said, and gave me fine leather gloves
And a red rose – for love.
It looked so rich beside the petals in my book,
As if it would live forever.

A coincidence maybe that you gave me a pottery urn,
As after nine years we looked again at a baby girl.
She was taken from us and we put ashes in the urn.
We cut marigolds for grief.
I pushed my book to the back of the shelf,
And we held each other under the weeping willow.

Twelve years went by and you gave me a linen cloth.
Next year the lace that should have been mine
Coincidently you gave to someone else.
A deep red carnation in my book
Alas for my poor heart.
For slighted love I filled a vase with yellow
chrysanthemums.

Redemption

The aspen tree in my garden laments my lonely years.
In vain I hoped for ruby, sapphire, golden gifts,
But more precious still were co-incidents of festivity and children's laughter.
I snip the fading pansies, and relinquish bitter thoughts of you.
As life's puzzle is accepted,
Let the scarlet geraniums be my comfort.

Is it a coincidence that the day comes?
Sixty years you would have remembered with a diamond,
Instead I stand amidst the falling yew leaves
And place an olive branch on your grave.
Peace I hope for both of us,
As I brush the faded memories from my book

Pro Publico Bono
Courtney Smith

IRENE Andra cannot be around syringes.

She addressed this with her therapist last week, shaky hands running through a blunt bob. Dr Newman informed her that given her circumstances this was completely normal, if not an accepted part of recovery. *Why yes,* Irene thought bitterly, *living in constant fear and paranoia really is the status quo in this society, isn't it?* Dr Newman knew that in Irene's line of work she would only need the gleaming, steel point in dire circumstances, which she would not encounter often in the narcotics department. Irene knew this too, and yet she continued her mantra, 'I can't, I can't, I can't.'

She was told that if she thought more positively about the idea, then maybe it wouldn't seem so terrible. *What a load of bull. Positivity?* Alright. She could talk about positivity. What about the positive terror that arises in her stomach? The addiction she had faced, how it had positively ruined her? *Oh!* What about the withdrawal, the positive hell she went through to become clean again? That just *has* to be the least terrible part of the whole ordeal, *right*? Pure positivity, *aren't I the cynic?* Oh, the more Irene thought of this, the more she thought about the point of a needle. What Irene was terrified of had nothing to do with a fear of syringes.

Irene was terrified because she was *aroused* by the thought of the needle sinking through skin and into her veins, the rushing of pestilential chemical concoction under her skin. She was aroused by the prickling sensation in her arm, the numbness that comes for hours after. She was irrevocably seduced by the droplet of blood that is wiped away after the needle is pulled from freckled skin. The second her eyes landed on the gleaming point she could never take them off it, positively fixated by the memories of the rush.

Call it the effect of severe heroin addiction. Irene briefly wonders if she should get a raise for this.

The undercover operation had been a success (if you used the loosest definition of the word). She had completed the mission she was given, no questions asked with countless arrests filed. It had resulted in the arrests of junkies, dealers, and producers alike, with sentences pending for months. Overall, the praise the operation received from the public and media made Irene sound like one of the biggest heroes the city could produce. Rehabilitation facilities were receiving those who were addicted to the poisonous substance and helping them through withdrawal and relapse periods.

Irene was one of those people.

She tapped her foot incessantly, fingernails finding their way between her teeth without even realising it. She knew she was being watched closely, she knew their judgemental eyes were condemning her as she sat. It had been too long since she had a hit. Irene knew it, it'd been too long, too long. She was getting nervous, sweating in her position despite the weather being barely at a comfortable temperature. It wasn't supposed to be this hot in this room, she doesn't remember it ever being this hot. Was it just her? She snapped three nails clean off.

The two inspectors in front of her were holding a guillotine above her head. They questioned her without any hesitation, and Irene answered with the knowledge that any wrong move would end in certain damnation.

She had done all the right legal procedures; she didn't lose her cover and identity.

Irene's hands were shaking like leaves in the autumn breeze, although she could not feel any sensation in them. Her hollow eyes followed the shuffling of paper on the table in front of them, the sound like nails on a chalkboard in her head. Words seemed too loud, even the quietest whisper like screaming in her ear. She could feel bubbling in her stomach, something close to nausea as the one she had mentally labelled 'Big Nose' tapped a pen against the metal table, bolted to the floor. This room was used for questioning, and here she was, being drilled like a common criminal. She wasn't. She wasn't. She was a good person. The other, 'Owl Dude', was speaking but Irene couldn't quite make out the words he was saying, even though it seemed like the words were being screamed in her ears.

'I'm sorry, could you repeat that?' Her words slurred together like she was sleepy, and Owl Dude raised a bushy eyebrow. His expression caused a tsunami in Irene's stomach, and she knew she was barely keeping her composure.

'Officer Andra, over the entirety of the undercover period, was there a moment where you smoked, snorted, or injected heroin? Or any other drug?'

The second Irene opened her mouth to respond she knew it was the end. She went to utter a positive response, the final nail in the coffin, but the bile rose up in her throat and—.

Irene was whisked off as if she was a junkie with a penchant for violence. As if she was one of the people she was supposed to protect society from. Talk about a drastic change in perspective.

She was given a dosage of methadone and a room that was more like a cell. There was a bed in the corner, with a metal frame and mattress that did not have anything more than a thin sheet on top. For a place supposed to aid in recovery, the lack of comfort astounded Irene in her half-lucid state. There was a porcelain bathroom set in the other corner, lacking a shower. The walls had old patterned wallpaper that reminded Irene faintly of stale cheese.

Three hours later the cold metal floor was decorated with the contents of her stomach.

It wasn't the same. They told her the methadone was the same as the heroin. They told her it had the same rush. They told her it would make her better, make her want to stop. They forced food down her throat after the pill and she had to be physically restrained in order to eat it. They had told her that eating would make everything better, make the pill better.

It wasn't the same.

They lied. They lied. They lied.

It was nothing like the euphoria she had once experienced. There was no rush. There was no blood, no bliss from the world. No numbing. She was sweating profusely, shaking even though her eyes could barely force themselves open. She kept vomiting over and over, there was nothing left in her stomach to keep down.

They lied. They lied. They lied.

It was hell. It was hell, and they lied and said it would be heaven. Irene pulled her knees up to her chest, and sobbed into them, begging pathetically for it all to stop.

In the past, Irene believed addicts to be troubled and dangerous. These people who got addicted, they had their own little devils whispering in their ears. They all had their own reasons for injecting, for snorting, smoking, and swallowing. Irene never would have grouped herself with these people in the past. She did not have a particularly troubled childhood, she did not go through emotional turmoil due to a horrendous abusive relationship, nor did she experience loss in her life. She didn't have any of this emotional, tragic backstory bullshit, and yet . . .

It didn't stop for days and days. She barely slept, couldn't eat because she knew that it would taste just as bad on the way up as it did on the way down. The vomiting kept going and going and Irene wasn't even sure that she had any stomach lining left after all she had expelled. She was clammy constantly, a thin layer of sweat coating her skin. Her room was a prison cell, and she now understood why people who were innocent were so paranoid of police officers entering. Every creak of her door was a year shaved off her life, and yet all she could think about was getting her next hit.

People don't always start because they have no other option. Sometimes, just sometimes, it's that tiny spark of curiosity. The spark that drives all rationality away. This tiny spark fills your veins and rushes to your brain, numbing all other senses. It consumes and replaces all other thoughts, and, once you finally give in, the satisfaction is like none other. The curiosity is replaced by the heroin streaming through your veins for those few hours before you need your next hit. There was a thrill in doing it, one that Irene would never be able to find the words to describe. Not that she was good with words to begin with.

The doctors in the facility were kind enough. They sort of understood. Not really.

Irene knew that they were thinking she was damaged, if not just plain stupid for taking the drug in the first place. She was a police officer, she worked in the department actively attempting to stop the practice. She knew all the repercussions of her actions yet she knowingly injected that first dosage and had gotten hooked. She had the full understanding of the consequences but she didn't listen. She didn't listen. She didn't listen.

They were trying to help her, though, and that's all Irene could ask for.

She banged at the door of her room at night and begged and begged and begged for even the tiniest of hits, that it would make her better, that it would make her better. Just one drop in her system would make everything better. It wouldn't hurt anymore. She wasn't addicted. She wasn't. She wasn't. She wasn't.

Dr Newman had tried to convince Irene that what happened to her was so like what happened to most young people who got addicted to the drug. It only takes a sliver of curiosity and one hit to become addicted. What she was feeling, the guilt and the self-hatred were what so many past users had felt. It was a completely natural response, and one that meant she had realised what she had done was wrong. It was a step towards healing, a step in the right direction. A step towards a life free of illicit drugs, free of the burden of addiction. It was a step towards leading a normal life.

It was a step towards redemption.

Irene wasn't sure she deserved it. After all, people who get redeemed weren't supposed to have a 90 per cent relapse rate. They weren't supposed to replace one addiction with another, going from heroin to methadone to cigarettes within the space of a month. People who received redemption deserved it because they worked incredibly hard for it, they persevered through all the horrific things the world could throw at them. But Irene?

Good people didn't take the drug in the first place, no matter how tempted they were.

Irene wasn't a good person.

It got better, of course it did. They told her it always does.

She knew she didn't need the junk after nine days. She knew she didn't need it, and she knew the methadone she swallowed every day was helping her. It wasn't the same, but it helped. Irene no longer threw up all food they gave her and she happily accepted carbohydrates in her system as soon as they were offered. She felt nauseous, but she knew the full feeling in her stomach was well worth it.

She wanted to get off the methadone, she didn't want to be dependent on it. She couldn't afford to get dependent on it because she knew the statistics, knew how easy it was to get hooked. This helping pill was far more addictive than any injection she could think of.

The second she was released, she bought her first pack of smokes.

The constant reminder of her past in her own workplace didn't help. First day back on the job, not even in the building, she heard other officers gossiping about her in the distance. She excused herself and pulled her bag open, revealing a rectangular carton. She popped it open and shuffled one stick out of it, and the red lighter wedged inside. The cigarette had become a comforter between her fingers. Slowly, she placed it between her teeth and she lit it. Irene inhaled the smoke and tapped her foot impatiently. She took a few more drags before stubbing the cigarette out against the wall and tossing it into the public ashtray. She inhaled a few breaths of second-hand smoke, and walked inside with her head forward.

She power-walked through the station, nodding politely to her superiors as she went past. Her desk was in the same place as always, and the closer she got to it the more she could feel her stomach becoming an ocean once again. She had finished all of the procedures for the undercover operation, and she knew she was almost entirely in the clear, but there were still whispers.

Don't mind them, she told herself, *they're just gossips who will have it bite them in the ass.*

In a cutthroat environment like this, the only one to get bitten will be her.

Irene did the best she could to ignore the stares she received on the way in, remaining composed as she did. She greeted those in the office and they all gave her odd stares, before wishing her well. Irene returned their stares, being completely unaware of what they had meant.

Then she saw the note on her desk.

You have been transferred to Homicide. All the official documentation is here, but this is the short form. I wish you all the best, and I will be checking up on you.

Sergeant G. Hanson.

'Oh,' she muttered stupidly, not entirely sure how to react to the news. She flipped through the wad of paper on her desk and sure enough all the transfer documents were there and signed in the right places. Irene let out a wheezy breath that was no doubt because of her smoking, and nodded to herself. She opened her bag and slipped the documents inside, looking up at the other officers in the room. 'Well, it was nice working with you all.'

The departure atmosphere was most awkward, and Irene fumbled with her possessions. She had nowhere to put any of them, and had no plan as to what to do. She knew she couldn't waltz up to Homicide empty-handed. Irene stuffed as much in her bag as she could, hoping that at least one person in Homicide would have a free box available. The bag was stuffed to the brim, and Irene fumbled with the clip. She clasped her bag shut finally, mind spinning with anxiety. Her reputation would proceed her, it would make things terrible and her chances of getting along with the other officers and her superiors were slim. She stood in place aimlessly for a few moments, her thoughts consuming her without her realising it. The slamming of a box on her desk shattered her train of thought.

Irene jumped and her head snapped towards the sound. She followed the arms that held the box to meet a smile as bright as the sun. It was almost blinding, and Irene found herself squinting at the sight. She offered a forced smile in return.

'I don't think you can fit all that in your bag,' he commented, and Irene found herself scowling deeply. The voice was too cheery for this early in the morning.

Her attitude didn't deter the man in the slightest, not faltering under the withering gaze she gave him.

'I do have eyes of my own,' she replied, voice tight. *Who the hell was this guy, anyway?*

'I'm Inspector Marco Fox, and I'm going to be your new partner. It's nice to meet you, Andra.'

Five Words that Echo through Time

Pauline Davies

THIS is a true story, whatever that means. Real truth is elusive, if it exists at all, but this is my truth, recounted as clearly as I can remember it; as a series of colourful snapshots that have played out in my mind in the same way for the last forty or so years. You know what early memories are like – they're fragmented, random, and mostly insignificant. We never know why some remain after most have faded. I remember falling through a glass door in England when I was three and the frantic rush to the hospital in a neighbour's car, and I remember a packet of crayons that melted in the Australian sun when I was six. But these are just moments, barely perceptible glimpses of a time lost forever. The memory I'm about to describe is as clear to me today as it ever was. The brief scene that took place on a warm afternoon when I was about eight-years-old always comes back to me in the same familiar way, and yet I'm no closer to solving its mystery.

I know how old I was because from 1972 to 1974 my family lived in an old green weatherboard house on the edge of a small town in rural Queensland. Murgon was home to a few thousand people and depended on meat, dairy and peanut farming for its survival. We had followed relatives there from a northern English industrial city whose noisy, narrow streets and bitterly cold winters were a stark contrast to the wide open spaces, dry heat and sudden storms of our new home.

The relocation from one side of the world to the other is a major disturbance in a child's life. Everything familiar is destabilised and has to be learned again: new faces, places, accents, routines. That wrench serves to divide childhood memories into either before or after, and the strangeness of the new environment crystallizes experiences into vivid memories. I remember the ancient wood stove that my mother fed every day, and its long chamber with the tap on the front that we used to heat water for baths and dirty dishes. Perhaps the contrast with the instant heat of our gas stove and hot water taps in England caused those memories to remain? I remember my father learning to drive so he could go to his new job at the abattoir; in England he had ridden a bicycle to work and we travelled everywhere by bus.

There was no public transport in Murgon; instead everyone drove cars – to me they seemed like strange, cavernous creatures with hard vinyl seats that scorched bare legs in summer.

We were a long way from everywhere. I remember a recurring dream: running wildly down a familiar street lined with semi-detached houses and stopping, breathless, outside number seventy-three. I remember the overwhelming rush of exhilaration as I realised I had found my way home, and the agonising disappointment on waking.

I already told you that my memory of the mysterious incident is clear, but what is perplexing is that I can't remember what I was doing before or after it. That's the beguiling thing about memory – it is selective. The event took only a minute or two in real time, and yet it plays over and over in my mind like a short film on a loop; the images colourful and the sound audible. I remember a tree in our garden with smooth silver branches and bright pink blossoms that fell on parched brown grass. Nearby was a curved corrugated iron tank that supplied water to the house. The tank stood on an ancient timber stand that was tall enough for me to step under without bending. I remember playing with my cousin in the garden between the pink blossom tree, the house and the water tank. An unruly 7-year old with sandy hair and freckles, Peter's arrival in Australia a year before us entitled him to an air of defiant cockiness.

This is the strange part.

I remember a voice. I heard it as we were playing. The memory commences with the sound of that voice. The images of the garden and Peter's presence only appear in my mind with the arrival of the voice. It sounded like my own voice, but didn't feel like me because I wasn't controlling it. It came from inside my head. It was loud and clear.

Authoritative. Uninvited. Intrusive.

'Get under the tank stand.'

Perplexed, but not alarmed, I heard my own internal voice ask why.

'Get under the tank stand,' the voice responded.

It didn't make sense. There was no reason to. My cousin would think I was strange. I proceeded to have an internal argument, resisting the necessity to move.

'Get under the tank stand!' the voice insisted, even louder than before.

Urgent. Hard to ignore.

Feeling foolish, I pointed to Boat Mountain; perched on the horizon, flat-topped and blue in the distance, nothing but paddocks and scrub between us and it.

'Hey! Look at those clouds over Boat Mountain. There's going to be a storm soon.'

There was barely a speckle of rain in our yard, and there was more blue sky than cloud above us.

'Let's get under the tank stand before it rains,' I said with forced enthusiasm.

I knew it was lame, but to my surprise, Peter obeyed and took one step backwards with me, to the shelter of the tank stand. My eyes were still facing forwards, focused on the space I had just occupied. In that instant I caught sight of a thin, vertical, white line, barely an arm's length away, at my chest height.

In the exact spot where I had been standing.

Silent. Harmless.

'Hey! Did you see that?' I shouted in surprise.

'See what?' He was still looking at the mountain.

'Lightning!'

It was gone in a moment, but had been about the length of a school ruler and hadn't touched the ground. Hadn't connected with anything. I laughed out loud in surprise, but felt sorry my cousin had missed it.

In the months that followed, I remembered the events of that afternoon, simply because of the novelty of seeing lightning up close. It was a minor oddity, an unimportant incident that would have slipped into the abyss of forgetfulness had I not learned soon after that lightning is dangerous.

Deadly.

I remember the feeling of shock as I absorbed the revelation. I replayed the garden incident in my mind, trying to reconcile the memory of a small and silent lightning bolt that had seemed so harmless with the notion that it had been dangerous. As the scene played over and over, so did the sound of the voice and the words that had saved me from either death or significant injury.

I had almost ignored that voice!

That's what was most shocking to me. What if I had defied that instruction? What would my life have been like? Would it have been snuffed out in that instant? I could not explain that intrusion in my mind, but I never doubted that it had happened exactly as I remembered. The significance of the near miss, and the repetition of revisiting the scene, ensured that the incident became lodged in my long-term memory.

I am reluctant to embrace the idea of the supernatural. Even as a child I found it hard to believe that a busy god would have bothered to save me from danger. What was it then; that voice?

Angel? Ancestor? Intuition?

Exploring any of these options opens so many areas of uncertainty and conjecture that it seems pointless to bother. Instead, I accept that I will never know and feel grateful that I listened to that inner voice.

I don't expect you to believe me.

I have shared my story with a number of people over the years, but it always seems to lose something in the telling. Perhaps the listeners have been too polite to be openly sceptical? I have the advantage of personal experience, but you must decide if my memory is accurate, or if time has caused me to become whimsically creative.

We all have occasional brushes with death. They remind us to appreciate how precious life is and to value our time here. Without the memory of the experience in the garden I think I would be a person who dismisses everything in life that cannot be seen, touched or proven. I feel extraordinarily fortunate, and not just because I narrowly missed being struck by lightning. Living with the memory of an unexplained phenomenon has allowed a window in my mind to stay open.

Just a tiny crack.

But enough for me to be occasionally receptive to the unknown possibilities of the Universe.

Finding Alisha
Jenny Woolsey

'NO! Dad come back!' Alisha cried, as she bent over the motionless body that lay on the velvet quilt in her parents' bedroom. Her long blonde hair soaked up the tears that drenched the pale face. 'Why Dad, why?' she moaned as sobs wracked her.

The day of the funeral Alisha felt completely numb. There had been no emotion. She'd gone through the process, been kissed by distant relatives she didn't know, listened to 'I'm so sorry's', even tipped a handful of dirt onto the oak coffin with its wreath of white lilies and baby breath. The coffin her mother had mulled over and taken hours to choose. 'Would your father like the oak or the pine?' she'd asked Alisha. 'And what handles? The silver or the gold?'

Alisha didn't care. Her dad was dead. Everything else meant nothing.

In the first term of Year 12, Alisha's report had shown all As.

'Keep this up and you could be dux,' Mr Allan, the deputy principal, told her.

'I'm so proud of you darling,' her father said upon hearing the news. 'You could be the first doctor in the family!'

But that fateful night, just before she blew out the seventeen candles and sliced through her chocolate birthday cake, what she knew as happiness was destroyed. Her father had staggered around the lounge room and collapsed on the floor. Alisha dialled 000 and her mother attempted CPR.

Distress crushed any joy in the household. The paramedics did all they could but pronounced her father deceased, and laid him on the bed for the funeral directors to come and retrieve him.

Part of Alisha perished with her father.

'I don't care that I'm getting Ds,' she told Mr Allan after he enquired about the deterioration in her marks.

'School is here to help you,' he said. 'You can have special provisions.'

But Alisha gave up on her career dreams, she slept a lot, arrived late to school or wagged it. The dark cave of her room was her sanctuary.

'I just want Dad back,' she told Billie, her closest friend.

'But you can't throw your life away,' Billie replied.

'Why not?'

'Your Dad wouldn't want you to. He wanted you to be a doctor.'

'I want to be dead like him.'

Alisha saw Billie starting to hang out with other girls. Her negativity wasn't understood.

'Great, I've lost my best friend too. She didn't want to stay with a loser. What's the point?'

Alisha stopped going to school altogether.

'You're throwing your life away. Your father wouldn't want that,' her mother said.

'I don't care.'

'Maybe it's time you went and saw someone,' her mother suggested.

'What? A shrink?'

Her mother nodded.

'No way! Everyone thinks I'm crazy. That'll just prove it.'

'We need to do something to help you.'

Alisha grudgingly attended the appointment.

'It'll just take time,' the psychiatrist said. 'You have PTSD. The medication will help.'

'Great, I am crazy,' she said with sarcasm.

Alisha's flashbacks lessened but her enthusiasm for life did not increase.

'Come on, let's go out and do something. You'll feel better,' her mother said, opening up her curtains.

Alisha blinked as the sunlight hurt her eyes.

'No! I don't want to go anywhere!' Alisha snapped, yanking the curtains back together.

Her mother hauled the curtains back open again. She grabbed Alisha's arm and tried to pull her up off the messed-up bed.

'Leave me alone Mum! I'm not getting up. I'm not leaving my room!'

Tears fell down her cheeks.

'If you're going to stay in here, at least have the light on,' her mother said quietly, flicking on the switch.

'Fine,' Alisha muttered.

The day the autopsy report came back, Alisha's mother sat her down at the kitchen table and taking a deep breath told her, 'It says he died from a drug overdose.'

'What? Why on my birthday? Why did he do that on my BIRTHDAY?' Alisha yelled at her. 'Did he hate me?'

'No, he loved you. He was depressed. I wanted him to get help. I'm sure he didn't mean to. Maybe it was an accident,' her mother told her, wringing her hands together. 'You were his princess, Alisha. He loved you from the moment we knew we were having you.'

Day after day passed by. Alisha stayed in her self-induced imprisonment, absorbed in online fantasy worlds.

'Alisha get off your phone! You need to hang the washing out. I've asked you five times!' her mother snapped.

'Go do it yourself!'

'Get up and do your job! This can't go on. I'm sick and tired of this!'

The wicker washing basket flew across the room and hit Alisha in her face. Blood trickled down her cheek.

'Sorry,' her mother squealed.

Alisha jumped up off her bed. 'Leave me alone! I don't want to live here anymore!'

She stormed out to the dining room and picked up the porcelain vase from the dining room table. She knew it was special. Her father had given it to her mother for their last wedding anniversary; their twentieth. She threw it to the floor and watched it smash on the tiles.

'I bet you poisoned Dad.' Alisha landed her final, twisted blow. 'You said he was a waste of space because he sat on the couch all the time. You killed him and I will never forgive you!'

'What are you talking about? That's insane! Go to your room until you calm down.'

Alisha rushed to her bedroom, grabbed her wallet, some clothes and toiletries and stuffed them into her school backpack. She surveyed the hallway for her mother. The toilet door was shut. Alisha left the house, ran to the train station and jumped on the first train. It was going south to Fortitude Valley. Alisha stuck in her earbuds and gazed out the etched glass window as the trees and houses whizzed on by.

At the end of the train station mall she'd turned left. The buildings loomed over her, sneering at her with their shadows. Buskers with guitars who collected coins in hats, glanced her way. There was no purpose to her wandering. She had no idea where she was going, not that it mattered. Inside she was angry. Angry at her mother. Angry at her father. Angry at the universe.

She had heard stories about the Valley. There had to be someone on the streets she could hang with for a while until her head cleared and she worked out what to do.

'Hey girlie, you new round here?' a scrawny guy with a wild sea of red hair asked her, as she strolled past him. He was casually leant up against an urban clothing store. 'Yeah, do you know where I can stay?' Alisha asked him.

'You a runner?' he asked her, a wry lift to his lips. Alisha nodded.

'All the hostels are full. You can stay over there.' He pointed his dirt-stained finger behind her, 'At the back of the park is a drain. That's where me and a few others hang out. But keep out of the way of the coppers or they'll take ya home.'

Alisha nodded. 'Um, do you have any money? I'm really hungry.'

'Sure but what are ya gonna give out to get it?'

Alisha stared into the eyes that had instantly lost their sparkle.

'I do-don't-don't give out,' she said, turning to walk back the way she had come.

'Ha-ha-ha. Just testing ya. You have to be careful here on these streets. There's lots of guys who'll want to take advantage of ya. You being a pretty girlie. Here,' he said reaching into his pocket, pulling out three two-dollar coins. 'It isn't much but it'll get ya something from the 7-Eleven. The Salvos bring a food van around later. Ticko by the way,' he said sticking out his hand.

'Ticko?' Alisha said, raising her eyebrow, ignoring his invitation.

He gave a lopsided smile and flopped his hand back to his side. 'You?'

'Alisha.'

A week turned into a month. Her anger mixed and gurgled with her depression, and spewed like an exploding volcano inside of her, consuming her brain and body. She didn't have her medication.

Nightmares of her father's lifeless body and his depressive moods before he passed haunted her.

Ticko became her best friend. 'I'll look after ya. I get how you're feeling. My oldie died too,' he said, giving her a ring he'd found.

A month turned into six months.

'I'm cutting my hair short,' she told Ticko. 'Time for a new look.'

'Lookin' good babe,' he had complimented her. 'You'll need tatts to cover those cuts on your arms.'

Twelve months passed. Alisha stared at her gaunt face in the mirror at the public toilets. The girl who stared back, did not resemble her. A vision of her father's face filled the mirror and she punched it.

'Damn you, Dad.'

The glass cracked and slithers cut her fist. Blood dripped into the basin.

Outside the take-away kiosk and on the pavements she searched for dropped coins.

'Hi darling I'll give ya some money if you sleep with me,' a guy said, interrupting her.

'Get lost,' she told him. 'I'm not a whore.'

Alisha sat in the gutter outside a donut shop. Her hair matted and her clothes worn. The sweet smells stirred her hunger. She counted her coins. She didn't have enough. She wondered if she should become a whore.

'Hey there,' a pleasant masculine voice said, interrupting her thoughts. 'Do you need some money?'

'Yeah. A couple dollars if you have it.'

'I'm Kai. I've got a van over there where you can have a shower or wash your clothes, if you want.'

Alisha looked to where he pointed. There were some other street kids there already. 'Thanks.'

'Um, did you go to Beerburrum High?' Kai asked her.

'Yeah, why?'

'Are you Alisha?'

'Yeah, why?'

'I was in your Biology class.'

'Hey. I don't remember you.'

'Are you staying around here?'

'Yeah.'

'Where?'

'Over in that drain,' she pointed.

'Okay. Well I'm here every Thursday if you need any help. I'll see you next week,' Kai said. He took his mobile out of his pocket and rang someone.

Alisha wandered over to the others at the van, took a shower and ate. It felt good to be clean and full. She'd lost a lot of weight. Then she meandered back to the drain to tell Ticko about the van.

'Ticko, where are you?'

Alisha walked around the concrete tunnel.

'Ticko!'

Alisha rushed over to the wall where a man was slumped over his backpack. She pushed him backwards and felt for a pulse. Alisha's howl like a tortured wolf filled the air.

'No, Ticko, no!' she shrieked. 'Not you too!'

Alisha took off. Tears streamed down her face, and soaked her embroidered t-shirt. Her sandal snapped and she flung it off her foot. She fled from the smell of more death.

The Story Bridge rose up before her. Alisha stared up at the curved metal giant. She thought if she climbed it, she could fling herself off and all this pain would be over. She could join Ticko and her father.

Alisha took some steps towards the narrow opening between the beginning of the bridge and the road. She slipped sidewards through it. The brown shimmering water swam before her eyes.

'On the count of three,' she whispered to herself.

'Alisha? Alisha?' A voice spoke to her.

She stared blankly at the lady.

'Alisha. Are you Alisha Evans?'

The woman whispered, 'Alisha, it's me, Renee. I was your neighbour in Beerburrum. I'm sure it's you.'

Alisha stared into the green eyes of the woman. They looked kind though tinged with sadness.

'Renee?'

'Yes, it's me.'

Tears welled in Alisha's eyes and tumbled down her cheeks. She collapsed into the woman's arms and sobbed.

A blaring siren was the last sound Alisha heard before she slipped into unconsciousness.

Alisha blinked her eyes and stared around her. The walls were cream and pale green. There was a side table and an oil painting of a bouquet of flowers on the wall opposite her. The sheets felt hard and rough. It had been a long time since she had been in a bed.

'Where am I?' she asked into the silence.

She brought her hand up to flick a strand of hair out of her eye. There was a hospital name tag on her wrist. Alisha stared at it.

She pulled herself up to sitting then swung her legs over the side of the bed and tried to stand, but wobbled with dizziness. She grabbed the table.

'You're awake,' a woman in a navy uniform said to her crisply. 'No getting up yet. Hop back into bed.'

Alisha slowly laid back down and stared at the ceiling.

'Where am . . .'

But the nurse had disappeared. Alisha slipped in and out of consciousness. Strange and psychedelic dreams whirled and swirled around her manic subconsciousness. Ticko and her father yelled and drowned, and rose as angels.

'Alisha. Alisha honey.'

A voice as soothing as warm milk, penetrated her mind.

Alisha's eyes fluttered open and stared into the face.

'How are you honey?'

Alisha noted that the hair of the woman was greyer than the last time she had seen her and there were wrinkles and bags under her eyes. She saw concern in the brown irises.

'Grandma?'

'Yes, it's me honey. Just rest.' Grandma reached for Alisha's hand and held it in her own. The warmth spread through Alisha's veins.

For a week Alisha lay sedated, and each day Grandma sat with her, holding her hand and stroking her hair.

'Let me brush your hair like I used to do when you were little,' Grandma said, picking up a brush off the side table. 'Can you sit up?'

Alisha slowly hoisted herself up while Grandma gently pulled the bristles through her hair.

'That's nice Grandma. How long have I been here?' she asked.

'Oh, a small while.'

Alisha relaxed as Grandma began to sing; her mind travelling back to enjoyable childhood times, baking cookies and playing in the backyard.

A sharp knock startled them both. The door opened slowly.

'Mum!' Alisha screamed as tears sprang from her eyes and gushed down her cheeks.

Alisha was crushed by her mother's arms. 'I've missed you so much.'

Alisha stayed in the warm embrace.

'I've spent every day trying to find you. If it wasn't for Kai and Renee I may never have. I could have lost you too,' her mother said as she released her.

Her mother sat on the chair beside the bed. Alisha grabbed her hand. It was squeezed tight.

'Kai?' Alisha asked, confused.

'Kai met you in the Valley. He and Renee help the homeless. Renee followed you to the bridge and rang the ambulance. And I'm so happy she found you,' her mother said wiping her red weepy eyes. 'She said you were about to jump!'

'I think so. I don't remember,' Alisha said.

'It's okay. You're getting the best help here.'

There was silence in the room.

The nurse came and checked Alisha's vitals. 'Will I be able to go soon?' she asked the nurse.

'Maybe, if you have somewhere stable to go to.'

Alisha turned to her mother. 'Mum, can I come home?'

'Yes of course! I've moved in with Grandma, so you can come and live with us both.' Her mother looked towards the nurse.

The nurse nodded.

Alisha looked at Grandma who smiled. 'Wonderful!'

'I have something for you,' her mother said, taking a gift box out of her handbag.

Alisha hesitated

'Go on, it won't bite.'

Alisha lifted the lid off.

She stared at the crystal figurine of an angel holding a heart. 'It's beautiful,' she whispered.

Another knock on the door made Alisha jump. She gasped.

'Kai, come in,' her Mum said to the young man shuffling awkwardly into the room.

'Um, I just wanted to see how you were,' he said to Alisha.

'I'm okay. I'm going back home.'

'That's good,' he said smiling. 'Wo-would I be able to come and visit you?'

Alisha's eyes grew wide. 'Sure.'

Home was at Beachmere, in a quaint cabin in the caravan park.

'I like it here. I like the beach and no one knows me,' Alisha told her grandma.

'That's good. Don't forget to take your meds and you have counselling at one today.'

Alisha nodded.

Kai visited often.

'Why are you coming to see me?' Alisha asked one day.

'I like you, and I had a secret crush on you at school.' A bright red flush filled his cheeks.

'Really? I didn't think any boys liked me.'

'Of course they did! You just had your head stuck in the books and didn't notice.'

Alisha gave a harsh laugh. 'Fat lot of good that got me. Now I have nothing.'

'You have me!' Kai smiled then nudged her.

'That's true,' she said smiling back at him.

Nine months later, Alisha's Mum handed her a large yellow envelope with her name typed on the front.

'What's that?' her mother asked.

Alisha pulled out the handbook and said, 'It's uni information. I've decided to try to get into paramedics. Maybe I could save someone's life one day. I've been thinking about Dad and I'm sure he would like that.'

'Wow. You've been keeping that a secret. Your Dad *would* love that.'

Alisha smiled.

'I know that you can conquer the world if you want to. You're smart and you're beautiful and you're strong. You can do anything you put your mind to. And I'm *so* happy that you're here.'

Alisha put her arms around her mother. 'I'm getting my life back on track and I want you to be proud of me.'

Her mother cupped Alisha's face in her hands, as tears spilled down her cheeks. 'I am already proud of you. And I love you with all of my heart and no matter what happens I always will.'

CITY IN THE MIST
William A Thomas

From the moment we kissed
We saw the city in the mist,
Surfers Paradise is its name
Sun, surf, and sand are its claims to fame.

Its beauty is beyond compare
As precious as the love we share
As we walked along the sandy beach
Its peace and tranquillity we felt for each.

Hand in hand we lay on the sand
The love we felt between a woman and a man
As sunlight turned to night
The love we made seemed so right.

As the sun dawned over the sea
The city glistened for you and me.
The dogs played with all their might
And we held each other tight.

The Deliverance
Max Miller

'MR Jeffries, the master wants you at once in the main hall!' boomed the butler.

'A half dozen jugs of milk... two legs of venison... and the satchel of parcels,' I muttered to myself, checking my horse's pack for the required supplies. Frost gave a brisk shake of her bells, eager to begin tonight's local errands. I leashed her to the stable entrance and strode up the steps to the main hall.

The grandiose foyer makes even the most noble of kings feel humble. My gaze wandered around the room, upwards to the chandeliers, along the stained oak dining table, and finally resting on the master's creased face, muscles tensed in thought. He looked up from his books to address me.

'It's going to be awfully cold tonight, Jeffries. The darkest evening of the year, they say,' cautioned the master, staring absently out the window as the first flakes fell, graceful heralds of a brutal and harsh winter.

'I'll be fine, master. I don't mind the woods,' I replied cheerfully, 'And Frost will keep me company.'

'Well, good luck anyway,' added the master, offering a curt smile.

As I turned around and walked towards the door, the master interrupted, 'One more thing, Jeffries.'

I stalled, frozen in my step. 'What . . . What is it, master?' I was scared to hear his response. Everyone knew the rumours about 'the missing': past servants of our house who have been tasked with a secret mission by the master himself.

I faced him cautiously.

'We've been on good terms for a while now, Jeffries. Enough so for me to ask a favour of you.'

The master shuffled around his papers on the table to reveal a small envelope.

'I want you to deliver this letter to the red brick house beside the frozen lake.'

'Under no circumstances are you to enter the house. Simply slide the letter through the mail slot on the front door. Do I make myself clear?'

'Of course, master. I shall depart at once.'

The master nodded affirmably and returned to his business.

The cold rush of air that swept across my face as I left the hall did little to put a chill on the thoughts that were racing around my mind. To whom was this letter addressed? Why was I not to enter the house? And most puzzlingly, why only now had the master asked this special task of me?

My troubles quickly disappeared as I saddled Frost and started off along the narrow road into the woods. I loved the feeling of riding in the woods – the feeling of being free, taking Life by the reins and forging my own path.

One by one, I unloaded the supplies at addresses scribed on my list: a derelict-looking farmhouse by the old flour mill, the majestic Robinson house, and Mr Grayson's cottage near the village outskirts.

Finally, when the moon was at its highest point in the starry black sky, I had delivered the last of the goods. Frost gave a dull shrug of her bells, signalling she was ready to return to the castle after a tiresome night.

'It's alright Frosty, we'll be heading home soon,' I said, patting her on the flank.

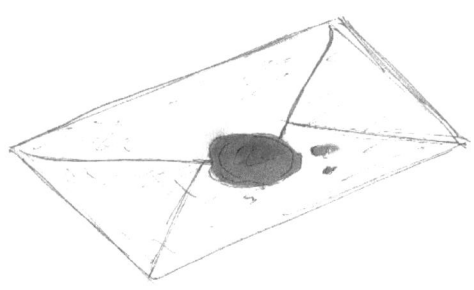

Our night wasn't done yet, however; I had yet to complete the master's special mission of delivering his letter. We continued along the road to the lake.

At first glance, the house looked perfectly normal. The gas lamps were turned on, illuminating the neatly trimmed hedge bordering the drive. The curtains were closed and the fence gate locked.

Everything was clearly in order, but even so, I could not help feeling a strange absence of life, as if not a soul was at home. I thought no more of it as I approached the front door. Remembering the master's instructions, I retrieved the small envelope from my coat pocket and reached towards the door.

I couldn't help but wonder what secrets that letter held. The stories of 'the missing' hung over me ominously, compelling me to hesitate for a brief moment before I placed the letter in the door's bronze letter slot.

'Well, that wasn't so hard, was it?' I said to myself, relieved, as I strolled back to the road.

My newfound pride and sense of accomplishment gave me a sudden urge for a taste of adventure. I looked ahead at the path I was following, then I gazed into the sweet darkness of the woods.

'Let's take the shortcut this time,' I grinned. Frost bucked in delight as we veered off the travelled route and through a narrow clearing, accelerating into a swift trot as we swept past branch and trunk. The swift trot quickly turned into a gallop, vaulting over fallen logs and weaving around rotting stumps as we rode. After a while, Frost slowed to a resting pace, stopping at the neck of a wider clearing. She let out a loud neigh in content.

In that moment, there was complete silence. Not a howl of wind scattering the leaves, no jaunty birds chirping. I turned my head around slowly, admiring the tranquillity of the nothingness surrounding me. That was why I loved the woods. I was able to let go of the minutiae of working life and delve into my true self, without the ceaseless distractions I was so accustomed to. I relaxed back onto the saddle and let my eyes close slowly, drifting into a doze.

My brief moment of peace came to an abrupt halt when Frost lurched forward violently, throwing me off onto the ground. The loud screech of an owl on a nearby branch had spooked her. As I looked up, all I could hear was the sound of her clattering hooves. I desperately tried to make out which direction she went, straining my eyes in the shadowy moonlight, but the sound was growing quieter and quieter.

Once again, there was total silence. This time, however, I felt alone and scared. I began to panic. My eyes scanned around the clearing hastily, brushing the mud and leaves off my coat. I began to walk in the vague direction in which I heard the sounds.

I tried to distract myself by thinking about what I would return to – the castle, my life, my home – but my mind was spinning out of control. Is this the punishment that fate had bestowed on me? Why was I to be punished for a decision out of my control?

A heavy snowfall was beginning to set in, and I was alone in the middle of the woods, lost, without a horse or even a lamp. For what seemed like hours, I battled through piles of snow and plummeting temperatures of the cruel night. My legs grew weary. Every footstep was both a step closer to home, and a step that could lead me to my death.

Luckily, my demise was not imminent.

At first, I dismissed it as a figment of my imagination – my brain's attempt to create a false hope to drive my exhausted body even further. When I realised that the splash of light I saw in the distance was real, I screamed out in joy.

My joy quickly faltered when I realised which building I had stumbled upon. It was the red brick house that I had delivered the master's letter to. I had to get out of this bitter, relentless cold. I had to disobey my master's orders and enter the house.

I stumbled round to the side door and knocked, but there was no response. What I found inside created an image in my mind so strong and so vivid, it will scar me for as long as I live. A young woman, slumped on an armchair, clearly dead. Her glazed eyes were stuck in a boundless stare, pupils widened presumably in fright or shock.

Beside her armchair was a pile of paper. I looked closer. They were envelopes – the same size and colour as the envelope I had delivered earlier this evening. Several dozen, all of them unopened, except one. The unfolded letter rested delicately in her lifeless open palm.

All of my years of dedication as a servant told me to dispel the temptation of reading that letter. But, like the woods, I saw it as an alluring fascination, drawing me closer. Against my conscience, it beckoned me. I couldn't resist reading the letter. Its contents, ingrained in my memory, shall remain a secret. But, after that night, I would never return to the castle again.

WAR GRAVES

Vera Murray

In this wartime burial ground,
So many graves in rows lie,
Like strings of broken beads,
Strewn across an ample breast.
Grim reminders of man's mortality;
The inevitability of many a man's fate
In this war of greed and hate.

The weak rays of the morning sun,
Pierce through the rising mist,
As the first sounds of closure,
Echo throughout air still moist,
As the melodic voice of a priest,
Begins the last prayers,
Over this newly departed.

As every methodical, monotonous thud
Of soil on wood reaches the mourners,
Although not audibly apparent,
The still air is pregnant with memories,
And thoughts of the bereaved,
As they tangibly entreat God for solace,
For explanation, for world peace.

Thus the circle of mourners present,
Swathed in their black misery,
Listen still in tortured silence,
As the priest finishes his prayers
For this departed fighter for world peace.
He knows many more are on their way,
As the war and those to follow, take their toll.

Wartime Memories
Vera Murray

WHEN the Second World War began in 1939 in Europe I was a naive and innocent school girl. We all led a secure and predictable life. Adults never discussed the war or other 'adult' subjects in front of children. It was remote and of no real concern to us, although some children made listening unseen a fine art. This was also a world where locking all doors when you left the house was unheard of. Delivery men like bakers, or tradesmen, had to go to the back door. A lot of families like ours also had chooks (fowls), and many grew their own fruit trees.

War came, created by Germany's leader, Adolf Hitler. Life at school became boring to us after we watched our weather-tanned soldiers in Brisbane's Army parades, all ready to join England in what was then a European war only. My best friend and I promised ourselves we would join the Voluntary Air detachment of nurses when it became possible.

The year of 1941 arrived, when most of our young men, except for many farm workers, became soldiers, and disappeared into camps.

War came closer to Australian shores when the Japanese attacked America's Pearl Harbour, followed by their onward, and it seemed unstoppable march, island hopping in the Pacific Ocean and southward towards Australia. We knew Darwin had been attacked, when a woman ran down the street screaming at each house that Darwin had been bombed by the Japanese. We children were not concerned as Darwin was thought to be a long way away.

It became common knowledge that the Federal Government would cut off any real assistance to Queensland if invaded. It would be known as the Brisbane Line, as only from the Queensland border south, was to be actively defended. No-one we knew moved south.

Trenches were quickly dug in backyards in case of bombing. When the sirens sounded, my mother, wearing a large sun hat, would sit on a wooden case, in our trench, and knit. She would happily chat through the gaps in the palling wooden fence to her neighbour who was also sitting in her trench. Places were built in the inner city for people in town to hide in whenever the sirens sounded for practice.

Only one family in our street had access to a private telephone, so listening to the radio was our only source of news. From it we learned that American naval ships had arrived. They were followed by General McArthur, in retreat, who immediately set up his headquarters in Lennons Hotel, Brisbane, not yet called a city. With him came American soldiers in tailored uniforms and with plenty of cash to spare. They seemed to be everywhere. When the opportunity arose and we were in town, my best friend and I, like many school children, took our autograph books and way-laid the passing Americans who happily gave us their autographs. We later compared them in detail with our school friends' collections.

The popularity of the Americans was so great that Australian soldiers conducted a protest march against them in the main town area. We heard it originally began when the ground sheets in Australians tents where taken and put in tents for the Americans. When they arrived, so many of our pretty young girls (particularly waitresses and other service staff) appeared only to notice the Americans.

We were amazed to discover that Americans were horrified when they found out how Australians used the smelly tall box called 'the dunny' in the back yard and that so many Australians had false teeth, quite rare in America.

A Japanese radio propaganda programme began in which Tokyo Rose, as she was called, told upsetting information and stories for American army personnel she named, about their wives, girlfriends, and family back home. The authorities did not take long to wipe her off the air.

Mothers of teenage girls forbade them to mix or be too friendly with Americans. Teenagers knew very little about the outside world and its people. The Americans appeared to know 'too much'. When my older sister made a date with an American soldier she was forbidden to keep it. Behind my mother's back my sister offered me six pennies to visit Hank, the American soldier, at work, and give him a note she wrote. After bargaining we settled on the grand sum of twelve pennies (a shilling.) That was amazing.

Saturday morning saw me on my way by tram to Perry House, on a corner of Elizabeth St. At the entrance I pushed open the door and found myself in a room with tables at which sat office workers. I asked for Hank and he rose and came forward. I handed him the note and he asked me to wait until he wrote a reply.

Suddenly someone close by whispered loudly, 'The Colonel's coming. I can hear his steps.' All, except Hank, were suddenly looking down at papers on their desks. Hank grabbed my arm and drew me to a door in the side wall. He swung open the door and pushed me inside. 'Don't come out until I open the door or we'll be in big trouble. Got it?'

'I won't,' I said as I was shut inside when the door closed behind me.

Time passed and boredom set in. I decided it would be fun to hide and give Hank a fright, but the only place I could hide was under one of the very large sinks that lined the far wall. Giggling with excitement I crouched down beneath one of them, my dark coat blending with the shadows there. This was real adventure to me.

Immediately after having settled, the door opened and I could see two pairs of male army trousers. I thought that it must be Hank and another worker, but one suddenly spoke in a deep authoritative voice and dispelled that idea. I became scared, and froze as they discussed what they referred to as developing film. Then the legs turned away and I heard the door close behind them.

Relieved, I squirmed out from my hiding place as the door re-opened and Hank and several of his mates rushed in. They laughed madly when I told them I had hidden under the sink.

I was rewarded for my cleverness by Hank taking me to the Pig and Whistle Milk Bar. (Called by us school children, The Hog and Toot.). He shouted me my favourite, a mint julip. Hank was shipped out shortly before news of the Coral Sea Battle was made public. I believe they could have been the photographs developed in the sinks.

My sister married another American and now lives in the United States.

One more of my many memories is when my school girlfriend, a few years older than me, discovered there was a dance in a hall in Adelaide St. Brisbane, for the Americans on Saturday nights. She decided we both should go. On our arrival we discovered there were rules. A group of stern-faced elderly ladies, seated at a table close by, made sure they were kept. The main rule was that no bodies touched when dancing, or you were OUT.

I got up with an American to jitterbug. It was a new dance only the Americans knew. Jiving was to follow later. To me, to jitterbug was to just jig up and down all the time to the music. I was doing great, or so I thought, when my American soldier partner laughed and said, 'You dance like my chooks fight.'

At the time I had a pet hen in our back yard fowl house, so I was not sure if it was a compliment.

To add a few more memories to this list: We found that all Negro American Army personnel were confined to South Brisbane. They were not permitted to cross the river into the city. Information came from somewhere that one attempted it, but was shot on the bridge for his disobedience.

After we settled into this different way of life for years, Japan was defeated. Our fighting forces returned, and we lined the streets to welcome them, shouting and screaming our thanks, especially when we saw a face we knew. If we didn't know them, we screamed out names like John or Bill, and were rewarded with smiles and nods from strangers who recognised their names.

During my upbringing, knowledge of the outside world was so limited it showed in many ways

On the south side of Brisbane, on the main road, there lived a man from the north of India. Each morning he sat on his front steps and had a long stretch of cloth similar to a bandage beside him. He would then begin to slowly 'twist' it in place around his head so it eventually became a turban and stayed on: a strange and fascinating event. There were those who, hearing about it, paid a few pence to travel on the tram past his house to see it. The tram riders had another look on their way back home. How our knowledge of the world has grown.

Those, and many more memories of those days, and the aftermath, remain unforgotten.

1945 – THE WAR IS OVER
Vera Murray

With the words, 'The War is over.
Have you heard the news?'
There came the first hope.
But was it true or just a rumour?
Though hating the suspense,
It made us wonder and to pray,
In that year of 1945.

As the news spread,
Those words still filled,
Our brains with doubt,
Until officially confirmed.
Then we gave shouts of joy,
While exchanging hugs,
With all those within range.

Workers deserted their jobs,
Helping to fill the main city roads,
By joining crowds drunk with joy.
Swaying this way and that,
Many discarded beer and drink bottles,
Which clattered down the streets,
Competed noisily with the shouts.

Many a mother watching,
Whispered, 'Thank God.'
A soldier, with the light of relief in his eyes,
Whispered in my ear to make me hear,
'It's been such a 'drag' but now at last,
I'm going home to wife and kids.'
He then disappeared within the crowd.

Redemption

Another from the States,
His face, yellow from malaria,
Began a story of his own.
'We have a ranch back home,
My sisters are trying their best,
To look after it for us. Now . . .'
The rest was lost in the din.

A loud band appeared from 'nowhere',
Sounding out with sax and drums.
Their playing helped to nourish,
Our joy and excitement
Although it failed to drown,
The many cries of 'The War is over.'
The memory of that day still endures.

Scarred
Maddison Lanham

THE rusted sign read *Midnight Screams*. From behind the thin tin walls loud music and ear piercing shrieks of laughter could be heard, and even from several blocks away the horrifying din could pierce innocent eardrums of a passer-by. Once entering the tin shed, one's eyes were met with the nightmarish image of couples grinding against each other in tune with the screams erupting from the speakers, underage drinkers vomiting in a vacant corner, and dejected people chugging down another shot.

Listening carefully, one could hear the sound of the heavy door opening and slamming shut, and a newcomer's stilettos tapping incessantly against the vomit-coated floor. Though it seemed natural that others would be unaware of a newcomer's presence, the girl did not go unnoticed.

Even with high heels, 18-year-old Grainne stood a head shorter than the rest of the crowd. Her skin was as dark as midnight and her curly black hair sat as an untameable knot on top of her head. Unlike the other girls in the club, her legs were not as thin as toothpicks and her chest did not fall as a flat terrain. Instead her short legs emerged from a curvy waist and her generous breasts seemed to explode from her top which clutched her torso like a second skin.

Unexpectedly, Grainne's colourless lips widened in an inglorious smile, revealing a mouth full of wonky teeth and tiny gaps. The source of her happiness, it seemed, was a blond-haired boy who was walking towards her. Reaching her, he bent down from where he stood like a tower above her, to give Grainne a smouldering kiss on her full lips.

'When did you get here?' he yelled, attempting to be heard above the woman singing about love through the speakers.

'Just now,' she screamed back.

Her voice was as different as her physical features were different. It was as deep as a grown man's and the strength of her Irish accent grated on the nerves of some. After giving her another quick kiss, the boy grabbed his girlfriend's hand, pulling her to the crowded dance floor. Once they stood in the middle of the grinding couples and other dancers, he spun around so that they were facing each other. The boy, Christopher, pulled her close to his chest and rested both of his hands on Grainne's hips as they swayed gently to the slower rhythm of the new song.

Grainne rested her head against Christopher's torso in contentment. From where her head rested she could peer curiously at the others. A frown which seemed to be filled with sadness and pure envy plagued her face as she saw that she and Christopher were surrounded by what society called 'natural beauties'. Their petite waists swayed to and fro with the music and their blonde hair seemed to cascade like water down their shoulders. Grainne felt her stomach contort and her breathing quicken into short rasps of air. Hurriedly, she pulled away and began pushing her way through the mass of people to the bar, leaving the boy standing alone, confused, in a sea of dancers.

After what felt like hours, with a few extra bruises from jerking elbows, the girl reached the bar. Quickly she made her way to a pitiful lone stool in a far corner. Motioning the bartender for a shot, she bent her head to rest it against the slightly cool bench, sticky with she knew not. Grainne breathed deeply, trying to calm her anxiety, gently rubbing her stomach in an attempt to halt its rapid churning.

As Grainne rested her forehead against the bench, memories flooded into her mind. Memories of a girl who had been abandoned by her mother in exchange for bottles and handsome men. Memories of a dark room with other young children who screamed for their parents to come back. Memories of staying with foster parents who beat her when she missed a speck of dust on the kitchen counter. Memories of staying with other foster parents who called her fat, ugly and worthless, while their children laughed along with them. Memories of swallowing a meal and then attempting to throw it up afterwards, because she couldn't bear to be called fat at school again. Memories of finally living with a family who she believed might find it in their hearts to love her. Memories of a white walled room with a stranger as he tried to fix her. Memories of deep cuts on her arms and legs, symbolising all of her deepest struggles, fears and secrets.

Finally a small glass was slammed beside her, its contents sloshing onto her hair, coating it in sticky liquid. Looking up she quickly grabbed the glass and tilted it upwards, swallowing its glorious contents in one gulp. The alcohol burned as it travelled down her throat making its way to where it would, hopefully, eventually, calm her writhing stomach. Finding the sensation both exciting and terrifying, Grainne motioned for another. And another. After her fourth, girlish giggles began erupting from her lips, she could no longer feel her legs that dangled from the stool beneath her.

Suddenly a strong hand rested on her shoulder and spun her around. In front of her stood Christopher, who was impatiently shaking off a few 'natural beauties', his eyes only for the drunk girl in front of him.

'What's wrong, Grainne?' he demanded, wrenching the small glass from her hand and putting it down on the counter, out of Grainne's reach.

'Nothing now!' Grainne slurred, reaching again for the glass to take another big gulp and swirl the contents in a dream like fashion

'This stuff is really good,' she said, lurching herself at Christopher and shoving the drink in his face. 'See!?'

Christopher tilted his head to the side, studying her face. Determination and frustration plaguing his handsome features, Christopher pulled Grainne from the stool, ignoring her cries of protest. He began half dragging, half carrying her to the entrance of Midnight Screams, all the while ignoring her drunken demands, excuses and questions.

They reached the outside of the nightclub. Britain's fresh cold air and the roar of nearby cars seemed to sober Grainne up, leaving only a girl still traumatised about her past. She leaned against the tin wall, forcing herself to breathe in and out, desperately trying to ignore the need to vomit.

'Seriously, Grainne, what's wrong?' he demanded, though his tone was gentle, 'Why did you just leave me?'

'Do you really want to know?' Grainne asked doubtfully.

Christopher just raised his eyebrows as if saying 'Well duh why else would I ask?!'

'Fine!' she said angrily. 'I don't get it, okay? I don't get why you picked me. Out of all the girls you picked me! You could have had any one of them.' Grainne yelled, while motioning back to the club's entrance. 'You could have had any one of them with their beautiful blonde hair, long legs and small hips. But instead you have me, the fat, Black girl with massive hips, big boobs and big hair.'

Suddenly a finger was pressed gently against her lips, effectively silencing her.

'But I don't want any of them.' Christopher laced with affection. 'I want you. I love the way your hips sway when you walk. How your chocolate brown eyes seem to be filled with infinite wisdom and questions.

I love the way you tuck your hair behind your ear and scrunch up your nose in frustration. And most of all I love how funny, smart and practical you are. And do you know what makes you even more beautiful?' The tips of his fingers tilted her chin upwards; forcing her to look at him.

Dejectedly Grainne shook her head, causing her dark curls to bounce slightly and salty tears to etch uncertain pathways down her cheeks.

Christopher's lips formed a soft smile. 'My darling Grainne, what makes you all the more beautiful is that you don't even know it!'

For a long time, neither of them said anything, merely studied each other's faces. Suddenly a small, shy smile spread across Grainne's face. Taking that as an invitation, Christopher swept her into his arms, resting his chin on top of the bundle on her head and whispered soft endearments in her ear.

Pulling away, Christopher slowly bent down and placed his lips gently on Grainne's. Their lips moved in time with the soft beating of their hearts, his hands resting against her hips, pulling her closer, and Grainne's fingertips playing with the strands of blonde hair that tickled at the base of his neck.

As they stood together amongst the streams of light coming from the lamps, Grainne's scarred hurt and anxious heart gave itself up. Finally she believed that Christopher loved all of her – the outside, the inside, her past and her present.

With Christopher she could forget the horrors of her past. With him she found herself worthy of redemption.

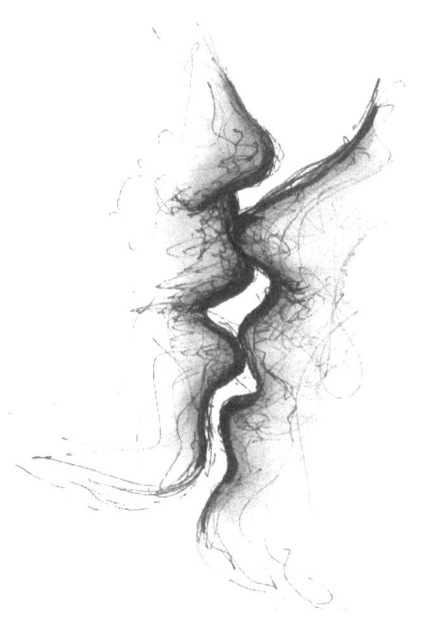

Withered Seeds
Jeanette O'Hagan

RILLA pushed open the side door of the mansion, hesitating before entering. The soft golden light of dawn painted the sandstone steps and reflected off the serried ranks of windows above her. Stepping inside, she slipped off her flimsy dancing shoes, damp with dew. Dangling them from slim fingers, she tiptoed down the narrow hallway toward the main staircase. Silence enfolded the house like a shroud. Mama was away on another trip and Papa, if awake, would be in his study engrossed in his latest project.

The corridor opened into the atrium where the stairs swept up to the higher levels. Rilla smoothed the gauzy material of her kameez and placed a hand on the rosewood balustrade.

A loud crash shattered the drowsy peace.

Her gaze darted around the room. Nothing was out of place, from the stuffed jaguar at the door to the large portrait of her parents standing in front of the moonflame flower on the wall. Had a servant dropped a breakfast tray in the kitchens? She pushed the strap of her gossamer blouse up and stepped onto the tread of the staircase.

A raised voice blasted from the opposite corridor. She stood still, her heart beating a rapid dance step.

Could the noises be coming from Papa's study? She was supposed to be safely ensconced in her bed.

Another thud, of wood on carpet, sounded from the study. No one else was stirring. What if Papa was in trouble? Her hands shaking, she dropped the slippers and grabbed a large candlestick from the stand. She edged down the hall to the study, her mouth dry.

This was a bad idea. Her ears strained at the smallest sound. The clop-clop of a horse-drawn carriage in the street. The soft tick-tick of the pendulum clock counting down the seconds in the hall. In the gardens, a karrabird gave a long chuckling call. Loud voices rumbled in the study.

The door swung open.

'Ridiculous.' Her eldest brother's voice blasted out in an angry tirade. 'Ten thousand kuzats on a mouldy old botanical collection, five thousand kuzats on tinted lens, two thousand kuzats on travelling ponies . . . ponies for sanity's sake . . .'

Slide it, what was Hekto doing here? At this hour?

'Yes, but—' Papa's soft voice sounded defensive.

Hekto, in impeccable morning attire, barrelled through the door. He threw a sheath of receipts in the air. 'It's extravagant. A vain attempt to recover your glory days on some foolish quest. It's got to stop, Papa. You are a joke to all of Kuza.'

Rilla backed against the wall, cradling the candlestick against her chest. Hekto stopped midstride, his implacable black eyes narrowing.

'Rilla, you're up early.' His gaze swept her from head to foot. 'Have you just now come in?'

Rilla stiffened her back and lifted her chin, defiant. ''Tis none of your business what I do with my time. I'm eighteen.'

'Seventeen.'

'A matter of mere months.'

'I doubt Mama thinks so and she funds your allowance.'

'She is in Kito.'

Hekto raised his thick eyebrows. 'I have oversight of her finances in her absence.' He pushed past her, his fine yarma-wool scarf whipping out behind him. 'Spend your evenings demurely at home, sister, or I will stop your allowance.'

Heat rose up her neck and seared her cheeks. 'Bully! Traitor!'

Hekto didn't break his stride as he headed for the front entrance.

The hot flush of anger left her and she sank to the floor, the candlestick rolling with a clatter from limp fingers. Oh, why hadn't she fled to her room at the first sound? Tears flowed down her cheeks to drip on the floor.

After some moments, she stirred and crept into the study. Golden light seeped through the gaps between the heavy window drapes. Exotic objects crowded the room; stuffed jaguars and yarmas, cases of botanical materials, journals and compendiums. Clutter spilled out from upended crates onto the patterned Tamrin carpets.

Papa lifted a crate. He sorted the scattered objects, placing each item with care into compartments and slots. His white hair flopped across his forehead and he looked thinner, his movements less sure than she remembered. When had he grown so old?

He looked up. 'Rilla!'

His fine lips pressed together as his gaze alighted on her attire. Before he could lecture her, she clenched her fists and launched a defensive attack.

'I'm old enough to decide how I live my life.'

He held out his hands as if to ward off her words. 'It's just that you don't look very happy, sweetling.'

'Why do you spend time and money on these mouldy old bits and pieces?' Rilla changed the subject.

Rummaging under a pile of small lacquered containers, he withdrew the plainest one. He slid the lid open and checked inside. His face relaxed. 'Ah, good. Not damaged.' He nodded at her. 'I'm sorry. I'm looking for something. Not all old things deserved to be discarded, Rill.'

His words pricked her like a sharp needle. She grabbed a coat from the wall rack and put it on. Its hem brushed the floor, the sleeves reaching past her fingers. The faint smell of plants, soil and chillied nuts, swept her back to when she'd follow Papa around the greenhouses and gardens like a puppy, confiding her secrets to his patient ears. How long since she'd done that? Not since her first ball and the soirees and picnics that followed. Shaking off the niggling sense of unease, she challenged him.

'Why do you let Hekto boss you?'

Straightening with a groan, Papa tucked the box into his coat pocket and gave it a pat.

'Since your mother deemed it best to put him, not me, in charge of her finances?' He raised a white eyebrow, his grey-green eyes gleaming with mischief. 'Still, he forgets that I use my own means to fund my affairs.'

'You're up to something.'

He put a finger to his fine lips. 'Shhh.' His face beamed. 'By the Maker's kindness, in this last consignment, I've found what I've long sought. All is in place for my last adventure.'

'Oh, Papa. You are too old for field trips.' Even though she now rarely saw him, the thought of being alone in this mausoleum of a house left her bereft. 'I will be alone.'

'I thought you were quite grown-up, mistress of your own destiny.' He scratched his chin. 'Well now. You could stay with your sister. I'm sure she'd appreciate some help with her lively brood.'

'How can you? You know we argue and Marra will watch me like a mother eagle. She's worse than Hekto.'

'Hmm, then with one of your many friends.'

'What is so important about this trip, Papa?'

He stood straighter, his face grave. 'I have to pay a debt before it's too late.'

'Silly, you have years ahead of you.'

He gave a tucked in smile and stared at the patterns in the carpet. 'Perhaps, but I have searched for this treasure half my life. Now I can do what I should have done four decades ago.'

Despite his fragility, she could see the determination in the jut of his jaw, the set of his shoulders. Who knew what dangers he'd walk into? She should tell Hekto or Marra. Then the realisation of her own humiliation hit her. Become a recluse or have her allowance cut off. Forced to watch her friends enjoy the whirl of social activities while unable to attend herself. She folded her arms across her chest. She wasn't going to tell Hekto a thing.

Papa squeezed her shoulder. 'Tell him if you must, but you better hurry.' He picked up his jaguar topped walking stick and took out his timepiece. 'The sixth hour. Adventure awaits.'

'You are not going to walk?'

He laughed. 'No, no, my sweet. I have arranged a spot on a horse train, leaving from the Singing Frog Inn in an hour.'

He picked up a pack and shouldered it. 'I'm sorry to leave you like this, though I hardly thought you'd miss me.' He dropped a light kiss on the top of her hair.

She grabbed his hand, a sudden thought taking hold. 'Take me with you.'

'But you are hardly dressed or packed for a journey.'

'Give me half an hour. What I can't pack, we can buy along the way. Please, Papa. I'm bored with Kuza. I'd love to go adventuring with you.'

He squinted at her between half-lidded eyes, then let out a long, slow breath. 'I will probably regret this. You'd better hurry. The caravan will leave without us, if we're too long delayed.'

A light, giddy feeling swirled up inside her. She grabbed him into a tight hug. 'I promise, you won't be sorry.'

Spinning around, she dashed out the room, along the corridor and raced up the stairs two at a time.

MANY days later, rain, cold and hard, sliced down from a grey sky, stinging Rilla's face. It dripped from her hood, trickled under the collar of her waterproofs. The mountain pony beneath her dipped its head and flicked water from its ears as it trudged up the mountain path. She was hungry, tired and flea-bitten. Papa had never said it would be like this. To be fair, she hadn't given him time to explain.

Around her, waterlogged plants bent before the onslaught. Water ran in runnels down the steep slope. A bedraggled child sat on a rock, long-necked yarmas grazing on the scrubby hillside nearby. A woman collected sticks and dung patties, carrying the load wrapped in a wet shawl on her back. After two-tendays, Rilla hoped they were nearing their destination and she could take Papa home.

His head bowed under a wide-brimmed hat, one thin hand on the reins of his pony, the other covering his mouth as he gave a deep, chesty cough. The journey had been hard on him.

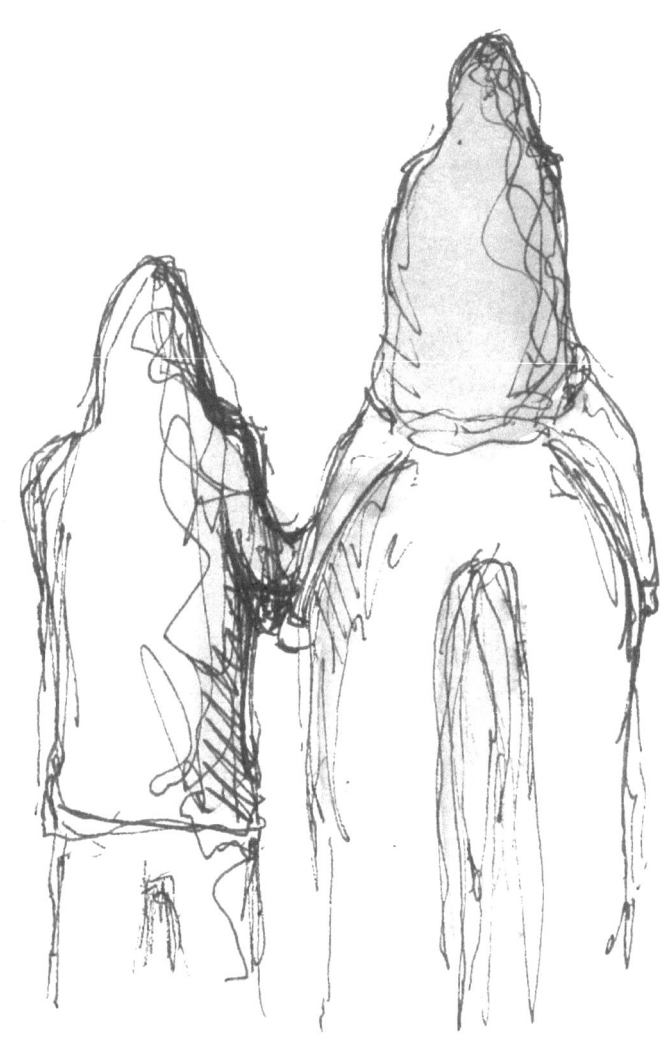

'Papa, we should find shelter.'

Not that there was much on offer. The sparse, uneven thatch and peeling painted walls of the mountain huts gave little comfort or warmth. The people were dull-eyed and gaunt.

'Papa.'

He shook his head, water scattering in all directions. 'We are too close to stop now.'

'If you say. Why do people live like this?'

'Do you think it is from choice?'

'Then why?'

'The Emperor's taxes take wealth and young people. The irrigation systems crumble and are not repaired. Landlords live in comfort. The traders give pittances for crops and goods, making a tidy profit, but charge high prices for anything from the city.'

'They seem so apathetic.'

Papa patted the neck of his pony. 'We were once a proud and fierce people.' His voice dropped. 'Though this is worse than last time.'

Something he'd said niggled at her. The pony strained as the path swept around a ridge before heading up the slope. Along the brow, a dozen adobe huts crouched like beggars.

The rain eased to a drizzle and the clouds lifted, giving a patchy view of the high snow-capped peaks surrounding them. Suddenly, it hit her.

'You said 'we', but we are Kuzi, our family goes back a thousand years, to the courts of the early Sulkans. We have nothing to do with these debased people.'

'Spoken like a true daughter of Kuza.' There was an edge to his voice.

Rilla frowned. 'What do you mean?' She met his grey-green eyes, still bright in his lined tan face.

'Your family, the Maedons, are nearly as illustrious as Mama's.'

'No doubt. Yet, I was born in this village before Hakan Maedon adopted me. My mother is buried beyond that ridge.'

Could this be true? 'Is that why you came, to honour her grave?'

'That is a good thought, sweetling. No doubt, she did the best she could, but, no. I come to pay another debt.'

He'd said that before. 'How could you owe these people anything?'

'I once took something that didn't belong to me.' His smile was grim. 'And though this theft brought acclaim and success, the harm I did has haunted me ever since.'

Rilla felt a ripple of unease at the intensity in Papa's voice. Why was this so important?

To Rilla's relief, the rain soon eased. A strip of intense blue-green twilight sky and the bright crescent of the silver moon peeked through the clouds. Papa urged his pony into a trot and stopped before the biggest hut. A young woman, a baby on her back, stood beneath the eaves, spinning wool on a hand spindle.

Papa swung off his pony. He staggered, gripping onto the strappy mane for balance. 'Good woman, we ask for shelter. Can you take us to the head villager?'

The woman's coffee-brown face settled into sullen lines.

When the woman didn't respond, he spoke a few words in the local language. A boy about ten came around the side of the house. 'I will ask for you, wananik.'

Papa inclined his head. 'Say, Zander Maedon wishes to speak with him.'

The woman spoke rapidly to the child. Together they entered the house. Voices sounded from inside.

Rilla shivered as the sweat dried on her skin. 'They don't seem friendly.'

Papa pulled a blanket from the pack and put it around her shoulders. He hunched forward, a deep cough shaking his thin back.

He took her hand, his fingers ice cold. 'I should not have brought you so far from city comforts.'

She lifted her chin. 'I'm not complaining.' And it was true. As trying as the long journey was, she had time to ponder how big the world was and how frivolous was her life in Kuza. Best of all, she and Papa had rediscovered their old ease together.

The door opened, the boy emerged. 'The Head Villager will not see you.'

Papa sucked in a breath. 'Please, ask again. I have something valuable to give.'

'She said you should go, wananik. You are not welcome here.'

'No.' He threw an apologetic look at Rilla. 'We will wait until she relents.'

'As you wish.' The boy closed the door, leaving them in the gloaming. Inside came the clutter of cooking pots, the smell of food, and the cry of a small child.

Stars sparkled like sequins against the patches of deep indigo sky. Somewhere, an owl hooted.

Rilla pulled her blanket tighter. 'What do we do now, Papa?'

'Let's tend to the ponies, and eat. Another villager may shelter you, but I must stay here.'

Noting the stubbornness in his voice, she sighed. 'Then, I will stay with you.'

RILLA roused from a doze, stiff and cold and hungry. The clouds had lifted and the half orb of the golden moon squatted on the western horizon.

Papa slumped against the door of the hut, his breath rasping in the freezing night air.

She touched his shoulder. 'Papa.'

He stirred.

'They aren't going to let us in.'

'I haven't come too far to fail now.' His words merged into a wheezing cough.

The door swung open and an old woman stood in the frame, her long white hair streaked with grey. Startling green eyes flashed from under white eyebrows joined over a strong nose.

'Go home, wananikas. Stop disturbing our sleep.' She cast a scathing glance over them, fists on her hips.

Papa struggled to stand, his hair flopping over his eyes. 'Asharilla?' Then his mouth firmed and he stood straighter, one hand on Rilla's shoulder. 'I wish to speak to the head villager. I have a treasure—'

'I am she. You have nothing we want, Kimsak.'

'But—'

'Do you see what good your kuzats did?' She swept a hand in a circle. 'With the taking of the moonflame, our valley lost its heart. You have done enough damage.'

Papa's hands gripped hard on Rilla's shoulder. He coughed, his body shaking with the force of it.

'Papa!' She put his arm around him. 'You need proper shelter.'

He waved a shaking hand. 'I'm fine, Rilla sweet.' His eyes glistened and his shoulders slumped.

The woman looked at her and then to Papa. 'Rilla? She is your daughter?'

Heat flared through Rilla, flaming her cheeks. 'What did you think? And what kind of place is this that leaves an old man out in the cold night? If he dies, it will be on your head. We can pay for our lodgings.'

'I don't want your cursed money.' The old woman's fierce eyes fixed on Papa. 'He doesn't look well, but surely from his own stubbornness.' She clicked her tongue. 'Come inside, but tomorrow you go. You do not belong here.'

RILLA'S cheeks burned from the fire's heat. Her hands and feet stung as feeling seared back into them. Papa sat hunched over, his hand on his breast pocket. The woman sat opposite, her fierce gaze watching them like a jaguar its prey. The young woman brought a tray of food and placed the bowls and beakers on the mat between them.

'Eat,' the old woman said.

Rilla picked up a bowl of roasted maize and offered it to Papa. He waved it away.

'You need to eat, Papa. Or at least drink.'

He took the beaker she offered and sipped, his eyes fixed on the fierce woman, Asharilla. That was her own name, shortened to Rilla. Had Papa known this woman as a young man? There seemed an intensity of feeling between them.

'You were right, Asharilla, and I was wrong.' His voice was low, strained.

Her wide mouth twisted. 'Much good it does now. What was done cannot be undone. You took the last flower spike of the moonflame, quenched its fire, or can you tell me otherwise?'

'I've searched all the valleys from Kito to Kuza and found no other.'

'And did winning the Empress's prize give you happiness?'

Rilla looked up. Papa had won the prize a few years before he met Mama. His name had been on everyone's lips and the Empress appointed him head of her botanical gardens. Had the moonflame come from this valley?

Papa took Rilla's hand, gave it a squeeze. 'Yes, some. And grief and regret as well. Asharilla, I remembered seeing seeds of *Killaris Agni* among a botanical collection in my first days in the Academy.'

The woman's eyes widened. 'Seeds?'

'It took years to track them as they passed from one owner to another.'

'But you have them?'

He pulled the box out of his pocket. Bowing his head, he offered it with two hands to the woman his daughter was named after.

The woman took the box and opened it. Her face softened then hardened like ice-rime on a bowl of water. 'What good is that to us? No one has grown them.'

'Remember, you said we could learn how.'

'It takes money and time. I cannot even feed my village.'

'I have willed much of my estate to this project—to train workers, local young men and women. It needs to be in the mountains where the moonflame once grew. I hoped it could be here.'

Asharilla cradled the box. 'It will be ten years before both moons are full at the spring equinox, ten years before the moonflame can flower again.'

'This is what my tinted lens are for, to mimic the dual light of the moons.'

Rilla clapped her hands. 'Such a project could bring hope to the valley. Papa, will you oversee this task?'

He smothered a cough. 'With what time I have left, despite my doctor's predictions.'

'You listened, Kimsak. You are the defender of the moonflame.' A tear slipped down the woman's withered cheeks.

'No, you are, Asharilla.'

'When can you start?'

Papa's pale lips twitched into a smile. His eyes shone. 'As soon as I arrange for my daughter's safe return to the city.'

'Oh?' Rilla bit her lip. She didn't want to go back to the round of senseless parties. That life felt frivolous and boring now. She touched Papa's hand. 'I could stay and help you.'

'You mother won't approve.'

'Yes, but she'll come around. Besides, you really are quite reckless. Someone should look after you.'

Papa smiled, a mischievous look in his green-grey eyes. 'I would like that, sweetling.'

Old Asharilla gazed at the withered seeds in the plain box. 'But what if we fail?'

Papa squeezed Rilla's hand. 'At least we tried.'

Larkspur

Inspired by the Kate Llewellyn poem *Finished*

Tyleigha Collins

THE clinking of plates and utensils irritates my ears, exacerbating the constant echoing ring that's resonating through my head. My family is talking around me but I can't seem to hear them over my own indecision. It's an odd sensation, being clearly able to hear the shrieking sound of a wooden chair, drawn across the floor yet unable to put words to the delicate movement of my mother's mouth. As her red lips move lightly, she is the picture of perfection, happiness, independence and love.

When I was a child, I'd looked up to her. She was my role model; always so calm, kind and beautiful with a capacity for love that was too large for me to imitate. Soon, my admiration led to jealousy and, shamefully, spite. I was envious of her and knew that I could never live up to her radiance. So I compromised. I could never be as beautiful as her, or as smart and kind, so I found someone who could.

I look around the table as everything moves in slow motion. I observe my family – my mother, brother, father, and husband as if I am watching from afar, viewing their silent exchanges but unable to take part in them. Why is that? Why are they free to enjoy so much while I can only endure? I stare at my untouched plate, contemplating. I guess the answer is simple. They are free, void of any poison hiding behind flowering facades, snaring victims with beauty while slowly releasing deadly toxins. I, however, am not free.

My eyes tread a slow path up the table to my love. He is handsome, so much more beautiful than the vivid stretch of colour thriving in my garden. More beautiful than the lush grass, forming glistening blossoms which dance in the breeze. Even when birds of all colours soar, performing joyous acts of song and dance as they choreograph their own musical with the sky as their stage, I'd rather be looking at him. My flower.

He is talking, but there's a notable difference between him and my family. He smiles, but his eyes tell me he's grinning. He laughs, but his lips are shadowing a smirk. Suddenly, blue and brown clash. His azure eyes meet my amber.

My heart, so slow – so *dead* – only moments before, comes to life in an instant. An influx of information invades me. I hear my mother's teasing words, my father's chortle, my brother's defensive disdain and my love's honey-soaked chuckle. Am I the only one who can see his lies? I feel sick, dizzy and alone but I came here with the purpose of changing that. I have to do it now or I never will.

'Love, could you join me outside for a moment?' All eyes are on me, layered in surprise and confusion. I nod towards the door before rising slowly, careful not to show my trembling unease.

Redemption

The veranda's swinging chair rocks back and forth in the wind like a yoyo in the hand of a bored child. My love sits across from me, only a hair's width away. *My love?* I suppose only habits preserve my affection towards him, the most magnificent flower I have in my collection. My hands are clenched together in my lap. I'm scared. A chill wracks through my body that has nothing to do with the weather, and I struggle to hide my shiver so that he doesn't offer me his arm. If he did, I know I wouldn't have the strength or will to do what I'd been conflicting over for months.

He's staring at the stars with that look of wonder and admiration in his eyes. I would know; he used to look at me that way too. Like the time when we would sleep in the same bed. My head would lay on his shoulder, and our gazes would connect desperately as if we were searching for our world in the other's eyes. That was before he relocated to the couch, so as not to miss the late night footy games. We used to have dinner together too, on beautiful starry nights such as this. I'd share a bottle of sparkling wine with my love while the veal was almost forgotten in favour of our flirtatious teasing.

An Arctic breeze shuffles my hair, arriving with another memory in tow and blowing away the distant memory of our laughter. I remember my legs wrapped around his neck, his hands warm on my thighs in the chill of the night, holding me off the ground on his shoulders like a child. Echoes of our howls yelled back at us from the cavernous drop just a few feet ahead. Remembering the weekend of our honeymoon was like ice to a burn in my heart. Though I know the burn will always be there, I can't stop myself from pretending, for just a moment, that my love is still my world and I am his. My home is still in his arms as I imagine he also believes that of me. My heart is still in his grasp, held lightly, not like the pressured force of a vice, capable of squeezing the life out of me. No, my heart is beating cheerfully in his gentle palm.

My family's quiet laughter shatters my wonderland. The image of my knight in shining armour and I, his princess, fractures and crumbles, tumbling into a void of swirling black pain and fear. A movement to my right snatches my attention. His eyes, so passionate only moments before, are now glazed and stare into mine. My cheek, carefully concealed with a thick mask of makeup, aches painfully, reminding me of the purple discoloration I was given not two days ago. My hands constrict tighter at the memory of me crawling sluggishly across the floor, haunted by his laughter.

The aftertaste of champagne lingers on my tongue as my jaw clenches with determination. I'm running out of excuses, I'm running out of breath, I'm running out of makeup and I'm running out of time. I open my mouth, beads of sweat rolling down my forehead, but before I can speak, my love begins in his honey-lathered tone.

'Why did you ask me out here?' In the silence, after his probing, he questions me with his eyes and

I struggle to find the right words to say. *Can I do it? Am I really willing to let go of the only man I've ever loved and the only man who will ever love me?*

He continues. 'Listen, I don't know why you wanted to interrupt dinner, but if you're not going to say anything, we might as well go back inside. Ok?' He smiles at me, a hint of menace hidden behind his carefully assembled smile. As he stands, the swing shakes but I can't let him go back inside. If he does I will lose my only safe opportunity to end this.

'Wait!' I hesitate, breathing in panting gulps of air as if I'd run a marathon. His dark eyes search my face as he melds with the darkness. I struggle to swallow, rubbing the sweat off my palms as I stand with him, trembling. 'I can't do this anymore. I want a divorce.' When the words leave my mouth, I'm surprised by the relief that surrounds me. There is no way out of this situation for him. My family is just inside, enjoying their meal in perfect hearing distance if anything unpleasant should occur. He couldn't hurt me here. He couldn't refuse my demand either. I've held silent long enough but I won't wait any longer and now, he knows that. I can be *free*. I slip my ring from around my finger and let it drop with a smile. It clanks onto the wooden boards beneath my feet with finality.

Only when his hands wrap around my neck do I look up with wide surprise. My fear returns. I struggle to escape his grasp, kicking, punching and squirming for breath until finally, the pressure loosens enough for me to scream.

I hear my family's chatter stop and feet running towards me.

'Candace!'

I sit up screaming. My hands are grasping at my neck to defend against my now invisible assailant.

My love stands over me. He is the one who called my name. He speaks with fabricated concern, making my heart ache. 'Be more careful around the plants, Love. I think you hit your head when you fell. Let me see.' I shiver at the word. *Love.*

My family gather around us, my mother's hand on his shoulder in support as she peeks over at me.

Larkspur is a beautiful and vibrant flower, once the most prized flowers in my possession. Only the foolish dare to touch its dangerous, blue blossoms and ignore the warning signs. I was foolish once, and now there is no anti-toxin that can save me from this poison. I am completely at his mercy, forever regretting the time when, to me, beauty was everything.

A young elf's atonement
Kasper Beaumont

'I ALMOST killed my nurse-maid. I must be a monster.' Shari-Rose shuddered.

The ten-year-old elf felt cold inside at the memory of pushing Neline-Dawn away with her powers, then seeing her sprawled unconscious on the floor. She shuddered at the hairs rising on her neck. *I didn't know she was there. It was an accident.*

The queen had whisked her away to the South Lands on urgent magical business, but the young elf yearned for her nurse-maid. *I hope she doesn't die. Oh, why did my father let them take me away?*

It then sunk into her consciousness that she was to be the shield keeper for all the South Lands. 'But I'm only a child. How can I possibly protect all these halflings?' She could feel tears prickling at her eyes and her heart was beating fast with something close to fear. She looked to the ground and her hair fell forward to hide her face.

Delicate hands swept her hair back and raised her chin to meet the kind eyes of Queen Liara-Star. A warm rush of energy and positivity came with her touch. 'Come my dear. Melita is keen to show you your new home, and Garleon-Sun too eagerly awaits you.'

Shari-Rose nodded first to her aunt and then to the halfling and tiny fairy who waited patiently at the foot of a grand staircase. They gave her a tour of the castle before climbing the tall tower.

The stairs were rather dark and shadowy as they climbed, so the fairy glowed to show them the way. The princess gasped to see the fairy's body and iridescent wings turn a bright pale yellow.

Melita-Li smiled at her reaction and made two pirouettes in mid-air. The bell on her cap tinkled.

'Wow. That is wondrous, Melita-Li.' Shari-Rose felt a smile forming and she bounded up the stairs ahead of them all in excitement. Her melancholy thoughts of the nurse-maid were forgotten.

She burst into the room at the top of the stairs and saw that it was filled with hanging crystals. A large round window in the ceiling was high above a raised pool in the centre of the room. It was identical to the room her father worked in, far away in the West Lands. She had peeked inside, but it was a room which she was forbidden to enter.

After taking in the beauty of the crystals, her gaze came at last to rest upon a cloaked figure lying upon an ornate settee in one corner. Two guardians stood beside him with impassive expressions, but neither prevented her from approaching the resting elf.

She tip-toed up to him. 'Ah, hello my Lord. Are you Garleon-Sun?'

The elf rose slowly to a sitting position and blinked as he studied her. He was the only old-looking elf the princess had ever seen, with cloudy blue eyes, skin an unattractive grey colour, and a look of fatigue on his countenance. 'An elf child in the Shield Room?

What is the meaning of this intrusion?' His face grew dark with anger and Shari-Rose backed away, scared of his sudden temper.

She bumped into Queen Liara-Star who put a long-sleeved arm around the child for comfort, before stepping forward to present the princess to him. 'Lord Garleon-Sun, it is a pleasure to see you again. Surely you have not forgotten that you bade me find a replacement shield keeper for Lakehaven, for you could feel your life-force waning. May I present to you, the Princess Shari-Rose, daughter of my brother Celdar-Moon, Shield Keeper of the West.'

Shari-Rose curtsied as the elf rose to his feet resting on an ornate cane with both hands. He studied her from a distance and shuffled forward to frown down on her. 'This will never do. I don't have time to wait for a child to grow into her powers and be trained. Go back to Conlaoch Diarmada and return when you have a suitable candidate.' He turned his back on the princess who stood there for a moment in stunned silence.

'Um...Aunt Liara, if I am not wanted here, can I go home?'

The queen shook her head. 'There are no others, Shield Keeper. The shield talent has not appeared since Celdar-Moon many years ago, until now. Come Shari-Rose. Show Garleon-Sun what we have been practising.'

If I can't do it, will she let me go home to Father and Neline-Dawn? She sighed.

The queen pointed at a crystal. Shari-Rose closed her eyes and released a tiny drop of her power into the gem. It flared alight for a split second, but was extinguished.

Garleon-Sun hmphed and sat down. He almost looked pleased as he addressed the queen. 'No, she doesn't have the strength required. You must ask Mage Nnarndam for one of his mages to replace me. I cannot work with this child.'

The princess felt joyful at the thought that she was not going to have to stay here. A big grin spread across her face.

The queen's lips tightened. 'I know what you are doing, child. It won't work. Show Garleon-Sun your power now please, for I do not wish to be cross with you.' There was a hint of steel in the queen's voice and Shari-Rose sighed.

'Fine. I'll do it, but I won't enjoy it.' With a deep sigh and roll of her eyes, the princess placed her hands upon her crystal rose jewel at the base of her neck. She breathed slowly and calmly. Her eyes closed as she concentrated all her energy on filling the crystal with magical power. The energy flowed through her and built in intensity until she pulsed with power. She opened her eyes and could see the aura of light surrounding her, many times brighter than the fairy had going up the stairs. The feeling was wonderful and exhilarating.

'More, more, let it flow through you. Light up the crystals.' Garleon-Sun was beside her, watching with shining-eyed jealousy on his ancient face. He urged her on and the princess gathered more and more magic into her.

She reached out a hand to the first crystal and poured magic into it. The fountain of magic inside her emptied into the hanging crystal which radiated with power.

'Good, good. Now the next one.' The old elf encouraged her and a satisfied smile appeared on his face as he realised she could indeed perform the shield spell.

The young elf had never felt anything as wonderful as the magic which flowed through her. Each time she filled a crystal she felt emptiness, but she concentrated hard to build the magic again.

After the second crystal was lit, a hand grabbed her own and she looked to see Garleon-Sun beside her. His eyes lit up like blue sapphire flames as her magic flowed to him as well. An expression of sublime peace came upon him and she felt a small amount of magic well up inside him and join hers to light the remaining crystals. Magic grew in exhilarating bursts, receded and was renewed once again. Each time took a little longer to create and Shari-Rose felt herself becoming more and more tired as they went along.

'Come, my dear. You are going splendidly. Only two more to go.'

She felt as though Garleon-Sun was contributing only a tiny amount of the overall force, but his encouragement spurred her on. When the last crystal was lit, the room glowed with incandescence as

Redemption

beams of light criss-crossed between each crystal to form a magical net, rather like a spider's web.

Garleon-Sun turned to her. His eyes were still aflame with power as he showed her rather than taught her how to push the magic upwards with the force of her mind.

The luminescence rose above the crystals and poured upwards through the window in the ceiling. Together they pushed the shield higher and higher until it joined the existing shield. The magic spread sideways now, flowing out to cover the entire South Lands and northwards to join the north, east and west shields above Conlaoch Diarmada at the very centre of the continent. In fact her magic was so powerful that she felt it even overlap the other shields and enhance the entirety of the Relorian shield.

As the last drop of magic was released, Shari-Rose saw Garleon-Sun collapse and felt her own legs give way. Her fall was broken by strong arms. She saw the green flames of her eyes reflecting on Daeron's face, then the light was extinguished and sleep overcame her.

WHEN Shari-Rose awoke, she felt tired, but also excited to have performed a shield spell, magic that only she, her father and two unknown mages could produce.

She felt a smile grow on her face and she opened her eyes to see the raised brows of Liara-Star and

Daeron as they looked down on her. The queen's expression was one of complete shock and Daeron's was surprise mingled with pride.

Liara-Star patted her cheek. 'Are you well, my dear? You gave us all a great surprise with your powers.'

Shari-Rose nodded and Daeron helped her into a sitting position. She was now on the velvet settee where she had first seen Garleon-Sun. Daeron sat beside her and the queen and several guardians stood in front. As Shari-Rose craned her neck to look past the elves, they moved aside and she could see the entire room. The old elf was nowhere to be seen.

'Where is Garleon-Sun? I am so happy I was able to help him.' The princess felt a flutter of fright in her stomach as though something dire had happened to him, but she did not understand it.

No-one answered her, but they all looked up through the glass window above them where a rainbowed mist could be seen in place of the blue sky.

'I don't understand, Aunt. What is going on?' Now the princess was really scared, for she knew what that mist meant, but she was loathe to believe it. 'No! He can't be gone. He was right here with me. I . . . I . . . need him. No . . . no . . . no . . .'

Her cries ended with a shriek and she threw herself sobbing into her guardian's warm chest. His steady arms were a comfort as held her close; maintaining his silence.

Shari-Rose cried for what seemed a long time, but would have been just a few minutes. Thoughts ran through her mind of the unfairness of everything: the accident with her nurse-maid; her father blaming her and sending her away; having to travel to live in a land of halflings; and now the death of the elf who was to be her mentor. It was too much for her to bear.

She beat her fists against Daeron's chest and he made no move to stop her. His shirt, soaked with her tears, clung to the well-formed muscles.

After a time, her strength gave out and Daeron lowered her to the settee once more. Her hair was matted to her face in places and in a disarray. Her eyes felt swollen from the tears and her lips trembled. She felt as though everyone must be staring at her and she looked to the floor, too embarrassed to meet the gaze of a room filled with guardians. *They must think I am mad, or a spoiled brat.*

Daeron sat beside her and she felt his arm around her. 'I'm sorry Daeron. This has all been a terrible shock and I'm so tired from the magic.' He pushed some tangled hair from her face, but remained silent. She looked up at him and saw unshed tears shining in his eyes. 'Thank you for looking after me, Guardian Daeron. It would be so much worse to bear without you.'

He laid a gentle kiss on her forehead and Shari-Rose felt her eyes go wide with surprise at his boldness in front of so many people. She glanced away from him and discovered that the shield room was empty except for them.

'I'm not going to like this, but I can see there is no choice but to stay here and be the Southern Shield-Keeper. Maybe helping Reloria will stop my regret for what I did to Neline-Dawn. Thank you for staying with me.' Shari-Rose sighed. She sneaked a glance at Daeron again and saw pride in his eyes. She knew that she had made the right decision to accept it.

He came over and knelt on one knee in front of her. His pale blue eyes looked steady and sure into hers as he recited the guardian pledge. 'By my life or death, I will protect you, Your Highness.'

MY GRANDMOTHER'S ROOM
Margaret Dakin

The sunlight strikes the ruby glass and jug,
It stains the lacy folds with crimson light,
And settles there upon the woven rug.
The room is shaded, musty, cool as night.

I look towards the gloom where lies the dread,
My aunt behind me pushes at my back.
I drag my feet and slowly touch the bed,
Afraid of what I'll see on pain-filled rack.

Old lady reaches for my cringing hand.
Dry skin and brittle nails enclose my arm,
Her toothless grin and shrunken gums demand
A struggle to retain my fragile calm.

But then I see that eyes show love the same,
As on her trembling lips familiar is my name.

Lifetime Regrets
Roz Glazebrook

JULIE walked along the cliff edge on her 70th birthday. She knew she only had a few more years and she wanted to make the most of them. She couldn't do any of the things she used to love most anymore, like bushwalking and kayaking, but she could still walk in wild places. She had sold her Brisbane home and moved to a small coastal town in Tasmania last summer.

As she walked along, she started thinking about her life. She felt she had had a good one. There were a few things that were still on her mind from many years ago. Things she still worried about, where she hadn't done the right thing. They weren't major things, but they had affected her. She felt she would like some redemption from them.

Her best friend Brenda was turning twenty-one and had planned a big party. She promised to be there, but she never made it.

A few days before the big party she was invited by a group of other friends to go horse riding for a couple of days at a riding farm at the foot of the mountains on the Tasmanian Central Plateau. She had never been riding before and really looked forward to the trip. They drove down to Deloraine late on Wednesday night and settled into the cabins on the riding property. She was working as a nurse in Launceston and had a long awaited four days off.

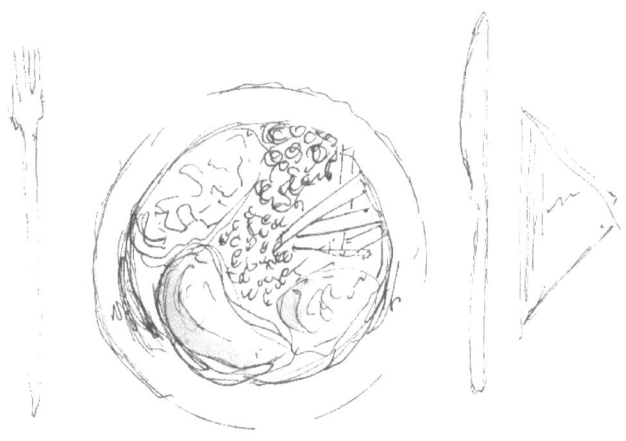

The birthday party was on Saturday night in Launceston

Redemption

The rides on Thursday and Friday were wonderful. The instructor taught them horse riding skills and took them on a couple of short rides around the country village. The big ride was on Sunday up into the mountains. Julie really wanted to go on that ride, but was torn because of her promise to her friend.

In the end Julie chose the ride over her friend's party and had regretted that decision ever since. She rang Brenda on Saturday morning to tell her she wouldn't be able to make the party. Brenda sounded disappointed. Their friendship was never the same afterwards and as the years went by, they drifted apart and lost contact. Julie moved to Queensland to continue her nursing career and Brenda stayed in Tasmania. Brenda never married. Julie married and had one child.

Maybe Julie was punished for breaking her promise. The ride was really great until the horses turned for home. On the way up the mountain, they followed the head horse docilely and the scenery was spectacular. When they reached the plateau, the horses galloped in the snow beneath fantastic snow-covered peaks. Betty, the horse school owner made them billy tea and damper and as they sat around on the islands of grass. Julie felt she had never been happier.

She nearly died on the return trip home. The docile horses suddenly took off down the mountain. Julie was inexperienced and before long lost her footing in the stirrups and could not hold the reins.

She clung to the horse's mane and tried her best to stay on. The worst part was when the horses reached the highway and bolted along it to the farm on the other side. At one point Julie's horse was galloping along the highway on the wrong side of the road. It was normally a busy road with numerous log trucks screaming along it. It mustn't have been Julie's time to die because no trucks came around the bend when she careered around a blind corner. A bit further along, the horse raced across the road and up the long dirt driveway to the farm. It went from a full bolt to a halt at the farm gate. Julie managed to stay on the horse somehow, but she never rode again after that horrific ride.

Years later, having moved interstate, Julie worked in hospital labour, orthopaedic, and surgical wards and loved the jobs, but she got sick of working shifts, particularly night shifts. She applied for and was successful in getting a job as a community health nurse, which was a normal 9am to 5pm, Monday to Friday job.

She mostly visited elderly and disabled clients in their homes. Her office was on the sixth floor of a high-rise building. She had the use of a government car to do her home visits. She worked with a large multidisciplinary team of occupational therapists, physiotherapists, psychologists, social workers, and health promotion officers and was very happy in her work. Their main role was to keep people out of hospitals and nursing homes by putting in services to keep people at home as long as possible. They all worked very hard and on Friday nights used to go down to the first floor of their building for happy hour at a piano bar.

Julie usually had only one glass of wine before driving home to her house, in a small beachside suburb thirty kilometres away from the city. She was allowed to garage the government car at home because there was no safe parking at the facility.

One night after a particularly busy and harrowing day Julie stayed on after happy hour with a few friends. They were all much stressed because their health organization was being reorganized again and they all feared for their jobs. A new Health Minister was threatening to reduce 'fat cat' public servants.

Julie left the hotel at 8pm after having three glasses of wine. When she got to the government car park, she did notice there was only one other car in the car park besides hers. She jumped in her car, reversed around and crashed into the car. As she got out to survey the damage she saw a man walking up the street towards her. It was his car and it was smashed in the side. Julie was very apologetic and told him it was all her fault. She gave him her work phone number and told him to ring on Monday and speak to John, the finance officer, and he would sort everything out.

She drove home very slowly after that and promised herself she would never have more than two drinks and drive again in her life. When she went into the office on Monday morning, she went straight into John's office and told him about the accident. He listened and then said the man had already called him. He told him there was nothing the Government could do because he shouldn't have parked his car in the government car park. There was a large sign saying it was a private car park. Julie felt absolutely terrible. That poor man. She didn't tell John she had been drinking and she had felt guilty ever since.

She did keep her promise and now, more than forty years later, she had never had more than two drinks and driven afterwards.

There was one other instance she regretted. Calling a handsome young priest *"Father What a*

Waste" to his face. She felt she was just saying what everyone was thinking and saying behind his back, but when she saw the devastated look on the priest's face she regretted it.

Julie wondered as she walked along the cliff, what had become of those three people whose lives she still felt guilty about. She lost contact with her old nursing friend, although she did hear through a mutual friend that she still lived in Tasmania and had done a fair bit of traveling since she retired. She never heard any more about the man whose car she wrecked, but she did hear the young priest was still in the priesthood. He was middle aged now and had overcome some health issues. He had moved to a country parish.

I guess many people have worse things to seek redemption for. Maybe Julie will find redemption in the next life, if there is one. If Julie could go back in time, she would attend the twenty-first birthday party and contact the man whose car she wrecked and offer to pay for the damage. She would also keep her mouth shut when she met that good-looking young priest.

THE BOARDROOM
Anne Olsson

John entered the room to attend the meeting
He smiled at a friend and extended a greeting.
The eight men sat around the board,
Here to discuss a plan that was flawed.

'We're here to keep the company stable,'
Cried Paul as he thumped his fist on the table.
'This plan will lead us into disaster,
And our problems will grow, and grow much faster.'

Tom argued the business was in a plight.
'This plan will save us and set us right.'
Soon the talk was intense and loud,
The mood in the room had quickly soured.

John looked on, saying little,
Watching as tempers became more brittle.
Soon the men were judging each other,
Angry and stern, brother against brother.

Blame was cast about the room.
The wrathful words built a pall of gloom.
But still John sat and quietly gazed
Upon these men so seemingly crazed.

Soft were the words John then spoke.
He told them blame was a pointless joke
'You only blame what you fear to see
Lies within yourself, as you truly be.'

Redemption

He then suggested a simple solution,
An idea to stop the verbal pollution.
'Listen,' he said, 'and heed what is said.
Hear with your heart and not your head.'

He described a new plan that was clear and concise.
He spelled it all out and stated the price.
So simple it was that all were surprised,
And much cheaper than they had surmised.

'Twas more than they thought to expect,
As they looked on John with a new respect.
The lesson was there, for life is a game:
Listen, and say little, and never to blame.

The Potty Curse
Bernie Dowling

Steele Hill's flat, Hendra, Brisbane, spring 1998

WE called him Potty and the name stuck. I was probably the one who coined Garry Potter's nickname as I usually bestowed new monikers on members of our racing crowd who gathered at the bar before the first race and after the last.

That was more than a decade ago as I was barred from all Australian racetracks in 1987. For quite a while, I kept in contact with many of our punting mob outside the track but I had not laid eyes on Potty for five years before he sat on my couch on that lazy Sunday arvo.

He continued to sip on herbal tea I keep on hand for guests while I finished my cooling coffee with a draught.

'I suppose you're wondering why I'm here, Steele,' Potty asked.

'Actually I was thinking about you just the other day.' I went to re-boil the jug for one more cup of coffee. 'I figured my thoughts conjured you here.'

'That could be right.' He brushed a finger across his left temple. 'I been thinking stuff like that meself, these days.'

I looked hard at him and saw a stranger. Not only did Garry Potter seem intent on indulging in gooey conversation certain to discomfort me. But he had not cursed since he arrived. I had called him Potty, as in potty mouth, for his habit of swearing like a politician. In the old days he could not go three words without a cuss. You like people to return to you in the same condition as they left even when the two events are years apart.

'I was only kidding.' I raised my palms upwards to show I was the same as ever, unable to resist a smart remark. I did not say any more in the hope Potty would forget why he was here and leave after drinking my tea.

'Why were you thinking about me?' Potty had the good sense to change the subject. He looked to be in his mid-30s, a few years older and a few inches shorter than me. He was conservatively dressed in light blue shirt and dark blue slacks.

I grabbed a glossy magazine off the coffee table in front of us. 'I was reading about this Pommy author in one of Natalie's arty mags.'

'Is Natalie still with you?' His voice could have done with a bit less incredulity.

'Sort of. Anyway, this Pommy author won an award for a fantasy book with a character called Harry Potter.'

I did read the story most of the way through after I found this J. K. Rowling author sheila, at high school, was a fan of the Clash and the Smiths. I figured she had peaked culturally as a teenager and she would be going nowhere, writing about boys and girls at a school for budding witches and wizards. She probably paid someone to get the award.

'That's funny,' Potty said in a peculiar unamusing way. 'A book brought me here, too.'

I knew he had to unburden so I waited for him to continue.

'You might remember, Steele, I was a bit wild when I was young. I did some things I am not proud of.'

'Is this about Alcoholics Anonymous, Potty? If it is, I forgive you.' I stood and went to take his teacup, even though he had not finished.

Potty shook his head. 'Remember when I would still visit you sometimes during the years after you were banned.'

I remembered vaguely, if at all. 'Yes,' I said. 'I appreciated that.'

'Anyway, a few months back, I was bored and began reading a book you lent me.'

'I lent you a book.'

'I actually stole it from your drawer years ago but I know now God meant me to have it.'

I stood again now the conversation was veering into icky territory. 'Awlright, keep the book.'

'There were two 100-dollar bills in it.'

Deja-bloody-vu, this was something I did not want to hear. 'Was this about 1991, 1992, and did you run into a furniture removalist's offsider named Lance who found two fifties in one of my books?'

'Lance is my brother-in-law and he is not an offsider any more. He owns four trucks and a storage shed. But yes he did tell me about the book with the fifties. But this was a different book. This one was called *Waiting for Godot*. You had two copies but only one had any money.'

'How did this happen?'

'I guess you put it there after a win on the horses or at poker?'

'No, how did you come to nick it?'

'Nothing much to it, really. I was around here, one day, and remembered what Lance had said. When you went to the toilet, I quickly flicked through a couple of books and found the money. When I heard you flush, I put the book down me shirt.'

'Go on.' I said.

'I had that book for six or seven years before God told me to read the bit about one of the thieves being saved. Do you remember it, Steele?'

'No.'

'Shall I tell it to you, Steele?'

'No.'

'Fair enough. But the thing is there were two thieves and only one of the four Evangelists documenting the crucifixion mentions one thief being saved. You know what that means, Steele?'

I shook my head and he continued. 'The odds of that thief being saved was seven to one.' He paused. 'Not good odds.'

I could see how Potty had worked out the odds of 7-1 but I was not sure of the mathematical rigour of the formula. I gave him the benefit of the doubt. 'Not good odds for either of the thieves,' I agreed. 'So what conclusion did you draw?'

'I decided I needed to redeem my past bad deeds starting with the worst one.'

'I was the worst one?'

'Of course not. Two years ago, Arthur Choker's wife Emily and I ran away together.'

A big mouthful of coffee went down the wrong way and I coughed the liquid back into my mouth. I thumped my chest with the side of my curled fist to regain composure. 'When you say Arthur Choker, do you mean Artichokes?'

He nodded.

Arthur Choker was a huge man, a standover merchant who had graduated from collecting debts for bookmakers to working for much nastier career criminals. I did not give him the nickname Artichokes which he had before he appeared on my radar. It was from an old joke about 'artichokes three for a dollar' and was a reflection upon the enthusiasm Arthur Choker had for exacting serious harm on people.

'You know, Potty, before you redeem yourself in the eyes of Artichokes, you should seriously consider giving me back my $200. Think of that gesture being a warm-up.'

'You don't understand, Steele. I want you to ask for Arthur's forgiveness on my behalf.'

Garry Potter might have given up swearing but I let loose with profanities under my breath. 'Why on earth would I do that?'

'I will pay you.'

That made me refigure the odds of my fronting the dangerous Artichokes. 'How much?'

'I'd like to give you more but I can only give you the $200 I took from you. Any other amount won't work.'

'That's ridiculous. I'm not risking being severely maimed for $200. Besides the last I heard Artichokes is still living in Sydney.'

'He is flying up to see Emily. Arrives day after tomorrow.'

'Emily'

'She's his wife. Or ex-wife. Or soon to be his ex-wife.'

'She's the one who ran away with you.'

'Yair. She left me three months ago. She might be able to give money for you to see Arthur before she does.' He turned over a business card to show me an address and phone number.

'I'll think about it,' I said, as I opened the front door for him.

He walked a few paces down the concrete path before he turned. 'One other thing, if Arthur asks, I haven't got any of that twenty grand.'

'What twenty grand?'

'The $20,000 Emily and I took from her and Arthur's joint account.'

As I drove to the outer-western Brisbane suburb of the Gap, I pondered another fine mess I'd gotten myself into. I am easily led; that's my excuse.

Garry Potter had given up swearing but I was not buying that redemption malarkey. He would have me believe he wanted to square the ledger with hired goon Artichokes. I could understand Potty not wanting to face Choker personally. I could even wear him being worried what the big bloke might do his ex, as in Choker's ex and Potty's too. But as a betting man, I had my money on Potter figuring that a vengeful Artichokes would come looking for him next after dealing with Emily. My A-plan after distilling all the info was to advise Emily to split and break her date with Artichokes. If she rewarded my gallantry good and well. If she told me to piss off, I would. Any fair person would concede I had tried. That was my A-plan. I had no B-plan.

Real estate brochures describe suburbs like The Gap as 'leafy'. At one level it means lots of trees. But what the brochures are really hinting at is the place is full of middle-class stiffs and, if you're one, you'll get along fine. It's the sort of space which makes a northern suburbs lad like me a little nervous. Technically the Gap is a north-western suburb of Brisbane. But we people who live in suburbs such as Hendra and Nudgee and Nundah and Toombul and Northgate and Wavell Heights and Virginia regard them as the true northern suburbs. We do not really approve of mucking about with a compass to come up with the concept of north-western suburbs. Our philosophy is kinda complicated even though My Cucumber Natalie calls it geographical primitivism.

Redemption

Still Robert Forster of the glorious, and now defunct, rock band the Go-Betweens grew up in The Gap as a kid. It couldn't be all bad.

House number 89 – I won't tell you the street was a largish low-set brick house of recent vintage. It exuded neither wealth nor modest means. It exuded The Gap. I had rung earlier not out of politeness but to make sure Emily was home. As soon as she answered, I had hung up.

I heard dance music from behind the front door. 'One-two-three-four, two-two-three-four . . .' a voice chimed above the music.

I rang the bell.

Emily Choker looked about 25, a decade younger than either Arthur or Garry. She was wearing grey and purple leggings and a grey sweat shirt with a purple wombat on it. She did not ask who I was. Just invited me in, turned off a CD player, and went to fetch a gun from behind the television on an oak table.

I am used to people pointing guns at me. 'Please don't shoot, Emily,' I said casually. 'I bought this T-Shirt only last week.'

'Who sent you? What do you want?'

I glanced at a pile of leaflets beside the TV. 'I heard you were a good aerobics instructor. I want to join your class.'

'You want to join my class?'

'I did but that's before I learned shooting was involved.'

'You're Steele Hill.' She put the gun on the table. 'Garry said he was going to ask some smart arse from his past for help. I told him not to bother.'

'If you are planning to meet with Artichokes tomorrow, you *need* help.'

'Arthur's a sweet sensitive guy.' She put two fingers on her mouth and removed them quickly. 'He won't harm me.'

'You really believe that?'

'I have to.'

We sat on two chairs at her dining room table. It seemed more proper for strangers to share coffee there than in her lounge room.

Emily Easton was 19-years-old when she married 32-year-old Arthur Croker in Sydney's Hyde Park. She was attracted to his aura of menace combined with his continual sentimentality. That was five years ago. It took three years for the attraction to wear thin. She grew to suspect Arthur was lying when he said his profession called on him to frighten people and to rarely harm them. She ran away with Potty when he made the offer, first to Hobart and then to Garry's home town of Brisbane.

'Where's home for you, Emily?'

'Sale, a country town in Victoria. I don't want to go back there. My parents left years ago and I have not kept in contact with them. I'm a city dweller now.'

I knew Sale was in Victoria as it had a racetrack, and the betting area code was VR which stood for Victorian Racing. I had never been there.

'And why are you meeting Artichokes tomorrow?'

'Are you a friend of Arthur's? How'd you know about that awful nickname?'

'We've met, Artichokes and I.'

'I don't think he's mentioned your name.'

'That's awlright, it's not up on billboards.' In a way it was, as I had made up my name from a billboard promoting a company touting itself as the Big Australian. 'The name Arthur Choker on the other hand is written in a lot of police notebooks and seared into the brains of people he has encountered in a professional capacity.'

'Arthur's violence is exaggerated.' Emily went to a drawer and withdrew a framed photograph. She showed to me. The huge Artichoke cradled a tiny koala in his arms. A note at the bottom right said the photo was taken at Lone Pine Koala Sanctuary in Brisbane. I couldn't help but think Lone Pine was a famous Wold War 1 battle at Gallipoli in the Ottoman Empire. Half the Australian soldiers were casualties.

I watched as Emily carefully replaced the photograph.

'Funny you knew where to lay your hands on that picture,' I said. 'You planning to show it to Artichokes? Yair, that'll fix everything up.'

She blushed slightly. 'I'm not running any more, Steele.'

Emily explained she had a mortgage on the house we were in and she was in the process of doing up the garage to conduct her exercise classes, saving money on the rent she was now paying for a hall.

She had got into the exercise game by watching 1980s Jane-Fonda videos, copying everything: the moves, the music, even the dress style. Her business started to pick up after one of her clients reminded Emily her workout songs were all a decade and more out of date. She updated, keeping some energetic tunes regarded as classics, and was getting by without making a huge amount.

'I swear I'll pay back Arthur every cent.'

'The twenty grand.'

She looked down at the floor and did not speak for a while after she raised her eyes. 'It was forty thousand,' she said softly.

'How'd you manage that? Surely your bank rang Artichokes?'

She had Potty practise forging Arthur's signature on a number of withdrawal forms which she co-signed. Luckily Arthur never gave the bank his mobile phone number which was for business purposes only, Artichokes' industry being threatening and maiming. She took the money out on three days spread over a month, on days when Arthur was working. Potty was waiting by the phone to pretend to be Artichokes but the bank never rang.

'What did you do with the money?'

'Garry lost $10,000 gambling in no time. Gambling was why I told him to leave in the end. After that, I put a deposit on this place and I was able to convince the bank I could afford to pay off the loan.'

Who knew you could sway a bank manager with a philosophical discourse on the financial power of aerobics. I swept an outstretched arm across the room. 'And you're gambling all this on your being able to persuade Arthur Choker, professional standover merchant and doer of physical harm, to forgive and forget. Half you luck, sweetheart.'

'You got a better idea, Steele.'

I didn't. But an idea which could not be much worse popped into my head. 'Lemme talk to him. I can say what you just said to me, about starting over.'

'That won't work. I think Garry was about to offer the same thing but he got scared before the words could come out. Arthur will think you're my new boyfriend and he won't like that. You will be even less safe than me.'

'Not if I can convince him you're paying me. He understands that sort of transaction.'

'But I can't afford to pay you.'

'That's awlright. You can take me down to the Paradise City, teach me a few moves to stay fit and healthy during the downtimes when I am not putting my life at risk.'

'I doubt'll work, but . . .'

My sentiments exactly. I was far from confident as I drove towards the Crest Hotel the next day. With luck, good or bad, Artichokes would be in his rented room in the hotel bordering one corner of King George Square in the Brisbane CBD.

I waited until the woman on reception was busy with guests and slipped around to the lift to ascend to the floor Emily had told me Choker's room was on. I knocked as a familiar odour filled my nostrils.

A soft, kinda squeaky voice barely penetrated the wooden door. 'Is that you, Em?'

For my turn, I spoke loudly so as not to stress the hired heavy when he answered the door. 'It's me, Steele Hill, Arthur.'

The door opened slightly and Artichoke's big head poked around it. I saw his eyes were red and the flesh above his cheek-bones was loose and puffy before the head retracted.

He pulled the door further open but it was stuck on something. Entering I saw two white bath towels wound tight and wedged against the bottom of the door. Choker motioned me to move in further. As you do I followed the direction of his hand and down the barrel of the Smith & Wesson towards a round table with a glass top on which sat a block of hashish, a pile of tobacco, a chillum pipe, a box of matches, and an ashtray.

'Who are you?' The soft squeaky voice had added a quaver to match the shaky hand with the gun in it. 'I seen you before.'

'I told you, Artichokes, it's Steele Hill. We've met a few times.'

'Yair, that's tight. Only don't call me Artichokes.' He pushed the gun further out towards my chest.' 'I don't like it.'

'I didn't mean anything by it, Arthur. You wanna shut the door?' I turned over my hand in the direction of the hash. 'The neighbours mightn't understand.'

He shut the door, locked it and asked if I wanted a cup of tea. I asked for coffee and Arthur said it was not good for you and I said tea would be lovely. All during our conversation, he pointed the Smith & Wesson at me while I tried to see if the safety was on, though I barely knew where on the gun the catch was.

He brought another chair over to the round table. Bringing the teas, he had to leave the gun in the kitchenette. Not that he needed it. The giant could break me in two with his bare hands.

He chewed on a biscuit, tiny between his thumb and fingers. 'I knew Em wouldn't come. I didn't think she'd send someone like you, but.'

I guess that could have been an insult but it did not bother me. 'It was my idea,' I said. 'I know she robbed you and ran off with another man but . . .'

I wasn't sure what the 'but' was so I shut up to hear what Artichokes had to say.

'I was going to kill her when I found she had taken $100,000 from our account.'

A hundred grand she had taken, not the twenty she had told Potty; not the forty she said to me. It had seemed odd a bank would lend an aerobics instructor enough for a house in The Gap. Having nearly a hundred grand deposit might swing it for you.

'She says she will pay you back.'

'How?'

He had me there.

Thankfully he changed the subject. 'You want me to fill you a pipe?'

'No thanks, but you go right ahead.'

He did and, after a big toke, he coughed. 'But she did leave the rest of the half-million.'

Ah, some more light shed on the situation. One reason the bank was not suspicious at the withdrawal of $100,000 was 400 grand was left. Artichokes had a lucrative business even if it was not very nice. 'Steele,' the astute businessman said. 'I still love Emily. When she left, I realised my Arthur was out of synch.'

Of course. His Arthur was out of synch. Arthur Choker's Arthur was out of synch. I might have a pipe after all. I sensed I was to be overpowered by a wayward sentimental conversation that could only end in tears. Mine. Tears of pain.

Redemption

'Do you know what I'm talking about, Steele?'

I hadn't a clue but I wish I knew whether admitting it was the right or wrong answer. I said nothing.

'I always shielded Em from the less attractive parts of my profession. But I think she knew and it affected our karma.'

'Karma as in Buddhist karma, retribution for doing bad things.' I asked feebly, trying to keep up.

'No, kama as in physical pleasure, as in Kama Sutra.'

Ah, the penny dropped. Artichokes was a convert to Hinduism, a religious movement I associated with Ravi Shankar and sitar music, and not much else. Still I was prepared to have a go at translating the world according to Choker. 'So you think your job does not represent your inner self, your true Arthur.'

He laughed at me. 'You think I'm saying Arthur?'

Obviously I needed it spelt out for me.

'A-R-T-H-A. My artha *is* my job, what I have always thought of as my life's calling. But when Emily left, and I began to think about everything, I realised my artha was out of sync with my dharma, my kama, and my moksha.'*

'I don't know much about that sort of stuff,' I said. 'But it seems to me you want a career change, a different jobska. And you think it might lead you to a happy life which will include Emily.'

Artichokes stood up and looked down at me with a strange expression, almost of awe, on his face.

'That's exactly what I am thinking. You put it so clearly, Steele.'

'I stood too because it was eerie to see him looking down on me with that worshipful look which should be reserved for rock-music sages. 'You know, Arthur, if you need a different kind of artha, maybe you shouldn't carry a gun around. Like a gangska.'

I didn't tell him Emily had one too in case it got him thinking guns might be divine.

'You're right, Steele. Now please take me to Em.'

That wasn't in my future. 'I don't think so, Arthur. Emily's left Garry Potter and she is rebuilding her life. If you want to be a part of that, come back in a year when you have changed your life and found a new artha, Arthur.

We struck a deal and the former Artichokes was so grateful he insisted I take the hash and the chillum pipe. If Arthur thought I was some sort of Holy Man he was way off beam. To tell the truth my premonition was that he would become Artichokes again within a few months. But I had bought Emily some time, had some hash to smoke, and should get back my $200 from Potty. Not a bad result.

I told Emily about what happened, the version without Hinduism and hashish, and she said she would contact Arthur in six to 12 months.

I asked my smart mate, the Gooroo, about Hinduism and he ran it down for me. Some of it sounded quite cool.

I did get my $200 back from Potty who had given up swearing on his path to redemption.

Redemption

I guess the three of them were after salvation. Potty wanted to be saved from the wrath of Artichokes who wanted redemption through a happy life with Emily who wanted shelter in The Gap from turmoil.

Potty was most surprised when I told him he was safe from Artichokes who had found religion. 'Well, I'll be buggered,' Potty said.

**Dharma (righteousness) artha (career), kama (sensuality) and moksha (spiritual freedom) are the four correct paths of human life. It is doubtful that Artichokes has a sophisticated understanding of Hinduism. Almost all Australians pronounce the name Arthur as Artha with emphasis on the first syllable. The usual abbreviation is Artie not Art.*

A LIFE GIVEN
Pat Cannard

History records through ancient writers that a strange event occurred
In the east some 2000 years ago, an event that shook the world.
A child grew up in Nazareth and lived for thirty years
a quiet life as a carpenter until one day a voice he hears,
an inner voice that prompts him to set out to journey wide
throughout the land of Moses' heritage; a voice not to be denied.

He found some friends to travel with in this dry and dusty land.
He healed the sick with touch so soft from that gentle loving hand.
He tried to teach them how to be kind and gentle with each other;
how to live in peace and love with friend and kin and brother.
His life was taken violently as he hung upon the cross,
He gave himself as sacrifice. Oh, what a tragic loss.

But when the women went to visit, no body could be found,
The tomb was empty; their hearts began to pound.
So Mary asked the question – Where have they put him? Tell me please,
And then a gentle voice addressed her: 'Mary' and she fell upon her knees.
For there before her stood the man whom she thought had died
Now risen back to life and to forever be life's special guide.

Redemption

And so each year we commemorate this deed – it's called the Easter season.
It's not only death that claimed him, but he did it for a reason.
The reason was to save our souls from being forever lost,
So we honour him this way and honour what it cost.

Lessons Learnt
Lucy Pilgrim

AT a crossroads I stand. A tall but brittle signpost erupts from the ground; an arrow pointing left and an arrow pointing right. To the left is a busy, smoke-infested town filled with the hum of everyday life. To the right a semi-desolate town that echoes the unknown.

All my life I have lived in the city and, while I admit it is dirty, loud and filled with the hustle-bustle of workers, it's familiar. It's home. Every junction, every old oak, holds the precious memories of a lifetime. The endless noise that crept in through classroom windows, newfound encouragement from a previously cold father after a teenage heartbreak; and the twinkle of the city that lit up every night, rain or shine. This place and these memories have made me who I am today – an individual moulded by the cruelness of the city.

That's not to say that I'm a bad person, I just prefer the more reserved things in life, like security, respect and the right to a good lawyer. That's what the city has taught me.

When I was 11, I remember seeing a murder case on the television where a man was sent to jail because he had a cowardly snob as a lawyer. This man was my neighbour; accused of brutally killing his wife. I knew he was innocent. It was a misty

Tuesday at dusk when I was on our rigid swing set outside, looking at the sky. I heard him screaming for help as a man in black ran out of his kitchen and into the woods. Next thing I knew he was in court being sentenced to 15 years to life

I told my Dad what I saw but he simply pressed a finger to his ice-cold lips. I didn't know it then, but that was the first lesson I learnt from the city: never get involved in things you should not.

The second lesson came on a summer morning just before I was due to start high school. I was riding down the boulevard, allowing the cool breeze to take me where I wanted to go. In the back of my mind I could hear the honks and yelling of inner-city road rage. I ignored it, but I shouldn't have. I was irresponsibly happy, and self-indulged, as an infant in a red dress was hit by a Corvette right in front of me. The worst thing was, I didn't even realise I was there when it happened until Dad showed me the front page of the paper the next day. The photo showed the infant lying on the ground, the Corvette covered in her blood and me, riding on my bicycle in the background smiling aimlessly. That was my second lesson: always be aware of everyone and everything for what you do not notice in the moment could be your downfall.

The third lesson I learned was by far the hardest. I applied to Harvard Medical School in hopes of someday becoming the outstanding doctor my father always hoped I'd be. So much pressure was on me to be accepted and I, stupidly, actually wanted to get in.

I thought that if I was accepted, I could do anything. I could say that I achieved something in my life; something that both Dad and I wanted so badly.

The exams were coming and I studied hard. Every night I stayed up into the dark hours fuelling my body with caffeine and Hersheys. Every night I quietly dismissed the whispers of doubt in my mind that I couldn't do it.

After the exams were finished I knew that Harvard would have no choice but to accept me. I had studied so hard my grades were going to be outstanding – the best they'd ever seen.

The lesson came on Christmas Eve 2004 when the letter arrived, stamped with a crimson red seal. I was denied. Dad was furious and so was I. At first. Then it started to make sense, that sometimes even when you really believe with all your heart that you deserve something, you still don't deserve it.

That's the third lesson the city taught me: never expect anything and presume nothing.

Those three lessons from the city are how I got here today. Now, standing at the barren crossroads, a suitcase in one hand and a briefcase in the other, I turn to the right. I am ready to enter the world of the unknown, a world without familiarity, security and life lessons. I am ready to leave everything that I have behind, to move forward and seek redemption on a journey of self-discovery in the city of desolate echoes and minds.

First Impressions Are Deceptive
David MacLaughlin

LAURENCE Harvey looked out of the nearest cabin window of his company owned twin-engine aircraft as it was flying to Broome where he was to have a meeting. No ordinary meeting as the Indigenous owners of a cattle property larger than any of his wanted a face-to-face discussion. It was all about his proposed purchase, with a Chinese and Russian consortium, of this pastoral property.

Laurie, as he liked to be called, folksier than Laurence, he reasoned, had come a long way since his early life in country towns. His father had been a veterinarian, his mother a special needs teacher. Both were caring parents and community minded. Laurie and his younger brother and sister spent a childhood in meeting rooms and draughty halls where their parents and others had gatherings.

The meetings were about the disadvantage of others and the lack of opportunity in health and education in country towns and the bush. Laurie and his siblings got used to being on their own and mixing on a daily basis with other children whom they did not know. Even then, Laurie could not see the sense in getting benefits for others when you did not get anything in return for your efforts. 'Mum and

Dad earn good incomes but it's peanuts if you want to buy a cattle station. I want to own something not just waste time helping sleepy country towns.' Laurie was destined to be an entrepreneur.

He had then no idea of what his future would be when he was young. As he was an intelligent lad he went to university and studied economics and animal husbandry. His siblings took a different path. His sister did medicine and his brother high-school teaching. However, he did know that what he would do in life would be for what he wanted to do not help somebody else's agenda.

Laurie at first could not see the point of Monetary Theory or Friedman economics in relation to owing and running pastoral properties. He had thought it was just a means to an end. If he wanted to get capital to buy large holdings, he must know about the flow of money as well as how breeding stock would make a pastoral property profitable. He knew plenty of good owners of individual properties who knew about breeding good stock but had little financial knowledge. The consequence was an unprofitable holding, which would eventually end up in loan defaults and loss of the property to the banks. Similarly, he knew financiers who could buy property at the right price but failed to make them profitable, as they had no knowledge of stockbreeding and management.

As you have now come to realise, our Laurie from the bush is single minded and is or will become ruthless in his pursuit of his dream of being an owner of large pastoral properties throughout Australia. Why just stop at pastoral properties? Why not own the whole production chain of properties: transport, meatworks, and shipping for export? Why not indeed, Laurie was beginning to think.

Skip forward a decade after his graduation with honours in his double degree from a university in Brisbane. Initially he worked for a merchant bank and travelled the world negotiating company mergers and takeovers. He earned a small fortune in fees for himself and his employers. However, if he was to buy a pastoral property, he needed more capital. His chance came when a large family-owned pastoral property came on the market. Its bankers who had repossessed the cattle station were offering the property for sale as mortgagee in possession.

Laurie knew the owners and the property well. It was in a good rain belt area and had the potential to double its stock holding and be very profitable. Now it was for sale at a forced price. Laurie organised a syndicate and launched a public share offering.

The company was successful and Laurie became the chairman and managing director of Felix Pastoral Properties. He began a breeding program and doubled the number of stock on the property. A large international private-equity firm made an offer of three times the original price. The Board of Felix Pastoral Properties recommended that the shareholders accept such a high offer.

They did and everyone made a huge profit. None more than Laurence Harvey. He had no qualms about the ethics of this transaction. He was adding value for the nation, the shareholders, and himself by buying low and improving the property then selling high. Simple economics with a social purpose according to his logic. The fact that the property no longer was owned by an Australian entity was just slight collateral damage.

Laurence did not stop at buying pastoral runs at distressed prices. He bought slaughterhouses, sale yards, transport companies, and minority holdings in new port developments. He had control from the farm gate to where his markets were. He let nothing stand in his way. His brother and sister would chide him about his apparent lack of scruples. Their aim was to help others and if any major financial reward came their way that was a bonus. Laurence did not see it that way. That is until the political climate changed five years later.

A minor political party rose, led by a feisty Jennifer Johnston who also came from rural Australia. An attractive brunette with an honours degree in political science, she was now the Darling of the Australian media. Buy back the farm and keep Australia for Australians were her political mantras. Her messages worked, as she became a Senator in the Federal Parliament. Repeatedly she targeted the way Laurence and his like preyed upon the distressed and bought pastoral properties only to sell them to foreign interests and pocket millions of dollars for themselves. Her message was a bit simplistic but it worked for her.

MIDNIGHT SCREAMS

At first, Laurence thought she was just one voice in the political wilderness looking for an easy target. He was working on his present project to buy through a Chinese-Russian consortium the largest pastoral property in Australia. The traditional owners of the land had bought this property with government assistance and it was never going to be easy to buy it from them. Laurence's enticement was that with the proceeds they could buy one of his improved properties at a discount and still have money left to use for housing or other infrastructure activities elsewhere. Jennifer used parliament as her forum to deride the sale as a sham and betrayal of Australian national interests.

Social media was viral with posts and tweets: *Harvey bullies traditional owners to sell, Harvey's interests come first, Australia for real Australians.*

Laurie had met his match in the form of attractive Jennifer Johnston. Laurence's past bullying tactics and backstabbing did not work in his favour this time. His backers distanced themselves from him. The Chinese-Russian consortium was having second thoughts on the proposal. The adverse publicity and scrutiny of buying the pastoral property were not worth it.

If Laurence was the villain. Jennifer was no lily-white do-gooder herself. She was as clever as Laurence and just as ambitious and manipulative. She knew she was on a winner that just happened to be part of her political platform. Australians were uncomfortable with their agricultural and grazing land being owned by foreigners especially the Chinese. Or more precisely, how the Chinese Government controlled their communist private sector companies.

In the dim recesses of Laurence Harvey's mind lurked an admiration for his parents and his siblings' community service involvement. Not the normal way to achieve power and wealth. Or was it? He had missed his dream of owning the largest pastoral property in Australia. Maybe he did not need it after all. He could redeem himself in the eyes of the masses by forming an alliance with Jennifer's political party and the various Indigenous land corporations to buy and manage Australia's pastoral industry. Redemption in Laurence's mind was entrepreneurial.

Jennifer and Laurence had a meeting. A working lunch in a private section of a Brisbane casino. The champion of the people Jennifer and the bush capitalist Laurence were guests of a multi-national entertainment company which owned casinos worldwide. William O'Brien the Australian CEO sensed correctly what his guests' ambitions were.

On a personal level, Laurie sensed a chemistry between Jennifer and him. She seemed willing to listen to his business case. He did likewise. Laurence needed redemption and Jennifer needed a major political cause that would have popular appeal. They agreed that the Australia Unlimited Party would back off from opposing the Laurence Harvey purchase of the Indigenous pastoral property. In exchange, the Harvey consortium would ensure total Indigenous staffing and operational management as a condition of purchase. The Foreign Review Board would not block the sale under these conditions.

So redemption for Laurie and political kudos for Jennifer were now assured. Or were they?

The Indigenous elder who was chair of the corporation that was owner of the largest pastoral property in Australia was miffed that these white Australians had not consulted him personally. John Blackman identified with his tribal grouping 'The Karajari mob from the Kimberleys. He was the chair of the Indigenous body that owned the property but he knew other committee members were partial to the idea of selling for a good price and buying more properties cheaply from the Harvey consortium.

John Blackman had been the beneficiary of a scholarship to go as a boarder to an exclusive school in Sydney. As fate would have it at the same time as William O'Brien. The pair had formed an unlikely friendship. John Blackman being used to tribal communal ownership had no trouble in accepting the Irish-Australian O'Brien's growing commercial entertainment empire. William O'Brien admired John's loyalty to advancing the cause of his tribal allegiances.

John and William combined to thwart Laurence Harvey's ambition. Defeating Laurence and his alliance with Jennifer's political aims was paramount to the interests of both men.

O'Brien reported to John Blackman the outcome of the lunch meeting between Laurence and Jennifer. John and William then came to an agreement. The casino enterprises would lend the Kimberley Indigenous pastoral property money at no interest to fund new infrastructure and breeding improvement programs. This would take care of the future of the property and leave the Indigenous owners free to purchase other properties when and if required.

The media and social media had a Twitter day. *William O'Brien the white knight helps Aboriginal land holding, What's in it for Bill, more casinos? Blackman trumps Harvey bid.*

Laurence and Jennifer were outbid by this new alliance of Indigenous Kimberley peoples and the capitalist O'Brien enterprises. John Blackman was ambitious for his own people but was every bit as ruthless as Laurence Harvey and Jennifer Watson.

Laurence had been hit for a six. He had not even thought that the Indigenous owners would ever consider arranging a deal with the growing O'Brien entertainment enterprises.

Jennifer's fledging political party quickly distanced itself from the Harvey proposal and continued to gain popular support.

John Blackman continued as chair of the Indigenous corporation that owned the largest pastoral holding in Australia. Now flush with O'Brien funds, the breeding and re-stocking of the property started in earnest. Within five years, John Blackman won a Federal Senate seat as an independent on a preference deal with Jennifer's party.

As the saying goes, `there is no such thing as a free lunch'. William O'Brien was expanding his Australian entertainment complexes, known by you and me as casinos. He reminded his friend John that the success of the Indigenous pastoral properties was in part due to his philanthropic generosity. In turn, John reminded his friend that his apparent generosity had been repaid in full due to the favourable publicity he got as the White Knight. Both men understood each other. William needed approval from the Competition Control Board. John needed influence and financial backing to achieve his ambition of becoming the next Prime Minister of Australia.

His opportunity came when the ruling Federal Government, which was a coalition of Labor, The Greens, and Jennifer's party, had a leadership spill. By default, John Blackman became the first Indigenous Prime Minister of Australia. He was a considered a short-term choice that the party could dump nearer to the fixed four-year term election date. However, John Blackman remained leader of the new coalition when it was returned to power at the next election.

Laurence continued to expand his agricultural empire. He craved redemption but actually did not need it. He was making Australia into the richest agribusiness nation in the world.

Jennifer Watson had never sought redemption. Just as well as she was never going to get it.

John Blackman rose to the highest political office in the country. He was only a professional politician but the electorate tolerated his misdemeanours as he put Australia first in all his policies. As for William O'Brien, he was as always the king maker. He prospered at the expense of addicted gamblers but that is life. Who needs redemption?

DEATH IS AN ESCAPE

Bakthi Ross

An unpaid debt,
No deliverance,
Except the gallows.

A deep trench, he buried himself into,
His contrition for his sufferings,
He killed people.

He couldn't make amends for his sins,
He left home, hid in many dark places,
He mingled with the dark and the destitute.

He was reduced and impoverished,
He had no values, His quality of life diminished,
He degraded himself in many things.

Class and status are no longer a concern.
He hid from the law, his family and friends.
But his conscience was a big load, he couldn't redeem himself.

He travelled from place to place,
One day he was a swaggie, next day he was a layabout,
He changed his appearance and his name,
But still there wasn't any redemption from his conscience.

He was good for a while with new people,
Then when they asked questions about him,
He had to pack and leave. He was like a rodent, ran from place to place.

Redemption

He couldn't even stand his own odour,
He dunk himself in the river,
And waited naked until his clothes were dry.

If he knew how to handle abuse, he wouldn't have killed,
He lived a dreadful life and suffered even more than the abuse,
No exchanges for his sins, he was old and wounded.

He could hardly breathe,
Death is the only redemption for his sufferings,
A deliverance from his sins,
Angels waited for him.

Running
Margaret Taylor

MY name is Brendan O'Hara and on the morning of 20th February 1852 I killed my brother Sean. It was an accident.

I can never forgive myself so how could I expect forgiveness from my Ma and Da.

Since the Great Famine in Ireland we were struggling to eat, pay rent and with no prospects of work Da said we should to go to America. My two older brothers, Michael and John, had already left for New York with the Lafferty family, our neighbours from the next farm. Ma didn't want to go to America, insisting, 'We will all be killed and scalped by them red injuns.'

My sister Mary went to England to live with Ma's sister in Liverpool. Kitty had sent word to Ma that Mary could find work in a laundry to earn her keep.

With Ma, Da, me and my younger brother Sean left at home, Da sat us down one day saying, 'If we don't leave Ireland we'll all starve. Look at poor Seamus O'Malley and his family, they're all skin and bone. I don't think any of them will see the year out.' Ma nodded in agreement. Da continued, 'We're all helping each other but most of us have nothing else to give. The potatoes are not growing and neither is anything else.' Ma started to say something but Da stopped her. 'I know what you're thinking, but we can't all go and live with Kitty in Liverpool.' Da looked at me and Sean, 'Ma won't go to America so if we want to stay alive, and together, our only choice is to go to Australia to find our fortune in the goldfields.'

Our family left Ireland in 1850 and boarded a boat for Victoria, Australia. We were in steerage because it was all Ma and Da could afford after we had sold everything we possessed. All we had were clothes and what few items we could carry.

The journey by sea took nearly four months and I swear to God I've never felt so sick in all my life. Sometimes the storms were so bad we had to stay below deck for days without any light and not much fresh air. The smell of unwashed bodies and vomit is something I'll never forget, although I'd like to. There were times when I thought we might die. Some people did. Most of them were children.

After the long sea journey we finally arrived in Hobsons Bay, Melbourne. We thought our journey had come to an end but soon found there was still days of travelling by road before we reached the goldfields.

We had made friends on the ship with the O'Sullivan family and on arriving in Melbourne stayed together to pick up our digging supplies. We were given tents, prospecting pans and cradles, tin pots, picks, shovels, crow bars, and cooking pots. After getting all the supplies we found a drayman to take us to the goldfields in his cart. Da had always been good at bargaining so he got the best price for us.

Back in Ireland we could never have imagined what life was like on the goldfields. The heat, dryness, red-back spiders, flies that got into your eyes, ears and nose, white ants and mosquitos were just a few of the things we had to learn to live with.

Work on the goldfields was hard. Not many women were there. We had tried to get Ma to stay in Melbourne until we made enough money to send for her. She was having none of it, 'What would I be doing in Melbourne all by meself?' she asked, 'and who would look after you three eejits?'

The four of us lived in a tent in Canvas Town which was on the south bank of the Yarra River. We slept on mattresses stuffed with leaves. Outside the tent we had a bucket of water and a cooking fire. Ma cooked mutton, made tea, and baked damper on the fire. At least we had food every day which was more than we had in Ireland. The O'Sullivan family were in a tent further down and sometimes we got together for our meal if either family had managed to get a few vegetables to go with the mutton.

One day, coming back from a day's backbreaking work Da stopped in his tracks and pointing to the tents spluttered, 'What's me shirt doin' hangin' on the tent pole?' Sean and I looked in the direction of Da's pointing finger and saw his threadbare, green cotton shirt flapping in the breeze. I looked at Sean who shrugged his shoulders. We hurried after Da who was striding towards our tent. Although we stayed outside the tent we could hear every word and probably everyone else could too. 'For the love of God woman...me favourite...' and '...it was auld anyway.' The brief argument came to an end as Ma stepped outside the tent followed by our red-faced Da.

'Look,' Ma said, 'how can you tell our tent from anyone else's?' She made a sweeping movement with her arm over the field of identical tents, 'They all look the same.' Hands on hips and smiling smugly as if she had just made a discovery that would change the world said, 'Now you won't have to go searching for our tent because you'll be able to see it for miles.' There was no arguing with Ma once she made up her mind about something so we did what we knew was best. We kept quiet.

I was sixteen and Sean was fourteen when we started working in the goldfields with Da. Usually the three of us would work together, standing in a stream using the cradle and the gold pan to separate gold from the gravel and water. We would laugh and joke with the other men who were from all walks of life, all ages, all nationalities, and all with the same hopes of something better for themselves and their families.

We were making a decent living from digging and Da said, 'If our luck holds out for another year we'll have our own home.' Da also wanted to start a business as a carter. One of the diggers he had worked with had bought his own cart and was making good money transferring stores from the seaport to the goldfields. The thought of getting out of the goldfields, into a proper house, and working together in a family business kept us going through the drudgery of each day.

One day, while working in the goldfields, Da told us, 'I've heard there's a spot downstream where a man struck lucky. He found a gold nugget the size of a potato so I'll try me hand there. We didn't have potatoes in Ireland but we might get some here.' Da chuckled at the thought. 'You two stay here and carry on.' He was still chuckling as he walked away.

As soon as Da was out of sight Sean took it as an excuse not to do any more work. 'Come on Sean, give us a hand', I asked, 'put your back into it.' Sean sighed, 'Me back's had enough for today. I'm sick of it.' He put his gold pan down into the stream and made to step out of it.

The hot sun and tiredness had got to me. I lost my temper, lunged forward and pushed Sean. He lost his balance and I grabbed for him but it was too late. He slipped on the stones and fell backwards onto a small boulder. I'll never forget the sound as his head hit the boulder. It was sickening.

Sean was a joker, always playing tricks on us. My mind went back to the time when Da had killed a chicken and brought it into the house for Ma to prepare. A short while later Sean, who was ten years old at the time, came rushing into the house shouting, 'Me finger, me finger' and held up a bloody hand with a space where his first finger should be. Ma rushed towards him, 'Oh, Jesus, Mary and Joseph,' she said crossing herself, 'how many times have I told you not to play with knives. Here, let me see.' As Ma took hold of Sean's hand his first finger popped up and he started laughing. Ma looked at the finger, the blood and then at Sean. You little divil. Do you want to give me and your father a heart attack?' She lifted her hand to give Sean a playful clip around the ear but he dodged it and ran out of the house laughing. Da started to laugh but a 'look' from Ma soon stopped that. We all knew that look.

Remembering that time I thought, for a brief moment, this might be another of Sean's pranks and wondered how he had done it. As I saw the blood from Sean's head seeping into the stream and looked into his lifeless eyes I knew it wasn't a prank. I watched as my brother's blood, mingling with gravel and water, trickled into his gold pan.

There was screaming inside my head but no sound came out of my mouth even though I was crying. Fear was strangling me. I didn't want to think about telling Ma and Da what had happened, that it was an accident. They would blame me because I was supposed to look after Sean. That was my job.

I did the only thing I could think of. I ran away. It didn't matter where to because now I didn't belong anywhere.

When it got too dark to see I stopped running. I was hungry, thirsty and exhausted but the worst part was the sadness. It felt as if I was wearing a heavy, dark cloak which weighed me down. I dropped to my knees and prayed to God to wake me up from this dream, this nightmare. Then I slept.

Redemption

The morning light and bird sounds woke me up. When I realised it wasn't a dream I started running again over the rough uneven ground. Running was hard but I needed to punish myself. Being still made me feel worse. I couldn't stop thinking of my family. I missed Ma and Da, I wanted my brother back, our life as a family back and I wanted to go back to Ireland where we belonged. I wanted what I couldn't have.

Too tired and weak to run any further I lay down under a tree. Sleep came quickly and with it a strange dream which kept repeating itself. In the dream I was running over the same patch of ground which would change to me being inside a building, the likes of which I had never seen before. There was someone else in the dream, a woman, although I couldn't be sure as I never saw her.

I don't know how long I slept before hearing a woman's voice calling me, 'Brendan, Brendan.' I thought it was Ma but felt she wouldn't want to speak to me ever again. The woman kept calling my name. Looking in the direction of her voice I saw her. She was wearing strange clothes; a shirt, trousers, and had short hair. I blinked, expecting the vision to go away but instead she smiled. It was a kind smile but I didn't smile back because I knew she could not be real. 'Hello Brendan,' the apparition said, 'I am so glad we have finally met. My name is Emma.'

She told me to look into the distance to my left saying I would see Ma, Da, Sean, my brothers Michael and John and my sister Mary. I knew it was impossible and laughed. Not a real laugh, but one of those laughs when you know something isn't true.

I was about to run when Emma said, 'You are dead Brendan. You died in 1852 shortly after the accident with Sean. You ran into the bush, got lost, and without food or water perished.' I gave another one of those laughs. 'It's true Brendan. How would I know your name and about the accident with Sean?'

'Well how do you know?' I didn't believe what she was saying but curiosity got the better of me.

'Sometimes I see people who are dead and I see you because my home is built on the land where you died.' I thought of Ma who would have said, 'The poor woman has delusions,' so I nodded as if I believed her.

'I have seen you in my home many times but you have not seen me until now. That's because you have not been ready to let go of your guilt and sadness. It has kept you here unable to join your family.'

I began to feel uncomfortable. How did she know how I felt?

Emma continued, 'I have helped other lost souls find their way and I can help you reunite with your Ma, Da, your brother Sean, your brothers who went to America and your sister who went to live in England. They are waiting for you Brendan. It is more than one hundred and sixty years since you passed and your family know what happened to Sean was an accident.'

My sadness, shame, fear and guilt came rushing to the surface nearly choking me. I had to get away from this strange woman but mostly from the feelings which were swamping me. I wanted to run away but was too tired. I had been running for a long time and wanted to stop. What if Emma was right?

As if reading my thoughts Emma smiled and said, 'Look to your left Brendan.'

I did as she said and in the distance saw my family, smiling, beckoning me. There was Sean with his cheeky lop-sided grin, Ma in her best dress, Da in his favourite shirt, along with Michael, John and Mary. They were just as I remembered when we all lived together in Ireland. It caught my breath and I wanted to laugh, cry, wave, run to them.

I started walking towards them but stopped as the thought crossed my mind that it was probably a dream and I would wake up to reality at any moment. I turned around to look at Emma. Her kind face and eyes smiled as she said, 'Go.' and shooed me on my way with her hands.

Seeing my family, hearing them calling my name, smiling, waiting for me with open arms, I knew, without doubt, that I was forgiven.

I walked towards my family, eager to be with them. Turning around I waved goodbye to Emma and with hands on my heart said, 'Thank you.'

A Mouse in the House
Pat Cannard

Part 1: A Blind Date:

THE owners of a big old country mansion in the hinterland took the night off and drove to the Gold Coast for dinner, dancing, and a visit to the Casino. The only person left in the house was the man's valet who was quite ancient, cursed with creaky bones, and hard of hearing. Once he retired to his flat attached to the rear of the property even a Jumbo Jet roaring overhead would have sounded to him like an annoying mosquito. Silence then descended, apart from the few squeaks and groans that pervade all old buildings.

In the kitchen, a mouse's whiskers quivered as it poked its head out of a hole under the kitchen sink. It moved swiftly up the side of the drain pipe and into a space just big enough for it to squeeze through to get into the kitchen itself. It scampered across the tops of cupboards, into drawers that had not been completely closed, searching, searching for any tiny morsel to appease its appetite.

It spied a bowl of fruit in the middle of the kitchen table. Up the table legs, across the table it scampered, climbed into the bowl and was about to nibble on a juicy pear when a voice startled it. 'Get off me, you smelly rodent, go and find some cheese to eat.' With that, a chorus of other voices began jabbering at the mouse. 'Leave us alone; get out of here. We're the royalty of the food kingdom in this household. This is no place for you.' The mouse was scared away from the fruit. He scooted further into the house, knowing there'd be a few crumbs on the floor of the play room where the visiting grandchildren ate their meals, leaving the fruit grumbling and muttering about the vermin that dared to invade their space.

The Delicious apple then rolled out of the basket, closely followed by the orange. They tumbled across the table and down on to the floor. The banana slithered after them and one by one they joined the fruit already on the floor. They felt free as they romped around, rolling and sliding across the tiles. Then they gathered into a circle and began to talk. Only one fruit was left in the basket, small and dark in colour; it sighed. *Off they go. Perhaps tomorrow night they will let me join them.*

Light was spilling across the floor from a space under the door leading into the laundry. A security light had been left on when they began to share their stories, each boasting about its own beauty.

'Let's hear from you first, orange,' urged the pear. The orange was short of breath as it began. 'I wish they wouldn't squeeze me so hard trying to find out how much juice I contain. I know I'm ready for eating and not looking forward to it, but I have to accept this end to my life. It comes to us all. I was once a beautiful flower, sweet-smelling and pretty, high up on a tree. Then I evolved into a marble-sized ball. I loved the rain that quenched the thirst inside me to make me grow. I soaked up the sun that burnished my skin until the busy hands of the pickers selected me as a perfect specimen for the farmer to send to market. The only problem was once we got to the packing shed, the tumbling and twirling on the conveyer belt gave me a pain until at last I was plucked up by gentle hands and carefully placed with other beauties into a box. We were packed so tightly that the jolting ride to market kept us from bumping together and getting bruised. Just one of us was selected at the market to be tested for sweetness and then we were on our way to the shop where we could be sold. There I was passed over by several hands before someone picked me up and put me in a bag to take home. How did you get here, grapes?'

'Well, much the same way but we grew lower to the ground on a vine – not as individuals but as a group. We feel lonely when we are separated from the group. The difference in the shop is that people pick some of us off before leaving us and taking another bunch. This means we are less than perfect for the next customer so sometimes we are overlooked until we get so old and withered we are not suitable for sale.'

On and on the stories went from the pear, to the apple, to the banana, each of them being admired by the others for their perfect formation. Meanwhile the little dark fruit left in the basket listened with envy at their stories, wishing it could join in. *Why don't I try?* It began with a squeaky voice barely able to be heard by the group on the floor. 'Can I tell you how I got here?' it asked.

The other fruit rolled together whispering, and wondering where that voice had come from. Then the pear realised and said, 'Oh, don't take too much notice of that thing. It's only a blind date, and it's brown and ugly to boot. Just as well it can't see itself.'

The little fruit felt sad and worthless, not needed in the world of popular fruits.

While the fruit were having fun in the kitchen, the mouse was running riot through the house. Up the stairs it went – into the library to scurry into the corner beside a row of books, trembling with fear, when it heard noise and felt movement in the room.

Part 2: Frolics in the Library:
Stirrings on the bookshelves became rustling, then thumps as the books began to come to life, ignoring the comics on a nearby table that the majority felt were usurpers in their refined presence. Suddenly the door was flung open and the occupants of the music room rushed in – the instruments had arrived!

In lumbered the tuba, in danced the piccolo; the trumpet blasted in, the drums thundered in, clashing and banging, the violin sauntered in and the zither came on tippy-toe. It was party time!

The instruments tuned up and began their selections. Excerpts from Prokofiev's *Peter and the Wolf* excited the children's books which had been poked away in one corner but now edged forward all agog with the sound of the notes. They romped, squealing and giggling, until the music changed to *Brahms Lullaby* – the signal for them to scamper back to their corner and go to sleep.

The rendition of Strauss' *Blue Danube* had the romance books waltzing around the room and then into a romp to the sounds of the *Trisch Trasch Polka* until they retired exhausted when the travel books came alive to the sounds of *I've Been Everywhere* – their pages fluttering open on scenes of great beauty around the world.

A change of tempo with excerpts from Strauss' *Die Fledermaus* encouraged the joke books and other humorous stories to dance around the room.

Meanwhile the poetry books had been resting calmly awaiting the gentle sound of Christian Sinding's *Rustle of Spring*. They sat quietly in a corner, their refined and tasteful contents on display – devoid of descriptive violent scenes and startled when suddenly the music changed; the tuba and the drums recreating the scenes of chaos via Richard Addinsell's *Warsaw Concerto*:

This alerted the war books, standing straight and regimented in their shelves. It was their turn to tramp into the centre of the room, their very aggressiveness declaring they would not be trifled with.

When the instruments tired of this display of power, the lively music of Bizet's *Carmen* brought out the murder stories, their covers displaying gloomy back street scenes, knives, pistols and dead bodies, causing the religious books to huddle together, well away from such revolting scenes; some with downcast eyes, others with love and hope shining from their covers. The instruments noted this and changed over to music from Handel's *Messiah*.

The dictionary began interrupting, constantly correcting the wrong spelling and bad grammar it could see as pages from each genre were displayed – scurrying to and fro buzzing among the books to the violin strings' speedy tempo of Rimsky Korsakov's *The Flight of the Bumble Bee*.

Throughout all society there are those who consider themselves 'a class above' and, the book world was no different. The volumes of the encyclopaedia, surveying the scenes from on high, were making sure everyone KNEW they were the royalty of the library as the violin continued with the solo of Handel's *The Arrival of the Queen of Sheba* evoking the pomp and circumstance of a royal parade.

There was no class distinction among the instruments in this household regarding the type of music played. Their repertoire included everything from nursery rhymes to excerpts from opera. Therefore the theme from the TV show *M.A.S.H.* provided the medical journals, which had been piled on a table, an opportunity to slide on to the floor then scamper among all the books giving advice on treatments for asthma, arthritis, colds and flu but also giving advice on treatments for mould, rust and how to get rid of paper mites, which can all create health problems.

Heavy metal music which some of the other books could not bear to hear, crashed and clanged, bouncing off the walls with only the books on trains, cars and boats jumping for joy, the rest closing up and scuttling away.

The comic books were sad that any music that resembled anything that might appear in their genre had been forgotten. With all the activity, they had been pushed off the table and were scattered around the edges of the room. They began to think their part in providing reading material for the family was worthless.

At last the instruments decided that their finale would be given over to the violin to play Vivaldi's *Four Seasons*. First came *Autumn* that made the books think it was time to wind down their nocturnal activities. The notes from *Winter* made them shiver and shake with thoughts of snow and wind. Next came *Spring* where they could hear the songs of the birds and the tinkle of the streams. As the violin performance drew to a close with the final notes of *Summer* the books thought they could hear the coming thunderstorms. They began to return to their rightful places on the shelves. Only the comics and the sleeping children's books remained where they were, with the latter oblivious to all the noise and activity of adult fact and fiction.

The instruments knew it was time to go back to their room, the zither leading the way enthused by the reaction of the books to their visit to the library, determined to do it all over again in the future. The house settled back into peaceful slumber.

When the owners of the house came home they found the fruit scattered on the kitchen floor. They had no way of getting back into the bowl. 'Drat that possum, it keeps getting in somehow,' said one. 'We must have disturbed it before it could eat any of the fruit. Look, only the date is still in the basket. It's a perfect shape and I love dates. I had forgotten I'd put it there. It's the sweetest of all the fruits. It will be ideal for my lunch tomorrow.' On hearing this, the little date felt its self-esteem had been restored. *I'm best, after all.* There was silence from the floor when they realised they had been outdone by what they had regarded as an insignificant addition to the fruit bowl.

The next day, when the master entered the library he tut-tutted that his grandchildren had left their books all over the floor. 'And just look at the mess made with my comics,' he muttered. He began to tidy them up, but as he flicked through the pages he got absorbed in reading the contents of Superman and Batman and chuckling at the antics of Donald Duck and Mickey Mouse. 'I don't suppose most people would appreciate that they are my favourite reading material that help me relax at the end of a hard day at work,' he mused out loud.

This was a liberating moment for the comics as they now realized they were not the poor relations to the books after all, but they held an important place in the library.

And what happened to the little mouse? As soon as all the noise subsided it came out of its hiding place, skittered across the room, down the stairs and into the kitchen. It reached the cupboard under the sink and arrived safely back in its nest sighing with relief at having survived the night. It made a vow to move out to a normal household where it could nibble in peace in the quiet of the night.

Mothers-in-law
Margaret Dakin

ALICE Thorne, unmovable as stone, sat close to the aisle on the groom's side of the Cathedral. No one was beside her in the front pew.

The unaccustomed necessity to sit idle at this early afternoon hour compelled her, for the first time, to accept that she had no close kin other than her son, who stood now before the altar rail. The sorrows of the past few months were like a weight on her shoulders. She looked down at her hands clasped in her lap. A ray of light coming through a window, stained them red and blue, and she longed for a piece of embroidery or tatting, or even a column of figures to add up, to distract her from the occasion. Her hatpin pulled at the hair screwed into a tight bun. She had jammed it through her newly acquired black hat, in that moment when her son called to her, 'Come on Mum, we'll be late.' She had felt like crying at the exasperation in his voice.

'She's left her canary here, Robert. I presume I'm supposed to look after it while you're away.'

'No need to fuss with it at the moment, surely? And Mum, her name is Susan.'

SITTING in the church now, Alice wondered what her life would be in the future as she waited for someone to notice she was no longer of use, like a piece of old furniture, fit only to be consigned to the upper regions of the house. She looked at the broad back of her son in his new dark suit and saw him lean over and say something quietly to his best man who nodded and patted his coat pocket. Robert tugged at his bow-tie and ran a finger round his collar, and for an instant she felt a hatred for the other woman. He had come to her for help with that tie just an hour ago.

'Mum, can you give me a hand here?'

'Why did she have to insist on such a formal ceremony, Robert? And why the Cathedral?' She had frowned as she tugged at the bow-tie. 'Isn't our local church good enough for her – and your father just three months in his grave?' She tucked the white handkerchief a little further into the pocket of his jacket.

'Now Mum, don't be like that. She only wants everything to be just right. We've waited so long.'

'You could have married before and got your own place, Robert. There was nothing to stop you.'

'There was plenty to stop us. All these years the business has hardly been able to pay me a wage, let alone enough to support a wife. You should know that from doing the books. Father's useless pipe dreams have always kept us on the verge of bankruptcy. Now I should be able to run the place properly and Sue can give you a break from your duties in the office – at least for the time being.'

He'd looked away, and his mother could see he was embarrassed at even this oblique reference to his hope that, within a year or two, he might become a father.

'I'm not too old, am I Mum? Am I being selfish tying her down? She's twenty years younger. And the old house . . . but she says she doesn't mind moving in. We want to be on hand to make sure you're well looked after.'

Alice had reminded herself this was the most practical arrangement. 'You're only fifty, Robert, and you're a fine figure of a man. Susan's a lucky girl.' Alice had straightened the small sprig of orange-blossom in his lapel, avoiding his eyes. She wasn't going to let herself be excluded from the business altogether, but this was the last time she would be called upon to do any personal task for him. From now on he would turn to his wife.

Her mind was drawn back to the present as she saw the organist glance in the mirror and rearrange the music. Behind her she heard the congregation murmuring, then rising, as the strains of the *Wedding March* filled the church. Alice clutched her walking stick but did not stand or look round.

She was aware that the few relatives who were on her side of the church had never seen Susan before. Not many had been able to come all this way for the wedding, and those who had made the effort would be curious. Alice knew they must have been talking among themselves, wondering how the young woman would cope with her new life in the home of her mother-in-law. The charitable among them would say, 'Alice has always done her best.' Others might call her a 'sour old biddy'.

As the music swelled, Alice put her hand on the end of the pew. With difficulty she pulled herself half around till she could see the people on the other side of the church, all strangers to her. They were looking back towards where the bride would enter the church. Alice turned further and saw the fair young woman pausing in the doorway, her hand on the arm of a tall youth. Robert had told her that Susan's brother was giving her away, as her father was no longer alive.

The woman walked slowly down the aisle, her features, seen through the lacy veil, unremarkable in repose. She lifted her skirt with the gloved hand that held a bouquet of pink roses. As she neared her husband-to-be, her face was transformed almost to beauty as she smiled. Alice thought of her own wedding day more than fifty years before, but could recall nothing of her expectations or hopes. Would the happiness of this girl gradually diminish as the years passed? Certainly she would find herself a widow at a much younger age than Alice was now.

Susan finally stood beside Robert and they turned briefly to each other as he touched her hand. The man and woman, no longer naively young, looked into each other's eyes, and Alice could see the bond, so tender yet strong, between the two.

She rebuked herself for her resentful thoughts. Robert deserved a life as a husband, not always just the son. She must accept that things would be different. Perhaps it could be enjoyable to have a grandchild to liven up the old house. She saw herself sitting in the sun, hands finally still, her eyes on the child toddling on uneven feet, his hand out-stretched with something he wanted to share.

Alice recognised that her new daughter-in-law was a good person and would not be difficult to live with. On the few occasions when Robert had brought her to the house she had been quiet, shy, respectful, allowing Robert's father to hold the floor as he always did; showing interest as he regaled her with details of his latest scheme, eager to convince her, at least, that it would be a money-spinner.

Alice made up her mind to prove that those who shook their heads were wrong – two women could share the same kitchen.

Suddenly she saw that kitchen as she'd left it to come to the church – all tidy as usual, the cat's dish clean, the cat asleep in its bed. But something imposed itself on that scene which had been the same for so many years – the bird cage on its stand over near the window – the only thing other than a few clothes and personal treasures that Susan had brought to the house.

What had she done in that moment as she delayed leaving for the church? She was giving the canary water, then Robert, impatience in his voice, called her to the car. She'd turned to the hall-stand, secured her hat, then shuffled out, neglecting to latch the door of the cage.

Redemption

Looking at the crucified figure hanging high over the unfamiliar altar, Alice closed her eyes and sent an urgent prayer. *Please Jesus, look after her yellow canary. Forgive my moment of malice. Give me the strength to be patient in the years that I have left to me, because you know how hard they will be.*

Alice turned to look at the front pew on the other side of the church and caught the eye of the other mother, whom she had met for the first time a few moments ago. She smiled and nodded slightly.

Susan's mother smiled also, and put her hand on the arm of the pew. Alice noticed that the rays of the sun through the church window now washed that hand with red and blue.

On Top of the World
Jeremy Leung

I GAZED upon the glittering sapphire starlight that danced from light years away. My toes embraced the sand beneath my bare feet, and wondered if my career at NASA would ever take me beyond this tiny planet, Earth. My watch read 9pm on the 12th day of December 2067.

I come to Gordon Beach nearly every night.

Dazzling displays of astral lux flickered before me, complemented by crests of foamy white water that brushed my toes, and the faint crashes of the swelling tide. I inhaled the aromatic scent of sea salts and looked into my telescope. The transparent and unpolluted cerulean sky over this beach provided crystal clear views of many complex constellations. 'Cassiopeia, Aquarius, Perseus,' I whispered to myself.

The misty scent of soothing sea salt filled my lungs and I lay in the sand as the Moon gleamed with pearly beauty. Every night that I came here, I felt transcended beyond human potential. I knew that I was meant for more. But, every night, I returned to my high-rise apartment in Washington DC, alone.

My watch alarm rang and I jolted into reality from my unplanned nap on the sand. It read 1am and it was time to leave the beach. The 30-minute car ride, although relaxing, was lonesome. After an excruciatingly heavy day at work and more than three hours at the beach, gravity took over and I collapsed onto my bed. I was asleep within seconds.

Slits of sunlight penetrated my curtains like excess steam in a space shuttle's engine – my most recent experimental investigation. A few minutes passed of pondering about anomalies in my experiments, and then it hit me. I was late for work. Again. My heart rate elevated exponentially, a combination of fear and dizziness pumped through my arteries, multiplying with each heartbeat. A cloud of vexation consumed me and I ran to the elevator, repeatedly smashing the descend button.

After a race to work at the Washington NASA Headquarters, I arrived at my manager's door and prepared for a hurricane of fury. Before I could speak, Winston, my manager, vehemently released his wrath. His yells of rage were probably audible from Mars. I apologised with genuine earnestness, hoping to receive even the slightest of forgiveness.

After ignoring my apology, Winston exclaimed, 'I don't care. You've a job here at NASA with an exceptionally high calibre. You're worthless to us and I can't imagine you've any friends. I've lost count of your late strikes, too. I cannot believe you are a 2-I.C., just under me – it's embarrassing.'

'Worthless!? Speak for yourself. No one here likes you, by the way.' I retaliated, knowing I would regret it. The malignant look in his eyes pierced mine. I just poured gasoline over an open fire – a blazing, infernal and scorching fire. What seemed like minutes of eerie silence passed and in the corner of my eye I could see co-workers listening in. I avoided eye contact with Winston and looked at my feet and prepared for the worst.

'You no longer work here, Angus,' he commanded, desperately containing his anger. I sharply inhaled his strong cologne and hobbled to the planetary transport unit, receiving sympathetic looks. The planetary transport unit was where the spaceships and shuttles were stored and prepared for departure.

I thought about how vastly different 2067 was to my childhood in the 2010s. Interchanging transport between close planets and moons was more accessible, safer and cheaper than a few decades ago. However, rates of poverty, famine, drought and hunger were on the rise.

To relish my remaining few minutes at NASA, I went to sit in a small silver space-shuttle that was departing Earth in a couple of hours and pretended that I was about to go into space, a dream I had from as far back as I could remember.

I swirled into a whirlpool of melancholy, all my dreams and aspirations were going down the drain. Word spread quickly about my job termination, so the shuttle technicians let me savour the moment. A brief moment of reflection passed and I came to terms with myself that Winston was right; I have no friends.

I flippantly joked to myself, 'I should just take off in this shuttle and live in space. No one would miss me anyway.' I laughed at my own joke since I often had no one else to laugh with. But, for a while, I considered it seriously. I was nearly sixty and had never explored beyond Washington DC. The shuttle was mostly, if not fully apt for take-off. A spark flickered inside me and a light bulb danced above my head. I had never lived dangerously, so why not start now?

Lost in the heat of the moment, I spontaneously prepared for take-off. Like a lion's, an intensely low growl emitted from the shuttle's engine. Concerned yells from nearby staff blasted from every angle, accompanied by distinctly aggravated swear words from Winston. A gush of fiery light surged from the backburner of the shuttle and I clatteringly put on safety apparatus: a sealed oxygen suit, gravity regulator and a seatbelt. The shuttle rattled with a metallic rhythm and it ascended above the ground.

My heart was racing at the speed of light as I prepared the safety compressors and readied the lift-off procedure. Euphoric, I widely smiled from cheek to cheek. I looked down and saw engineers and operators desperately trying to remotely stop the shuttle. However, I had manually cut off major transmission points between the operations centre and my shuttle. After being distracted for a few minutes from flicking switches, regulating pressure and releasing the sub-shuttle, I saw the NASA headquarters as a speck in a sea of industrialism. Gravity became weaker and I was in the clouds – literally. Before I knew it, the shuttle had disconnected from the Earth's gravitational and magnetic fields. I was levitating out of my seatbelt. I was in space. I was free.

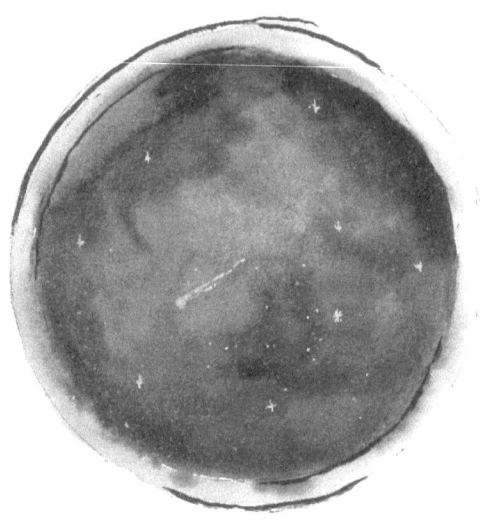

I turned off the movement engines and it was silent. The colour of the infinitely enlarging universe was the darkest black I had ever seen. Earth's atmosphere must have been tremendously polluted, even at Gordon Beach, for the blackness of space to be so hidden.

Every star, every moon and every planet exploded with colours. Every spectrum of colour was observable and glistened from every angle. The hyper-polarised windshield allowed safe viewing of the Sun, which was ablaze with hundreds of shades of yellows, oranges and reds. Extravagantly radiant solar flares combusted from its chromosphere and its luminescence lit up the entire solar system. Magnificent rays of corona thundered from the Sun's upper atmosphere and beams of golden energy blasted out from the photosphere.

After admiring the Sun, I floated towards a two-metre refraction telescope that had an immensely high magnification of up to 8000x. After minutes of searching for something other than planets in the Solar System and nearby stars, I detected a neutron star in the midst of a recently exploded supergiant star, which resulted in a supernova. It was like an eruption of rainbows. Colours that I thought did not exist, existed.

Next, I lowered the magnification and tried to find my apartment, but during the search, my attention was taken by something abhorrent. There were millions, if not billions, of people in inhospitably dry conditions without food or shelter. At least half of the Earth's population was poverty stricken and hordes of children and animals were malnourished, diseased or left dead, mostly in Africa, Europe and Asia.

Deforestation was ever-so-present, with countless rainforests appearing a parched brown colour from exposed and insect infested trunks. Australia was merely a wasteland of sand and its surrounding seas were browner than they were blue.

Thousands of deceased animals lay buoyant on the polluted waters. In contrast, some other desiccated environments seemed entirely barren, with no visible lifeforms whatsoever. Small villages and suburbs were ravaged from erupted volcanoes and assumedly their peoples were not warned about the natural disasters, regardless of the advanced technology that existed in foreseeing such disasters.

The issue of the rising sea level had come to such an extreme that small islands such as Fiji and Tonga were fully submerged underwater – a condition where mammal life was impossible to sustain. Countless aquatic organisms were beached across dry land and their dryness suggested they had been dead for a while.

Worst of all, once I had found my apartment, it was palpable that the USA was profoundly privileged. I always had a misconception that the entire world was the same.

I came to a distressing conclusion that advertisement and tourism had awfully untrue depictions of the world. The US Government had concealed the increasing and out-of-control problem of environmental destruction from its population for its own benefit, which explained why travel was very rare, if not banned for 'safety' reasons. It also explained the government's push on my ex-job at NASA for safe human transport and colonisation of

Mars by large populations. They expected an expedition that would be like an enormous Noah's Ark to another planet.

Humans were overcome by greed and gluttony and, as a result, Earth was nearly at its end. I planned on returning with photographic evidence of the conditions outside of America, so that I could expose the government.

I was disgusted at what the Earth had become. I was preoccupied with the appalling condition of the planet for what seemed like hours. Until, a piercing whistle-like sound emerged from the silence. It was getting louder as time passed. The louder it got, the more paranoid I became.

I took myself away from the telescope and looked through the windshield. One speck of grey, orange and navy blue – government colours – was getting larger and larger, and it left a trail of more greyness, like a smoke or dying fire. Its size and sound continued to increase and I thought that I was having sensory issues from the high astronomical pressures. I envisaged the worst case scenario, where possibly there was a gas leak, an oxygen deprivation event or a crack growing in the windshield. 'Calm down, you're being paranoid. Nothing is happening, Angus. The government wouldn't really do . . . *that*,' I reassured myself.

I was wrong.

LIFE ON EARTH
William A Thomas

On Earth many problems by human animals have been created

Which over the centuries have been discussed, argued, and debated.

Over issues such as poverty, pollution, disease, deforestation, animal extinction, wars and waste,

And if life is to survive they will have to be solved in haste.

My Obsession
Ronald Holt

MY finger paused and shook as I was about to hit the key on my computer. At last my time for redemption was here. In a few moments what I had craved for so long would soon be mine. It had become such an important part of my life, I needed to savour this moment.

Looking back I realised how many years it had taken to get to this point. Years that were often shrouded with self-doubt about both my personal life and ever achieving what I had worked so hard to acquire. If anything, what started out as fun had become an obsession. In reality I could have attained my goal without the trauma involved but where was the fun in that? It was really more than just fun, my obsession helped me through some of the darkest times in my life. I really wondered if all my struggles had been worth it, with the changing technology, but I had convinced myself that it was worth all that time and energy.

A lot of people, mainly my work colleagues, thought I was crazy or at least obsessed. I did not look at it that way but I suppose I could understand how others may have formed this belief. I had let my quest become all consuming. But not all the time.

I led a rather dull existence. I had no family and was not sportingly inclined. All I had was my work at the postal mail exchange sorting letters and parcels. My social life was watching television to break the monotony. I was from the country and after losing my parents in a motor vehicle accident, I moved to the city. I suffered depression and I could not stay in the country town where I was brought up as it had too many painful memories. The move had not really assisted as I knew no one. I felt very alone and lost in the big city. So I suppose to a degree my obsession had given me an alternative outlet and interest.

Everything changed the day I met Jenny. I could never see myself as ever being blinded by love or finding love at first sight. I had never met anyone like Jenny and my life was about to be turned on its head.

I was working on the office counter at the time when Jenny entered through the glass doors. She seemed to glide so gracefully across the floor to where I was standing. Jenny was about 160cm in height, was slightly built with long golden hair. Her beautiful brown eyes seemed to sparkle when she flashed her infectious smile. She was dressed in a casual shirt and jeans which clung caressingly to her shapely body. I could not take my eyes off her.

'I have been waiting for a parcel to be delivered but it has not arrived. It should have been here by now and I was wanting to check to see if anything could have happened to it,' she said in voice which sounded so angelic to me.

I told her that I would look around to see if there were any parcels for her. I did remember seeing something behind a sorting machine. I crawled underneath the table and there it was. I felt a sense of euphoria being able to help her.

'Thank you very much,' Jenny said gratefully as I handed the parcel to her. 'I was so afraid it had been lost. It is a gift from my parents for starting my course at the local uni.'

'You don't live far from my place,' I observed having noted the address on the parcel.

'I have just moved down from my parents' cattle property outside of Longreach and am living with my aunty. I have started a nursing degree,' she replied.

'I am a country boy too and have not been here all that long. I don't know about you but I feel lost in this big city.'

'Yes, I know how you feel. I really don't know anyone here except for my aunt. Anyway, thank you again for finding my parcel.'

Jenny hesitated as if she wanted to say more but then turned slowly to leave. She did not see a briefcase another customer had left on the floor and she tripped over it. I saw her start to fall and moved quickly to grab her. As I cradled her warm soft body preventing her fall our eyes met. The touch was like something magical had happened and I could see in her eyes that she felt something too. Or at least I hoped she did.

She thanked me profusely for saving her from the fall while the owner of the briefcase apologised for leaving his briefcase where it was. I am not usually forward being a rather shy person but I boldly asked her out. What was I thinking? A beautiful girl like Jenny would not want to go out with a virtual recluse like me. To my pleasant surprise she agreed and we commenced dating.

The next few months were the best in my life. We had both led rather sheltered existences and everything was new to both of us. We went to movies, band concerts, picnics and outings with other students. Many of these students were also from the country and I was accepted into the group without any reservations. My obsession faded into the background, although it never entirely went away.

Jenny's parents wanted her to have the opportunity to live a life away from the remoteness of the cattle property and, as a caring person, she decided that she would like to become a nurse. While we dated or spoke on the phone regularly I had to respect the time constraints imposed by her uni course. She was grateful for my consideration of her study schedule and we were getting along very well.

To me the world had become such a wonderful place and every time we met, I could not help thinking how lucky I was that such a beautiful person had come into my life. In the back of my mind I still had the fear, probably from the sudden loss of my parents, that something could go wrong.

One day when I was at work my mobile phone rang. I recognised Jenny's phone number but was not expecting her to call at that time. Her tearful voice on the other end of the line told me immediately that something was very wrong.

'It's my father,' she sobbed, 'he has had a heart attack while out working on the property. He is in the Longreach Base Hospital. He was fortunate that there was a visiting cardiologist there at the time. I have to return home immediately to help Mum on the property while Dad is in recovery. I don't know how long I will be away. I have contacted the Uni and deferred my course.'

Jenny's departure left me feeling like there was something missing in my life. We spoke regularly on the telephone although reception on the property was not great due to its remoteness. Every time she went to Longreach to visit her father she would call. She did not know how long she would be away as that would depend on her father's progress.

As the days turned into weeks, then into months, I started to feel that sadness I had felt after the deaths of my parents. It was then that I returned to my obsession which had helped me in my dark days.

As time passed, my telephone contacts with Jenny became less frequent. Her father had improved and had returned to the property. I put this reduction of telephone frequency down to telecommunication problems but secretly I began to fear that Jenny would never come back.

This fear and my concern that depression would follow, drove my obsession onwards trying to remove the anxieties which were raising their ugly head.

Taking every opportunity and offer available to me, I saw my target coming nearer.

The less I heard from Jenny the more determined I became to reach my goal and to beat the demons forming in my head. If she did come back, I did not want to be in such a condition to spoil our relationship.

With one concerted effort, my goal was reached and the only thing left to do was to secure my redemption.

I decided to wait one more day starting to think that once I had made the redemption, what was I going to do? I suppose I could just start again. While I sat pondering, my mobile phone rang. Jenny's number came up on the screen.

Unlike her tearful voice which brought the news of her father's heart attack, she was back to the bright bubbly person I had met in the mail exchange which seemed so long ago now.

'My parents have sold the property and are moving to Brisbane so that Dad will be near better medical care and I can continue my nursing studies. I really admired the work of the nurses who helped Dad and it makes me more determined to become one myself. I will be back in Brisbane next week. I can't wait to see you.'

My heart leapt for joy and the cloud of depression lifted. I felt so high I am sure that I could have danced on the ceiling.

It was in a state of high elation I had taken out my laptop in readiness for this moment and had gone onto the website. I had clicked on the appropriate screens until I reached the page headed 'Redemption'. I scrolled through the available rewards until I found the one which I had worked so hard towards.

I needed 83,200 fly-buy points for a Tom Tom Go 6200 which was more than just street maps. It had its own SIM which allowed hands-free calling, updates by WiFi and Smartphone messages. I hoped with this I would never again get lost in the big city.

My finger pushed down on the 'redeem' key and a message flashed up that my redemption had been successfully processed and that I would receive a message to my email address with redemption details including the order number 439761.

In hindsight I could probably have just bought the Tom Tom and maybe I had become too obsessed. I wondered how much it had really cost me. There again I had to buy that food and petrol, and to get my reward was a bonus. There was a certain thrill in chasing the points available on shopping and petrol and any other offers. More importantly, my obsession helped me through dark times and with Jenny coming back, my future indeed looked brighter. I probably won't need to chase the fly buy points anymore – well maybe not but old habits do die hard. Perhaps I may be able to use them towards a honeymoon in the future.

We Stick Together
Jessica Freiberg

I SMILE.

I am an absolute wreck. I feel like I am in the middle of nowhere and I am smiling like the happiest person alive. The noise of the cars flying past fades away. The tears continue to slide down my cheeks mingling with the rain. But everything will be okay now. I know it will.

Ever so slowly and cautiously I close the back door. The damn door lets out a squeak. I freeze. Goosebumps pop up along my arms as I wait nervously for any more noise. Minutes creep by before I decide it is okay to move. I sprint across the yard, the soft sound of Boo's paws on the grass follows me through the silent night. Under the dim light of the moon, the grass crackles dryly under my feet as my heart pounds in my chest. We reach the deep darkness of the bush and I finally slow down. Dry twigs snap and leaves crunch at my feet as I walk further inwards. I suck in lungfuls of the sweet, pure night air as I look down into Boo's precious, crystal-blue Husky eyes. Her tail wagging eagerly, she watches me contentedly as I begin the walk to our tree. The bush is filled with eucalyptus trees but ours is the biggest, most special one of them all.

By the time we reach our tree, tears are starting to blur my vision. My breath is starting to come in small little gasps as I pathetically gulp in air. My wild, dark curls hang about my face like vicious, frizzy snakes. I'm a mess. I throw myself into the little hollow at the bottom of the ginormous tree and begin to sob and howl as Boo curls up beside me and looks up with sweet sad eyes. She drops a large stick by my side and I know she understands, this is how she shows it – with big pointy sticks. Between us sticks mean forgiveness and sympathy and friendship. No words are said but she understands. I don't even need to tell her that my first day at high school was the worst day of my life, my Boo Baby just understands. I can't decide what the worst part was, but essentially the entire day was horrid. Ever since I was little I would venture out here to let out my feelings, rather than risk my parents hearing me and asking too many questions. This area holds a special place in my heart, it belongs to Boo and me. It is our tree.

The next morning, like a ton of bricks, Boo excitedly jumps on me and eagerly covers my face in kisses. This is the highlight of most days. Waking up to Boo jumping all over me at the crack of dawn. I don't want to, but eventually I roll out of my warm cocoon and slowly begin my depressing, mundane school morning rituals. Boo lays on my bed intently watching me as I get ready. The days seem to be growing more humid and unbearably hot.

Today will be the first day of rain in a long time. Dad says that this rain will stick around for a while, which is AWESOME! Boo loves the rain, she will beat down the back door if it begins to rain so she can go roll in puddles and make a total mess. I make a solemn promise to race back after school to grant Boo her wish.

She gives a small whimper as I grab my bag to leave, staring into my soul with her beautiful blue eyes, making me feel so incredibly guilty. I wish I didn't have to leave her. I walk out the door and already feel the crushing loneliness, away from Boo. I am alone. School is just an endless torturous time where I am surrounded by people but have this sinking feeling of drowning in my own isolation. I can't wait for the sweet sound of the bell at the end of the day signalling my freedom.

The minute I walk through the door after school, I am greeted by a frenzy of yaps and a smothering of excited kisses. I don't bother to get changed but instead slip immediately into my massive, bright purple raincoat and begin to hunt for Boo's matching lead. Shaking like a leaf, tail wagging a million miles an hour, Boo eagerly bounces after me barking madly. We love our walks together, we will take a walk rain, hail or shine. Today it is definitely going to be a rainy walk, Boo's favourite.

Racing out through the side gate, Boo yanks at the lead enthusiastically, so enthusiastically she nearly pulls my arm out of its socket. Busily rushing from side to side, Boo takes in as much as possible, the sights, smells, everything. Large drops of rain splatter around us as we continue down the street. We come to the corner of our street which of course sets Boo off yapping madly. Boy this dog is embarrassing sometimes. She begins to yelp and tug at her lead, spinning in circles and jerking me along. I glance left. I glance right. All clear. Yank! Boo lunges forwarding barking wildly, sprinting across this road like her life depends on it. We leap over the gutter on the other side just as a dirty red car roars past. 'Boo you nearly got us killed. Now I know you are scared but that was just ridiculous.' I sigh as I'm dragged along the familiar route.

Even now the excitement of going for a walk hasn't worn off. Boo scurries from tree to tree impatiently pulling me along. As I trudge up the streets of our busy suburb towards home the rain really begins to pelt down. Grape sized drops hammer into me and drench Boo as thunder snarls and growls overhead. The wind picks up and tosses leaves through the air. Oh God. Here comes another dog. The tiniest little dog I have ever seen. What on earth is anyone else doing out in this heavy downpour? I pick up the pace in the hopes that Boo won't see them as she hurries along. Suddenly she comes to an abrupt halt and notices the other dog. Off she goes. Like a maniac she howls and growls and lets loose a string of threatening barks. I hide my face in the hood of my raincoat as I jog past, attempting to control my dog. Once when Boo was a puppy she was attacked on a walk by a huge, sleek dog and ever since she goes nuts when she sees another dog coming, even when it is the tiniest pup like the one that just passed. I hang my head in shame and decide it is time to get home. I jog the rest of the way and race through the gate; in the rush to get out of the rain. A vicious storm is on its way.

I peel off my raincoat and soaked joggers and rush inside to the warmth of the kitchen. 'Mamma I'm back,' I holler.

'Oh thank God you're back, I was getting worried, this storm is going to be huge,' Mum says in her soft, gentle tone as her shock of dark curls, identical to mine, falls around her face in frizzy tangles. 'Now did you make sure you locked the gate properly? We don't want Boo running out in this wild weather.'

'Yeah, yeah Mum, it's all cool,' I say quickly as I race for a long, steaming hot shower.

Once I eventually crawl out from the glass box of warmth I wrap myself up in my bathrobe and plod down to my bedroom. All relaxed and warm I feel the tension in my shoulders release and melt away. I jump from the cold of the tiles and sink into the creamy carpet in my bedroom. I take in a long slow breath and close my eyes, tired from the day and my embarrassing damp walk with Boo. I hear a noise. Soft panting.

I open my eyes and sure enough there is Boo, stretched out on my bed like a queen. I push out my breath of air in a shriek. There is mud EVERYWHERE! I look to the floor and see large paw prints. I look at the wall she leant against and see a large patch of filth. Then with horror I look at my once clean bed and see Boo, proudly sitting there covered in mud and drenched from the rain.

'OUT BOO! GET OUT! GET OFF MY BED! GET OUT YOU STUPID DOG!' I scream in a high-pitched, hysterical voice. Anger simmers through my veins as I chase the damn dog out of my room and outside. Tail tucked between her legs, she sulkily sits down on the cold cement of the patio and pathetically looks up with big, sad eyes. I slam the door.

I spring out of bed the next morning. It was such a long unsettling night without the warm comfort of Boo beside me. Soft streams of sunlight drift through my window as I bounce around like a bunny eager to be reunited with Boo. I bolt straight to the back door and call out for Boo in a sing-song tone.

'Boo! Come get some brekky baby girl! Come on Boo. Boo?'

Where could that dog be? I walk to the edge of the patio and call out louder. My stomach drops. The gate. It's open. I'm paralysed. I can't move. I can't think. I don't understand! I swear I closed the gate yesterday when we got home. How could it be open?

A million questions create a whirlwind of confusion in my mind, guilt and fear creeping in. What if she ran far away? What if she can't find her way home? God this is all my fault! Poor Boo, I yelled at her and now she is gone. She loves the rain but once the thunder and lightning kick in she freaks out; and the storm last night was fierce. I shouldn't have yelled at her! My body goes into motion and I run inside, screaming for my parents to come. Shrieking as I shove my shoes on and yank my phone off charge.

Redemption

We slide into the car together and off we go. I anxiously tap my foot, nerves eating away at me. I urge Mum to drive faster. Surely she has to be somewhere. I roll down the window and scream out her name, trying not to choke on the massive wedge of guilt sitting at the back of my throat.

Five minutes. Ten minutes. We wind through the familiar streets of our suburb. Strategically we move from street to street. We leave Dad behind to go door knocking and ask if anyone had seen or heard Boo while we rush through the streets desperate to find her. It feels like everything is going in slow motion. I strain my eyes trying to see any sign of her, trying to not think of the worst. Up ahead I see it. A mound of fur. 'Stop the car!' I screech. I jump out of the car and sprint as fast as I can go. It's Boo.

As I look at her broken body my throat closes up. The weight of the world pushes me to the ground. My stomach swirls and heaves with guilt. The bitter taste of regret and grief choke me up. My heart shatters in this moment, all the love I have for this dear sweet dog pulses through my body and I break down. I am overwhelmed by the light, the noise of passing cars and the beating of my broken heart. I close my eyes and attempt to shut it out. The darkness is somewhat comforting but I know I will eventually open my eyes and the world will be a darker, colder place without my bubbly, sweet Boo in it. A world I never even considered facing one day, a world that I have been thrown into unprepared. Numb. Empty. Broken.

I kneel next to her and cry. I wail and howl, my chest heaving, my body shaking.

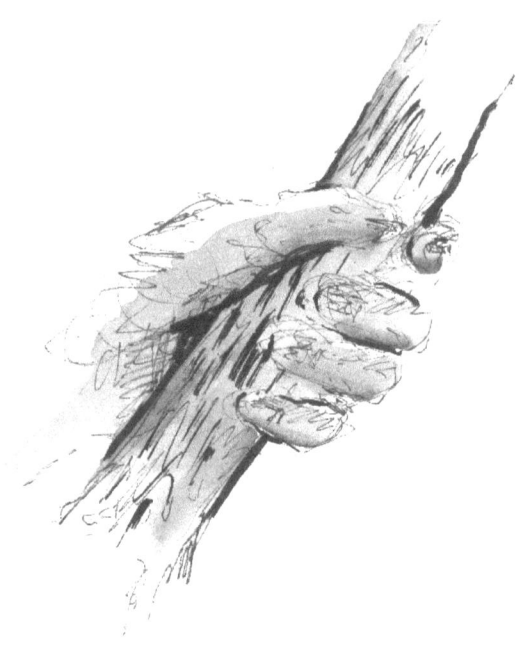

She was hit by a car. Then like a brave soldier she pulled herself off the road and came to rest on the grass. I put my head against her chest and feel no movement. Glassy eyes stare back at me. Glassy eyes that used to flood and sparkle with warmth and love, now empty and lifeless. I wail harder. This is all my fault. I hate myself.

I lose track of time. Minutes or hours later I am slowly pulled away as a drizzle of rain comes down. I stand up, clutching onto Mum and my body folds in on itself. I am hysterical. I loved Boo with all of my heart and she must have hated me for yelling and locking her outside. She must have been terrified.

Then I see what looks like a big stick. A massive stick. Almost as big as poor Boo herself. I fall beside it in amazement. In my heart I know it is a sign. She was bringing it home. Home for me. My parents look on bewildered, as I stop gasping and calm down. A wave of calm washes over me. I feel the self-loathing wash away as I redeem Boo's love. I clutch at the stick, the tears stream down my face in small rivers, mingling with the rain. I smile. Everything will be okay now. I know it will.

The Theatre of Life
Anne Olsson

WE had no suspicion, on the final night of the play, of the tragedy about to unfold that would threaten the very existence of our little company. On that night our little theatre was full. We had played to full houses for the past three weeks. *Fallen Angels* proved popular. The audiences had laughed and applauded with enthusiasm. That final evening had brought with it a wild storm, and looking back, I wondered if it had been an omen of the dark time that was to follow. The audience members entered the ticketing area dishevelled, shaking wet umbrellas. The rain continued to fall heavily throughout the night, but we were snug within doors and the performance continued without mishap.

Eileen, our prima donna, played the female lead. Our director, Ivan, favoured her because she was a convincing actress. I had no illusions about myself. I was competent in my role, but it was my ability to learn lines quickly, and assist the other actors when they faulted, that Ivan appreciated. Anita played the role that I had wanted. She was the proficient maid, speaking French like a native and playing the piano with assurance. Ivan had cast her well, and as the play progressed, she had only to walk on stage for the audience to break into laughter.

Redemption

It was after the show, as thunder boomed and rain beat on the windows, when we blithely lounged about on the stage, tired but exhilarated, that Ivan expressed his satisfaction. The weeks of work were behind us and the show had been a success. We were familiar with Ivan's crusty temper, but tonight he was exuberant. 'What do you say?' he asked us, 'Shall we have our party tomorrow at my place?' The after-show party was a tradition within our theatre group. It was the time to relax and enjoy a feast of food, make congratulatory speeches and present complimentary gifts to the stage crew. Thomas, our stage manager, suggested we dismantle the set first, but this was vetoed by the cast. We agreed to meet the next day at Ivan's house. 'Come at 2 o'clock . . . and bring a plate – with something on it!'

We gathered that Sunday afternoon at Ivan's mansion, innocently prepared to enjoy ourselves. His great white house stood on an acre of land overlooking Lake Kurwongbah. His wife Eve greeted us warmly as we entered the spacious, tastefully furnished lounge. There was food aplenty, and games had been devised to entertain us. Eric, our sound and lighting man, was true to form, coming dressed as a clown, complete with bulbous nose and a ludicrous orange wig. Alistair, the company's staid treasurer, came dressed in a crumpled suit. Eileen, over dressed as usual, looked resplendent in a Ralph Lauren gown. The rest of us were clad in our oldest and most comfortable clothes.

We sat about with drinks in our hands discussing the play. Eileen sat forward abruptly, spilling her drink, and merrily recounted the night she had forgotten her lines. I had been off-stage at the time, and unaware of what eventuated. 'My mind went completely blank,' she boasted, 'and I froze...hadn't a clue what my lines were.' She laughed gaily. 'After moments of deathly silence, I demurely declared I needed to go to the bathroom, ran off stage and checked the script in the dressing room.'

'Yes, damn you!' Alistair expostulated, frowning. He had played alongside her as her long-suffering husband. 'And those of us left on stage had to do some quick thinking and improvise. I am sure Ivan wasn't impressed, but I doubt the audience noticed a thing.'

We were playing charades, laughing at our absurdities, when Ivan suggested I come out to see the ducks on the lake. 'We'll leave that lot to wallow in the booze and bullshit,' he declared. We wandered down to the lake's edge, and he tossed breadcrumbs to the ducks that had settled on the water. Two black swans were sailing gracefully towards the far shore where a forest of eucalypts and casuarinas grew. It was peaceful and beautiful. 'Well, we'd better get back, or I'll be accused of being a bad host.' In the ensuing days, in the light of all the troubled events that followed, I was to wistfully recall that brief time by the lake with this man whom I admired so much.

Back at the house we did not appear to have been missed. The alcohol was flowing, and the games continued. Eve was carrying trays of food about, offering everyone sweets and savouries. 'They are a playful bunch,' I commented at Ivan's side. 'Yes, we are a family, we theatre people, and we like to have fun. We're not afraid to reveal who we are . . . No inhibitions. We have our little tiffs, but we'll stand by each through thick and thin.' As Eve led him away to open another bottle of wine, Eric approached me and lay his arm affectionately across my shoulders. I commented that Eve was a generous hostess. He responded solemnly, 'Yes, she is. A great hostess is one who makes her guests feel at home, even if she wishes they were'. I looked up into his smiling eyes and laughed.

Ivan now suggested we conduct the serious part of the afternoon's agenda. He and Thomas made their speeches, with Eric tossing in a few asides, and gifts were distributed to the backstage crew. Ivan then proposed an outing in the bush. No one thought he was serious. The proposal was greeted as a joke, but he was not deterred. The men were persuaded to take part, if somewhat reluctantly. 'It'll be a lark,' Anita declared. 'Our little group of thespians strutting dramatically around the stage of the great Australian bush!'

Eileen at first refused to consider it. Eric mocked her, prancing before her in imaginary high heels. 'The little princess is too dainty to touch the dirty soil of the land!' he mimicked. Having by this time consumed four glasses of wine, she was aroused to defy him. 'I am not afraid of anything,' she declared.

I remember those words, because naively none of us realised we had good reason to be afraid. The outing was arranged for the following weekend.

Showers were forecast for the Saturday, but it dawned cloudless and bright. We met early at Ivan's house, and drove off together in three vehicles, bearing backpacks carrying hats, raincoats, water bottles and lunches. We travelled north to the Glass House Mountains. The traffic on the motorway was congested, and it was a relief when we turned off onto Steve Irwin Way and headed through the pine forests towards Mount Tibrogargan, past plantations of pineapples and macadamia nut trees.

We met up with the others in the Mount Tibrogargan car park. It was strange to see the taciturn Alistair, without his suit and tie, sporting hiking boots and a hooded jacket. Eric gave me a friendly wink as he stepped away from his car, resplendent in a new Akubra hat. Alistair looked up at the summit of the mountain and grunted. 'It would be something to climb to the top of that,' he exclaimed. Eric raised his eyebrows. 'Knowledge is knowing that it is possible to climb that monolith. Wisdom is staying safely down below on flat ground.'

We set out to walk the Trachyte circuit, a distance of six kilometres. I relished being out-of-doors again, thoughtlessly unconscious of the drama that lay ahead. The fresh morning air was invigorating. The walk took us through open woodland and heathland. We saw delicate wild flowers growing among the grasses. Two kookaburras laughed at us from the tree tops, and little wrens and wattle birds darted amongst the shrubs as we passed.

Thomas and Anita were experienced walkers and soon outstripped the rest of us. By the time the main group reached the lookout, we were ready for a rest stop and a welcome drink of water. From this point we had a splendid view of the other peaks. Ivan looked flushed but happy. Eileen was complaining of being hot and tired. Cheeky Eric cupped her chin in his hand and looked solemnly into her eyes. 'Remember, little princess,' he said majestically, 'you're not afraid of anything!' She scowled, picked up her backpack and walked on. By the time we arrived back at the car park, we were all hot and tired and hungry.

It seems strange to recall how merry we became, as we sat about on rugs, enjoying our lunch in the shade of the trees. We had no intimation as to what was to come. Alistair sat apart from us at a picnic table, declaring, 'It is insane to sit on the ground when there is a perfectly good table to sit at.' This did not dampen our spirits.

'I'm starving!' Eileen declared.

'Then eat up, little princess,' Eric responded, 'we've got more walking ahead of us this afternoon.'

'What! Haven't we done enough?' she expostulated.

'How about we climb Mount Beerwah?' Thomas suggested.

'No way, Thomas!' Eric protested. 'It's too difficult.'

As we sat about contentedly, Thomas spoke again. 'Come on, you lot, we've got to decide where we're going next. Let's climb Mount Beerwah.' I disliked the idea, feeling uneasy about it. Thomas was insistent. 'Those that don't want to needn't climb all the way to the top.'

Alistair was scornful. 'The girls'll never make it,' he asserted.

'Speak for yourself!' Anita declared indignantly. 'I'm ready for it.'

Looking back now, I wonder – was it fate? Were we destined to climb Mt. Beerwah, or could the future that awaited us have been changed? I cannot answer this now, but the question still nags me. I lie awake at night, wishing we had made another choice.

As we set off again in the three vehicles, I was feeling some trepidation. I had not commented during the conversation, but I had heard stories of the difficulties Mount Beerwah presented, especially for the inexperienced. But I had said nothing and let the discussion run its course. I was in the third of the three cars as we left the bitumen road behind us and met the dusty gravel road leading to the base of the mountain. The cars ahead of us churned up the dust and we had to close the windows to shut it out. I was thankful when we had pulled up in the car park.

Ahead of us loomed the mountain. I looked up at it in awe. 'They call that a mountain,' Alistair said disdainfully. 'It looks more like a hill to me . . . We're pathetic in this country. If you want to see a real mountain, go to the Himalayas.'

Redemption

I shuddered, because I was surprised by his comment. This 'hill,' as he called it, looked very impressive to me. And there was something dark I sensed in that great monolith – it emanated a brooding presence.

We donned our backpacks and set off together, but Thomas and Anita soon forged ahead. It was hot in the early afternoon, and we felt the heat. A forest of trees grew either side of the rough path, but it was the mountain that soared above us that filled our awareness. We had not gone far when we passed a shelter. Eileen stopped abruptly before me, and declared there was no way she was climbing 'that thing'. 'I'm going to stay here in the shade. I've done enough!' she declared dramatically.

So we left her there and walked on. I felt uneasy as we started to climb. Warning signs depicting falling rocks were displayed beside the track, admonishing us to be cautious because people had died on the mountain. Steps had been built into the slope, and they seemed to go on and on. I was hot and tired and knew there was still a long way to go. I slowed my footsteps and allowed the men to overtake me. As Ivan passed me, his face was red with exertion but he stepped forward cheerfully. Eve stayed with me, but I was certain I would not reach the summit.

We continued quietly on together until a sheer wall of rock appeared ahead of us. The others were now out of sight. Sweat was trickling down my face. I turned to Eve tiredly. 'I've done enough, Eve. I'm going back now. You go on if you want to.'

She smiled in her quiet way. 'No, I'll come back with you.'

Though the steps downhill seemed unending, we eventually found Eileen, lying on her back in the shade. 'The ground makes a hard bed, but it beats walking in this heat,' she commented.

We waited in the shade, talking sporadically amongst ourselves, and as time passed I felt a growing sense of uneasiness. We waited a long time. Eve sat up suddenly. 'What was that?' she asked anxiously. 'Did you hear that?' I was drowsily resting against a tree trunk and had heard nothing. 'I heard a cry,' Eve insisted, 'I know I did.' I stood up and looked towards the mountain, straining to hear. 'Something's wrong,' Eve persisted. We were all looking back towards the mountain now, hesitant and fearful. 'I hear someone calling,' Eileen whispered. 'Something is wrong!' Eve asserted. 'I'm going back up.' Abandoning her back pack, she set off in haste.

Nothing was to be gained by following her, but the waiting game was now even more difficult.

We heard the thud of Thomas's steps before we caught a glimpse of him. He came running towards us, calling frantically between laboured breaths, 'Ring for an ambulance . . . Hurry! . . . Ivan has fallen!' In disbelief I grabbed my phone but had to rush back along the road until I found reception.

So began a blur of events that I hate to recall. The ambulance could not reach the site where he had fallen and a rescue helicopter was called.

When they finally reached Ivan he was unconscious and was airlifted to the hospital.

When everyone else arrived back at the car park, Eve was frantic. We quickly drove the long way back to her home from where Thomas drove her on to the hospital. The rest of us waited together in the house for news. When the call came through, Anita answered. When she put down the telephone, tears were welling in her eyes. 'Ivan has died,' she whispered, distraught. As though in a stupor, I made us all a strong cup of tea, and we sat there, unwilling to leave, numbed and incredulous. We waited until Thomas and Eve returned late that evening. Grief-stricken, Eve walked in as though she was in a trance. I took her in my arms and held her a long time.

Alistair stood up, preparing to leave. 'This is your fault, Thomas,' he snapped, 'If you hadn't suggested that climb, this wouldn't have happened.' I stared at him in irritation.

'Shut up, Alistair!' Eric retorted, 'that's not helpful.'

'It's true nonetheless,' Alistair retaliated. 'And Thomas was beside Ivan when he fell. So what happened? Did you push him?' I looked at Alistair aghast.

The look of anguish on Thomas's face was distressing. 'No!' he protested, 'You can't possibly believe that!'

'Go home, Alistair,' I demanded.

He left, unrepentant, and the others followed soon after. I stayed with Eve that night, to give her what comfort I could. She cried inconsolably when she rang her son to tell him of his father's death. I stayed on the next day, reluctant to leave her. I cooked and cleaned for her and but I could not ease her suffering.

Eric rang me with the news Alistair was spreading rumours among theatre members, blaming Thomas for Ivan's death. I was shocked, but more phone calls followed. The rumour was like a cancer, eating into people's mind, spreading doubt about the events of that afternoon. I kept this from Eve, for it would not have helped her to know. I left when her son and his family arrived. It was not my place to be there now.

Once I arrived home, I called Alistair, to convince him of the senselessness of his allegations. He would not retract them. 'I am at loss to understand why you are being so vindictive,' I remonstrated. 'Your assumptions are absurd. What do you have against Thomas? What's at the bottom of this?'

'I know what I saw', he declared pompously. 'I've reported the matter to the police, so there's nothing more to be said.'

The committee met the following evening to discuss how we could deal with the situation. Alistair had done his work well, and doubt and confusion reigned. I had been receiving angry phone calls from members declaring that something must be done. Most were convinced that Thomas was innocent, but some small and suspicious minds were feeding on the drama Alistair had created. It threatened to split our group apart.

When the police became involved, it cast a shadow over us all. We were questioned intensely, and an autopsy was ordered. I could hardly contain my anger at Alistair. Ivan's death had been sufficiently traumatic but now the pain of this confusion was overwhelming. The rumours could not be kept from Eve now. She was horrified by Alistair's assertions. The police questioning distressed her but she never doubted Thomas's innocence.

By the time of the funeral, an autopsy had revealed that Ivan had died of a heart attack. I was thankful that the true cause of his death was revealed. It was not the fall that killed him. The perfidious Alistair was proven wrong, and Thomas was exonerated. When we said our sad farewells at the graveside, I knew we had lost a great friend. Our theatre group was bereft of its star director, but I sensed his spirit would linger on within the walls of our playhouse, and perhaps heal the wounds of distrust that were still raw.

Mr. WILLIAM SHAKESPEARES

COMEDIES, HISTORIES, & TRAGEDIES.

Published according to the True Originall Copies.

LONDON
Printed by Isaac Iaggard, and Ed. Blount. 1623.

DARKNESS
David Bell

You twine your velvet fingers around my soul.
The balmy summer evenings and the cool
twilights of spring are near kin to you.
Close intimacy is your dear child.

Yet sinister intent dwells at your heart
and unknown evils frame your very walls.
Your canopy hides inhumanity,
and greed, and death – purveyors of despair.

O, darkest form of which I am a part,
are you a chasm for eternity,
or do your ill-lit corridors lead up
unerringly into eternal day?

Satanic forces gather in your sight
to wreak unholy magic on a world
of superstition. What lurks in your streets
has taken form from unreality.

You are the place where phantoms dwell, in which
my waking thoughts are hidden in their pain.
You grant me hours of solitude and rest,
where dreams and nightmares fill my resting mind.

You must not be ashamed of what you are,
for I have painted evil on your face
and in your eyes. I use you to escape
the day's facade, and nestle in your arms.

Redemption

Eternity, one day, will spread her wings
around me. Then, will darkness be no more
or is there flourishing in paradise
a shady glen where souls find solitude?

Pay-Back
James Barrance

HASTENED footsteps echoed throughout the vacant parking lot. Flashlights brightly lit the path ahead, while the moon's white beam cast a dim light over the city. The streets surrounding the block were dead silent. As the footsteps neared the top floor of the parking lot, a feminine voice emerged from behind a stone pillar, 'Oi, Jeremy, George, over here!' At first the two boys looked dazed, turning to see where the voice had once been. Eventually, a tall slender silhouette appeared from behind the pillar. As it walked closer, the moon's light revealed a girl whose hair flowed blonde out of the dark maroon beanie which snugged over her head. Her lips were chapped from the cold air that surrounded them all.

'So boys, what have you got for me today?' she said quite calmingly.

'Yes, yes, we uh, got more stuff Tiffany,' Jeremy responded, forgetting that they were supposed to be quiet.

'Keep your voice down man, we're not supposed to be here!' George whispered cautiously at Jeremy.

George opened his large coat and pulled out a handful of expensive nail polishes from the inside pockets. 'This is all we could smuggle out of the store,' he whispered.

Tiffany opened her large handbag and held it in front of George, gesturing for the goods. George's hand dropped a dozen or so bottles into the abyss of the bag. A small dainty purse emerged in Tiffany's hand from the side pocket of the handbag and $50 was carefully placed in each of the boy's hands.

'Now run along you two, don't want anyone suspecting anything. And remember, if you get caught, you don't know me. Got it?' she warned.

'Got it!' both boys simultaneously replied. Tiffany turned away to count the bottles, while both the boys hastily made their way out of the car park, back to their homes.

Jeremy was awoken by the loud siren of his alarm. His eyes tried to open, although they were blinded by the rays of light that pierced the room through the shutter blinds. The pain of having to go to school filled Jeremy as he slammed his head against the pillow. The waft of pancakes occupied the household and Jeremy reluctantly stood up, drawn by the temptation of food. His tired body carried itself to the kitchen where, slumped onto a stool, it slouched over the kitchen tabletop. His nocturnal 'job' made Jeremy more tired than any other normal kid his age. He was an average 10th grader, getting average marks. Jeremy's parents had taken him to the local doctor as they believed he had a sleeping disorder. Jeremy played along, anything to avoid being suspected of sneaking out at night. The pancakes disappeared one by one until stomach cramps stopped Jeremy.

After a quick shower and cleaning of his teeth, he said his goodbyes, jumped onto his bike and left for school. Every day, he passed the pharmacist which he had taken from, feeling a slight knife of guilt. When he got to school, he was reunited with his best friend.

'Oi, George!' was hollered out from Jeremy's lungs as he entered the school's bike racks. A surprised George would always turn to yell back. Their friendship dated back a decade. Nothing would ever come between them, nothing would ever be too challenging for them.

After the final bell, George and Jeremy darted off to the local skate park, where they would spend an hour, until heading their separate ways. The skate park was where the boys first met Tiffany a few weeks ago. Her appealing physique could not be given a 'no' from any teenage boy. The faint sound of a V6 engine could be heard from up the street. Louder and louder grew the engine, thundering its way down the road. The boys knew who it was before Tiffany had step foot out of the driver seat.

George was the first to approach Tiffany, quickly followed by Jeremy. 'So, did ya make the dosh?' George asked trying to sound sleek and cool.

'Yes, George. You know, you two boys are great!' she replied, wrapping her arms around George and Jeremy.

They both blushed slightly before George exclaimed, 'What do you want next, we'll get anything for you Tiffany, you know we will!'

Tiffany smiled and handed George a note with product names listed. They said their goodbyes before she raced off.

George turned to face Jeremy, 'Well, see ya tonight, my partner in crime!' They exchanged a handshake before riding home.

The sun had vanished from the sky and the moon's crescent beamed down upon the houses. Jeremy was now wide awake and ready for work. He put on socks to manoeuvre around the house so no thumping of his feet would disrupt his parents' slumber. He carefully unlocked the back door and made his way to his parked bike. He opened and closed the gate slowly as he wheeled the bike through.

After he was free, he made his way to the rendezvous location. George was already there, sitting on the stone pavement with his phone in his grasp. Both the boys left their bikes on the wet grass and darted over the road to the closed pharmacist.

Around the back of the store was a large hole at the base of the chemist. It had been cleverly hidden by the use of a large cardboard mascot inside. George crawled in first and pushed over the mascot. Jeremy soon followed behind him after George had given him the 'all clear'. They proceed to do a bit of late night shopping, the catch, they were not paying.

After going through the list of items on Tiffany's list, they crawled back out of the hole, placing the large cardboard cut-out back in its position. Both boys made haste, checking behind themselves every so often, for anyone lingering in the dark who may have seen them. They finally reached their bikes. George took all of what had been stolen and shoved it in his schoolbag, which had been emptied before he left. They waved goodbye and took off homeward bound.

Jeremy woke up, just like every other regular morning, although he felt bad, as if something terrible was about to happen. He shrugged off the feeling and sauntered out into the kitchen. He sloped over the kitchen counter. The cereal brought before vanished quickly. The local news station played faintly in the distance. Suddenly, he heard something alarming. His body twisted to the television. '... last night security cameras caught a glimpse of two thieves taking beauty products from the local pharmacist, which had experienced missing stock for weeks ... the owner believes that the intruders are young males, possibly mid-teens, are prime suspects ...,' the reporters continued on. Jeremy was deeply worried. 'I don't want to face jail. What will mum think? I'll be ruined for the rest of my life.'

He raced to finish preparing for school. He slung his backpack over his shoulder and furiously pedalled his bike to school.

On his way, he noticed two police officers talking to the owner of the store. Without looking in their direction, he quickened his pace. The bike's tyres skidded across the dirt below the bike racks. Instead of yelling to George, Jeremy bolted to him and sat uncomfortably on the bench which George was on.

'Why are you in such a flurry Jeremy?' commented George.

Jeremy catching his breath replied, 'Did you not see the news!?'

George shook his head, confused. 'They got footage of us, don't you see? The pharmacy's security cameras got a video of me and you breaking in and stealing.'

George stood up, dumbfounded and anxious. 'Well, did they see our faces!' he sharply replied.

Jeremy thought about it for a second. He shook his head.

George wiped his hand across his brow. 'It'll be ok as long as we don't go there anymore. Damn, man, I just realised Tiffany's gonna be pissed at us. She'll know it was us, and she won't come by anymore, man.'

They discussed it some more and decided to skip out on the skate park after school.

The day stretched out longer than usual, with every excruciating hour feeling like a millennium. When the final bell released everyone, George raced off back home, forgetting to say goodbye to Jeremy.

As Jeremy pedalled back home, he slowed down near the pharmacy. Guilt slid down his throat as he saw the owner sitting out front, his face in his hands, distraught. Jeremy looked at the path ahead and slowly resumed his journey home.

In his room, he opened a small cardboard box placed on the top shelf of his cupboard. Inside was a pile of cash from the heists. Jeremy held the cash in his hand and tightly pondered his actions. The guilt built up. He thought about the distraught owner. He thought about what he had done. He thought about jail. Shaking his head, he quickly strode back outside to his bike. He shoved the cash in the bottom of his backpack, slung it over his shoulder and hastily pedalled back down the path he had come.

The bike's tyres skidded as he sharply braked outside the pharmacy. Jeremy's legs forced his terrified body through the front door. The owner was behind the counter, tapping the desk anxiously. Jeremy tried to make eye contact, though the tired owner's eyes sagged downwards.

Jeremy built up his courage. 'Excuse me sir...I want to tell you something . . .' Jeremy went on to explain the truth and how he was deeply sorry. He unzipped his backpack and handed the owner the wad of notes. 'I know that is not enough to cover the damage. I'll work here for free for a while if you want – to make up for everything.' The owner looked deep into Jeremy's hazel eyes and gave a slight grin.

'You know, I'm deeply upset at what happened, although I greatly appreciate you coming forward. I'll tell you what, I'll accept your payment, although I want to bring your accomplice here and both of you can help out here for a week after school.'

Jeremy's heart lifted into the air and he revealed a large smile. Jeremy pulled out his phone from his pocket and proceeded to call George. He explained the situation to George, who at first, had a tremble in his voice. George finally was persuaded to come.

Twenty minutes passed. George arrived outside the store, resting his bike on the wooden bench. He sauntered inside, holding his share of the cash. After ten minutes of discussion, the owner had cancelled the police report and given his terms to the boys. They both left, relieved.

Jeremy turned to George, 'What about Tiffany?' he asked.

George replied laughing, 'I'm way out of her league!' Both boys laughed before a fist bump sent them their separate ways.

A Loud Room
Aaron Bowen

HE stood atop the black lonely building, the temptation to leap ever rising in his stomach. The solid block of nothingness filled his malnourished gut. Cold sweat stung his skin as the wind cut into his damp flesh. Below his feet, a swarm of tiny ants clumped in groups, all begging him to step back from the edge. The flashing lights, sirens, the whirring of helicopter blades, they were all silent to him on this gloomy night. *A loud room*; he was trapped, a deafening silence screamed 'jump' into his ears. No matter how hard he tried, nothing existed outside of his loud room. Nothing ever entered or escaped. It wrapped its slender fingers firmly around his mind, and he could never leave.

All of his strength, all of his vim, all of his – *himness* leaked through.

With shaking knees, he raised his eyes. The magnificent city skyline shone vibrantly and confidently, but only in his peripheral vision. Colours echoed around, shining and glimmering in the scurrying evening air. He looked at the grey path below him, not at the beautiful shimmering sky and neon, urban atmosphere; still trapped in the loud room.

The crowd below murmured anxiously at the sight of the cold-hearted being standing atop the building, not knowing that Death had just stolen his wife. She slept an eternal coma. A beautifully horrifying example of the Sun's power. It shone differently for everyone under its radiant gaze. Blackness crawled into the corners of the man's eyes. Remorse, despair, hollowness, leaked from his dying body through tears as thick as the river on the horizon. Tears of pain, anguish, but not of fear. He welcomed Death.

'What is left . . . ?' His shattered voice inaudibly cried to the world . . . There was no answer.

A calm zephyr nudged him closer to the edge. The street was in clear view from his position on the building. An updraught cooled his shaking body. Every step closer to the edge seemed to reduce the noise of the loud room. Violating monsters had chewed him up, and seemingly spat him out. The man was reduced to nothing. Like the nothing in his heart. Like the nothing in his person. . .

A tropical storm raged; it lurked across the evening sky, thick blotches of rain drenched his clothes, and his mind. His blurred, red eyes scanned the city, maybe for the last time.

The golden river flowed away from him, like his *hope*. The black clouds smothered all light, like his *soul*. Yet, the loud room didn't let up its mighty grip upon his weak heart.

The ominously colossal weight of social conformity had dragged him to breaking point. The man's bare feet pulled him closer to the ledge of the building.

Redemption

Bullies from his childhood tormented him consciously and in his dreams. The gravity of his mental illness had finally taken its toll on him. The school yard bullies were truly the founders of the man's psychologically unescapable loud room.

The last of the pink-orange light was shrouded by dark, menacing clouds. He thought of his two little girls he had only seen so recently. Their innocence, their beauty, their – cold skin.

An unfortunate accident it had been. The slow motion head-on replayed infinitely over and over and over in his mind; unable to erase it from his memory. Trapped in a loud room. The car sank to the bottom of the river off the bridge. He took another step closer to the edge, toes hanging off.

The man searched and searched for the light. But there only remained a black hallway. White noise filled every pore of his body. Photos hung on the walls of the hallway, and he did not have the courage to look away from them. His wife, his two, sweet girls; their sunken-eyed portraits suspended on the walls, slung up by hanging rope. It seemed like an eternity standing in the hallway. Tearing at his head trying to stop the sound. Muffled screaming. Unbearable pain. The familiar metallic taste filling his mouth until he couldn't breathe. But finally, *finally*! The loud room door cracked open and shadows leaked in. He made no hesitation.

All that remained in his vision was the silhouettes of creatures circling in the sky above, chattering, as if urging him to jump . . . and he agreed with the dark monsters. His skin was hot, his eyes stung, his ears bled, his black heart thundering away in irregular pulses . . .

With all of his strength, all of his vim and all of his *himness* he choked onto this moment. Away from his enemies, away from his fears and evils. This was a crack in his loud room; an opportunity to come back and overthrow his childhood nightmares, an opportunity to see his two sweet girls and beautiful wife, an opportunity for redemption.

The sensation of cold air punching him in the gut would be burned into his mind for eternity. His foot triumphantly tread heavily onto the emptiness below his weight.

In the eyes of his loud room, this was his chance to redeem himself.

The Wandering Jew
Virginia Miranda

I carried you on eagle's wings and brought you to myself – Exodus 19:4

THE first orange hued rays of sunrise kissed the treeless desert as Isaac stepped from his stony mountain home. He let the soft amber glow of the sun's rays pour through his fingers like gold dust, bringing warmth to his cold empty body. He pushed aside the reality of his despair and savoured the light radiating from the golden orb.

Today was Good Friday. Looking across the valley, far to his left, he could see the sparkling waters of the Dead Sea. Directly in front was Masada, Herod's desert fortress and last remaining site of the rebel Jews. A place of majestic beauty and intolerable sadness was now a pile of rubble. The cable car that transported tourists to Masada's lofty heights was visible in the sun's reflection.

He was connected to the desert. Was now, was in the past and would be way into the future. His was a connection to the beauty of the desolation of his surroundings and the desolation of his soul.

Was the desert in sympathy with him or was his soul sympathizing with the desert?

Many years had passed since he last spent time in his beloved Judean mountains. He had arrived in Tel Aviv three days ago. A bus ride to Ein Gedi and a day's walk found him high up on the eastern side of the mountains. The cave that had been his home on and off for an eternity had not changed. His meagre belongings were still there, hidden in the wall of the cave, protected from animals by a large granite rock.

On his first night Isaac slept in his twenty-first-century clothes. He built a fire, spread out his blanket and dreamed of a life with soft beds, food on the table and new places to discover. But Passover was in a few days. He had work to do, both inside and out – a cleansing of the soul and a cleansing of his surrounds.

The following day Isaac donned his monk's habit and leather sandals from centuries past, and set about finding food and water. In Ein Gedi he brought provisions: flour, salt, matches, and a warm blanket. His ancient arthritic joints needed the warmth. He collected herbs from the mountain ledges and water from the local springs. He set small traps above his cave home and along trails used by local fauna.

In the early morning and late afternoon he knelt to pray, praying from deep within his heart.

Isaac's visit to the Judean Mountains was no holiday. It was no camping trip into the wilderness, no getting in touch with his inner camper. This was his penance, his atonement . . . and it was long overdue. For Isaac was cursed to wander *till he sees the Son of Man coming in his kingdom.*

In the early years of his accursedness Isaac spent Passover and the Easter period here in the mountains in search of peace, praying for redemption. As the years turned into centuries he tired of the desert and began to roam the world, learning, teaching and praying.

In the thirteenth century he could be found in Forli Italy, a wandering monk with a grey beard carrying a long staff. He was known to miraculously heal the sick and offer redemption to sinners.

Stories of his exploits across the world appeared in folklore and literature. From Germany to France to Iberia people called him *The Wandering Jew*. He related accounts of history with conviction only an observer would know. He spoke fluently the language of the lands he passed through.

Once he saw a painting, named *The Wandering Jew*. Was this how people depicted him? A birdlike creature standing with a black hand pointed to the back of his head as if holding a gun. Another hand pointed down from heaven, using the motif *the Hand of God*, suggesting the divine origin of the curse? An empty chair in the foreground gave rise to the belief; the figure could not settle and was forced to wander.

In the 1500s he was seen in Hamburg – repentant and ill clothed. People reported he was distracted, disturbed at the thought of having to move on in a few weeks.

Farmers in England arranged the rows in their fields; so on the Sabbath Isaac might find a resting place. The farmers believed for every other day of the week his hands must rest on a plough. His only respite was Passover and Christmas.

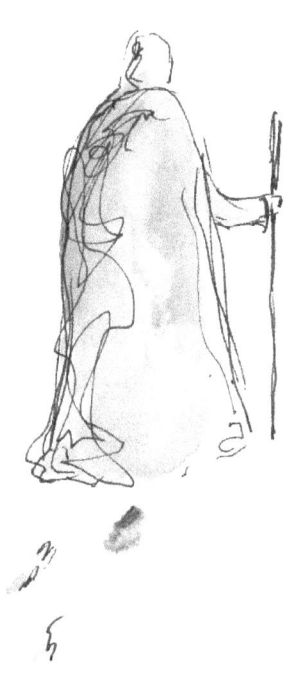

Redemption

During the seventeenth century he was a bishop in the court of King Charles II. For Isaac this was a time of civil war and great political upheaval.

In the eighteenth century he was a Trappist monk at Abbaye de Orval, Belgium. As a Trappist monk his silence was accepted, for idle talk was discouraged. Silence meant people did not ask questions or observe each other closely.

During his stay at Orval the French Revolution broke out. Isaac along with his fellow monks offered hospitality to Austrian troops. For this transgression French forces burnt the Abbaye to the ground. Isaac escaped, making for the English Channel.

Once when he was in New York in the 1880s, he read a poem about himself. It was a sad poem. After, he searched the mirror looking for those bitter unyielding eyes, eyes that remembered everything.

He had flinched at the reflection, a troubled soul with no foreseeable end to this curse and no forgiveness forthcoming. They were the eyes of a man who lived a life of anguish, eyes that forced the poem's narrator to look away.

Isaac saw deep within his own soul the many stories of his lives thus far, and he remembered everything.

He knew he could never stay in one place for any length of time. Always he must move. Never could he divulge who he was. People could guess, speculate, write stories and paint likenesses. For more than two thousand years he travelled as a monk, a friar, a priest – in search of a higher truth and of his self.

He brought his mind back to his mountain home, back to the ledge, reuniting his body, mind and soul. He sighed and felt the waves of a terrible loneliness sweep over him. How much more time must pass before he atoned for his sin.

He felt a gentle nudge. Like a returning friend the Nubian ibex stood beside him. Light tan in colour with a white underbelly, the sweet-faced animal appeared to remember him.

Isaac spoke to her of life, love, loneliness, and death. He told her of the day he stood in the River Armenia and became a Christian. Did the Lord want more, he asked. That had been long ago. He must keep going. He could not rest. He would stay for the customary time and then he would return to his world, a world he hardly understood, a world where death and hatred were daily events. Where his words were often mocked and more often ignored.

The ibex tilted her head listening to his soft words. Isaac smiled in spite of his thoughts. The morning sun spread its warmth inside the cold stone walls of his mountain home.

A group of eagles flew past his ledge. He watched them soar high above Masada, in a warlike formation. But Isaac knew differently. The eagle represented great power, balance, dignity and grace. Theirs was a connection to higher truths. In the sacred symbolism of many native tribes the eagle stood for power rising above the earth, above the physical and the literal into the heavens. They were seen as mystics with penetrating spiritual intuition.

Redemption

The eagles saw the overall pattern of our lives – the connection to spirit guides and teachers.

Isaac bowed to their creative spirit. He felt a flutter in his chest. Were they listening to him? Through knowledge, hard work and faith he hoped to achieve redemption . . . to balance heaven with earth . . . to communicate with his creator.

He could not forget his indiscretion and his ultimate punishment. He would continue his work, travel the world helping to shape its history, proselytizing spreading the Lord's word even in the face of great adversity. He would fly like an eagle above humanity's ignorance. He would continue to preach to the faithful and pray one day he would be forgiven for that indiscretion.

The ibex made her customary clicking sound and turned to leave. Isaac lightly patted her on the rump and returned to his mountain home. Yesterday, his traps were fruitful, capturing hyrax, lizards, partridge and ducks. He would not starve and with a steady supply of fresh water he would not go thirsty.

A soup of hyrax and partridge simmered over the open fire. Beside the pot was a collection of wild edible plants. He would add them once the meat was tender. Buried deep within the coals was his bread. The freshly baked smell produced a low rumbling from his empty stomach.

But now was not the time to eat. Now was the time to pray. He knelt before his ancient carved granite altar and began with the Pater Noster. His Latin words echoed off the walls. A shadow fell across the cave opening. But Isaac's eyes were closed, lost in the words he knew so well. With her ears upright, the Ibex appeared to be listening. Across the valley the eagles sat quiet, their sharp eyes watching, their keen ears to attention.

> PATER noster, qui *es* in cœlis;
> sanctificatur nomen tuum:
> Adveniat regnum tuum;
> fiat voluntas tua, sicut in cœlo, et in terra.
> Panem nostrum cotidianum da nobis hodie:
> Et dimitte nobis debita nostra,
> sicut et nos dimittimus debitoribus nostris:
> et ne nos inducas in tentationem:
> sed libera nos a malo.

The Lord's Prayer finished, Isaac spoke to Him of his transgressions and achievements, these many years gone. The love he found, but had left behind. He knew he couldn't stay . . . his choice. The people he helped, the people he saved, the work he did in far off lands, the wells he dug, and the buildings he helped build.

A great sadness overwhelmed him as he saw in his mind's eye a vision of Jesus as He stopped to rest outside the shop, the shoemaker's shop, Isaac's shop, the cross weighing heavy on His shoulders.

Then as every year for the past two millennia, he saw himself raise his hand in anger and heard his own words, 'Go on quicker Jesus! Go on quicker! Why dost Thou loiter?'

Redemption

There followed the words that would condemn him to an eternity of wandering. 'I shall stand and rest, but thou shalt go on till the last day,' the Lord said.

Slowly at first, in a state of grace, Isaac professed his faith. From his words came strength and understanding. He prayed one day his punishment of immortality would be over and he would taste death.

Soon, he thought, *the Wandering Jew would be no more.* He felt a quiver in his bones.

Outside, the group of Eagles flew high, their dark feathers contrasting against the blue sky. Had they heard his prayers? Would they carry his message to the Creator? Had they seen the pattern of Isaac's life, his continued hard work, his reclaiming of his faith?

Would they connect him to his spirit guide and send him home?

A great tiredness overwhelmed Isaac. He lay down to rest and closed his eyes. Outside, the flight call of the eagles resonated across the Judean Mountains.

The Ibex turned from the cave entrance and gently soft footed her way back up the mountainside.

COCA COLA AD

Mocco Wollert

Depending on the mood I am in
I smile or cry, sometimes both
every time the Coca Cola ad appears.
For thirty seconds I am young again,
swigging coke and dancing rock-an-roll.
I had forgotten all about it
but really nothing has changed.

Youth needs to dance, fall in love,
irrespective of time or place;
decades on, it is still you and me
against the world, only the tune changed.
The television blasts into my ears
'Coke's the best' - I was the best,
we all were, oh man we were.

I hum the tune, making nostalgic cow eyes.
After the tears have dried I decide
that you and I are still hanging in there.
I go and buy a king size bottle of Coke,
mix it with two stiff rums in tall glasses,
ready to give my old man a good time.

The Lost Wonders of the World
Giang Nguyen

IT was a sight he had never experienced. In a place like this, you could forget the colour of the sky – for the canopy spewed a million greens. Emerald, shamrock and jade ornamented the treetops, illuminating the space with vivid rays of lime. Shades of olive twisted and twined up thick trunks, slithering their way towards the interrupted sunlight. Even the forest floor was flooded by envious leaves, who longed to subside in the crown, where they were once vibrant and lively.

James held the photograph up to a dim light bulb swinging from the cabin ceiling.

'Grandpa, where did you take this?'

Michael swung around, and squinted his expiring eyes. As they rumbled over the abyss of greenery captured within the frame, the hole in his heart reopened. He thought back to a time when his joints could move freely. They carried him across the rolling sand hills of the Sahara in 2009, where the weight of the Moroccan sun beat down on him mercilessly. They hiked him to the tip top of Tianzi Mountain in 2016 to spectate its illustrious, floating sea of green. They even swam him face to face with a great white shark in 2024, the time he went diving through the exotic Bahaman waters.

Michael's biology career opened him up to an entire new world. He never had to work a day in his life, for he did what he loved – during the days he was on field, that is. After his discovery of Florapotestatem – or as it was commercialised, *FloPower* – he really didn't have to work at all. With the decline of fossil fuels in the 2000s, the discovery of a plant based source of energy was deemed revolutionary. Michael Butler painted a name for himself as the biologist who transformed living; not only was *FloPower* ten times more efficient than oil, but it was far more environmentally friendly – or at least it seemed that way. While Michael had been so caught up in the fame and fortune, he had not realised that he was slowly stripping the world of rolling sand hills, floating seas of green and Bahaman great whites. He even managed to take away . . .

'The Amazon Rainforest,' he nodded, zapping back to reality.

James twisted his head in confusion. He could remember Mrs Little teaching his class about the Amazon Desert, but did not recall anything about a rainforest.

'It was once filled with trees,' Michael said, noticing bolts go off in the 8-year old's head, 'trees that grew to the size of skyscrapers, and were filled with macaws, parrots, hawks, herons and swallows!'

'Birds? They lived in trees?' James' eyes widened with wonder.

Michael loved talking to his grandchildren about his past. The way they lit up reminded him of his childhood – days and days of running to the forest behind his house, and exploring to his heart's content. This very aspect is what drove Michael to fall in love with travelling in the first place; it let him feel young again. It put him in situations where he was magically lost in moments of discovery. Beautifully confused. It didn't matter whether it was waking up at 5am in Iceland to a sky illuminated by crystal blue ribbons, or the first time paddling out over the shallow reefs of the Caribbean. There was this feeling of invincibility that hit him like a drug. And all of a sudden . . .

'What happened to all the trees, Grandpa?'

Michael's heart sunk. It had never occurred to him that James' generation was living through a childhood that did not consist of reckless tree climbing, unsupervised exploration or daisy chains.

'Well Kiddo,' he paused, 'we had to cut them down to make sure everyone could enjoy a home with electricity and warm water. It's a growing population out there, you know?'

James didn't 'know'. He just shook his head, scrunched his lips and crossed his arms – the way he would when his mother said no to a toy at the supermarkets.

'Don't the birds deserve to enjoy a home with electricity and warm water too?' he simply replied, leaving Michael chuckling.

For the next half an hour or so, James ran around the wooden cabin roaring about jaguars, tree frogs and tarantulas the size of baseballs. Michael simply continued to filter through what was left of his Amazonian studies; since that was what he had been there for.

Binoculars, a compass, bug nets, an exhausted sketch book and stacks of land profiles. *Where was what I was looking for?* Michael thought to himself. He'd been searching for days and was starting to lose hope.

'Grandpa! Grandpa!'

'Did you find it, Kiddo?' Michael asked.

James shook his head, and held up a pair of flippers and a snorkel.

'What are these, Pop?' he laughed, flapping the flippers around hysterically as if they were wings.

Michael stumbled over the mountains of turned over boxes, and took the snorkelling equipment from his bird-mimicking grandson. He told James to sit down, and eased his weak body to the ground next to him. Michael slid the flippers onto his feet; and snorkel over his face.

'These,' he said pointing to the flippers, 'are just like fish fins. They let you swim real fast through the ocean.'

He moved his attention to the snorkel. 'This funny looking thing lets you breathe underwater. Just like a shark!'

It only took these few words for eyes to fill with wonder once again. James excitedly jumped up, forgetting about his 'fish fins', and in seconds, boxes were flying across the cabin. Michael swore he'd never laughed so much in his life.

'So . . .? Are you going to tell me about snorkelling?' James prepared himself for another one of Granddad's stories; crossing his legs and straightening his back.

With a grin painted across his face, Michael retold the story of his Great Barrier Reef adventure as if it were yesterday. He could still recall every last polka-dotted coral trout and could even remember winning the 'spot the octopus' contest – of course, if he tried to play spot the octopus today, a win would be impossible. The water was too acidic for man to swim in, let alone for animals to live in.

The truth is that Michael's life was now a series of memories which would never be relived. Not because they were so unique and therefore irreplaceable, but because the places in which they existed were no longer. They'd been dug up, thrown over and shredded to pieces by corporate businessmen who did not care for any more than their wealth.

There were many places where humanity had realised that they had done wrong – places which begged the world for a change. Perhaps when the coral reefs started bleaching, and marine life started suffering, someone should've picked up on Nature's cries of pain. But what happened? Man was too thick to bother, and instead turned a blind eye. Maybe when the islands began to drown in the tears of the Mother Earth, and people, themselves, were losing their homes, humanity might then have realised what the word karma really meant. That didn't appear to stop anyone, however. Once half the trees had been cut down for *FloPower* Inc., and the air turned into a thick smog, surely someone would've stopped there! Michael could have stopped there. But instead he, like the corporate business men he once despised, only thought about one thing. Himself.

Looking through his lifetime of work the past couple of days had brought back memories; ones which warmed him, but also ones which haunted him.

'I'll never find them,' he whispered to himself.

Michael had always been a dreamer, but in this moment, there was not a hopeful bone in his body. It was because of him, that all his hard work went to waste. It was because of him that the world fell apart. It was because of him that what was once in a lifetime for the older generation, would be never in a lifetime for James.

His joints felt numb and his throat like scurvy. With a single blink, his eyes were suddenly wet with tears. How could he have let this happen? Michael, of all people, should've known better. Experience is far more valuable than money will ever be. For money cannot buy back the Amazon rainforest, the Pacific Islands or the Sahara Desert. His weak hands, shakily attempted to cover the pain that ripped across his face – he couldn't let James see him like this. Michael had always tried to act bravely before his grandchildren, but in truth, he was terrified.

'Pop?'

'Oh, I'm so sorry, Kiddo!' he cried hysterically, placing his tear-smeared hands on his grandson's shoulders.

James opened his mouth to speak, but was interrupted by a weeping Michael.

'I swear I'll make it up to you!' he promised, even though he was unsure whether it was one he could keep.

James just giggled and called his grandfather silly. The boy pulled out a satchel full of various seeds and flower bulbs he had been holding, and instantly Michael's attention had drifted away from the promise and onto the satchel.

'I can't believe it!' He gasped.

With just one glance at the seeds, Michael saw a universe of potential. Some were smaller than grains of rice, and others, the size of golf balls. A few were red or green, and others were dull blacks or browns. But it did not matter how they looked, for they were ugly ducklings just waiting to happen. Perhaps one of them would grow into a grand Kapok Pine, who would grow higher than any other tree had dared to reach. Another could blossom into a bold Heliconia, igniting the world again with life and colour.

Upon an impulse, Michael lifted James off the ground and swung him in the air. After days of searching and searching, it had been here all along. This was it. This was how he would redeem himself.

Michael took his grandson's hand in one arm, the seed satchel in another and kicked open the cabin door.

'C'mon Kiddo,' he exclaimed, glancing back at the photograph, 'I'll show you what a real rainforest looks like.'

A TROPICAL REVERIE
David Bell

The rain beats on tin roofs intensely, loud
above the voices – droplet forming sea.
Precipitation and humidity
Inseparable – an interwoven shroud
of singular intent. Life's blood empowered
with frightening force in stream and tribut'ry.
The works of man bend in humility
before a wanton nature, free, unbowed.

Inertia is at one with tropic heat.
Quite imperceptibly the seasons pass.
The heavens are still – amphibians reply.
Life's rhythmic pulse, responding to the beat
of hearts, increases for a moment. Grass
forever green, awaits the monsoon sky.

Cleanliness is Next to Godliness

Bakthi Ross

AN unforgivable hatred Mason had towards the people he was living with. He could not get out of the situation because of the remoteness and he couldn't get a new job out of that place.

They had continually taken advantage of him. Whatever he told them they still behaved the same. Some days the abuse was unbearable. Total nonsense and petty things they argued about. They weren't even worth talking about. Sometimes Mason told lies to avoid confrontations and argument with people. 'Yes, I took the packet of papers and I will go and get you another pack,' and he drove to the shop and bought two packets of papers and gave them to them, before it turned into an argument. It was only two dollars for the packets of papers.

Arguments about two dollars would go for months and would be reminded of every day. 'Don't touch my stuff without asking for it,' Narina would say. If Mason said, 'No one touched your stuff,' she would not believe him. All the people in the house would have a comment over it as well. The tension in the house over two dollars was hard to take.

Someone may lose their temper and hit someone over two dollars. Mason had to put in the money to keep the calm in the house. He continually put out five to ten dollars and thought it was not worth arguing about.

Once someone had taken Narina's notepad. It was only fifty cents. She threw a book at Ray and hurt him. He had to go to the hospital to have two stiches. Continuous bullying and abuse over petty things. When someone left the door open and the cat ran outside meant it would be never ending abuse and foul language.

Most of them became scared of Narina. She was an anxious character and wanted everything to be perfect and clean. She would not relax. Being casual was a sin for her. Her home environment was worse than a work environment. You cannot do this, you cannot do that, she was full of orders. You cannot casually sit on the couch and watch television. Mason had to worry about creasing the couch and bed sheets. When you get off the bed it should look no one had slept on it.

It was dinner on time, lunch on time, sort of a place. Mason could not even relax in his own room. Music was a no-no, even with an ear phone. Some days Mason stayed out and told Narina he would not be there for dinner. He was happy to put his feet up and eat the drumsticks with his hands. He did not have to behave perfectly at the dinner table.

Once the little boy next door hit the ball and it damaged the rose plant. Narina walked to the neighbour and knocked on the door and told her off. The little boy was very scared and did not even want to play outside. The neighbour had to keep the children inside too much and became very stressful. The family moved out of the house.

The fear Narina created in people's minds was unbearable. Why they were so scared of her, no one knew. Their minds were controlled by her. No one stood up to her. Someone should punch the crap out of her, but no one did. Why people accepted these situations and lived under her rule, Mason didn't know. She was overpowering.

Mason named her Miss Petty. All the petty nonsenses became a big argument and big drama with her. One of them had moved out because they left the door open and the cat ran into the garden. Such a small incident and she put them through such abuse and hell they practically ran away from her.

Tension! Tension! This was the climate in the house. A quietness and silence took over the house. People feared placing a glass on the table. Any loud noise created havoc. Most walked quietly in the house. Their walk was so quiet they startled at anything. No one could come near them, they feared someone would hurt them.

Narina was a fat anxious bossy figure. No one sat near her or looked at her eye to eye. Each of the people transformed when they saw her. They were laughing, playing and joking away from her. When they entered the house, they became someone else.

Mason thought he wanted to do something about the situation. This cannot go on. He wanted to talk to her and tell her off. Life is worth more than this petty nonsense she argues about. She hurt many people's feelings and people are more important than petty things. He wanted to tell her off but she talked and over talked and never listened to anyone.

He feared she may hurt someone seriously over two dollars. He wanted to correct her and calm her down. Narina acted like she was crazy and hot tempered. When you left a cup on the coffee table and did not take to the kitchen sink and wash it meant the day would be ruined for everyone. '

'I am not going to clean after you,' she would yell. 'I am going to wash it in a minute,' is not good enough for her. You have to do it straight away. No one likes to live that perfectly.

Home is a place where you relax and let go the customs. How to eat? How to sit? All that is unnecessary when you want to relax. Narina would not let go of her customs and rules for anybody. It became so stressful people would not even sit on the couch. Narina was stressed all the time. She tried to keep everything perfect but she couldn't keep up with it.

Mason tried to annoy her by leaving the plate on the table. He brought out his shoes and left them in the middle of the room. Narina was like a mad woman. Mason looked at her while she was angry and she lost her temper. Mason stood still in front of her without saying a word. He waited until she stopped talking. She talked so fast without leaving any gaps between words. Because Mason didn't say anything or do anything, she stopped talking and looked at him. She came to a realisation that she was over concerned about tidiness and chased everyone away. Narina couldn't control her own temper and was obsessed with cleanliness.

He slowly helped her overcome her obsession. She needed to de-stress. She was cleaning day and night. She wanted everyone around her to be clean as well. No one did what she wanted them to do. Her obsession made her sick and tired but she wasn't aware of it. Why she was angry or how to control anger she didn't know.

Mason made her house dirty and watched Narina's anger rising. She was over tired and couldn't even sleep. Mason sat down and talked to her and told her when her house was dirty once in a while she didn't have to go mad. Take a rest before you clean it. You do not have to clean every day. Organise your time and make time for rest.

He noticed a slow change in Narina. She followed Mason's time management sheet.

After a month, for the first time, Mason saw her smile. Narina learnt to relax and cleaned only now and then. It was redemption from her clean-freak mentality. She behaved normally and made plans to have a holiday. She cleaned every week rather than every hour.

THE HAT

Mocco Wollert

The hat caught my eye,
as the old man put it down beside me,
on the rough, brown bench.
A small, feather was wedged in the hatband.
I suddenly saw it in my hand, picked up
from the sodden floor of an autumn forest.

We used to walk on Sunday afternoons,
he matching his strides to my small ones,
his face smooth, first wrinkles teasing,
my love for him warm and safe,
as he held my small hand in a mitten.

One day the forest no longer heard our steps,
gone his walks with a small child
who now cried in grown-up grief,
refusing to accept the inevitability of death,
subconsciously still holding his hand.

As I looked at the hat on the bench
my heart finally broke, acknowledged
he was truly gone, that other small steps
walked with a father on Sundays,
that different, tiny feathers
lay amongst the wet, brilliant leafs.

The Twilight and the Dawn
Nicholas Thomas

I'D never seen the woods from this angle before. From the edge of the forest they had appeared so tall, dark and frightening. Only the foolish would delve inside. However, from atop the hill on which the fortress stood, the snow-capped trees looked beautiful. The skies were empty of birds as it was far too cold for flying. 'Twas the evening of the winter's solstice, the darkest night of the year. I could see the trees stretch for miles like a green and white carpet rolled out across the land. Of course, they were still frightening, but from this point of view, they also beckoned.

"Dirhael, shields!" A voice cut through the chilly evening air like a sabre. The familiar whistle of arrow flight sounded in the distance as a cloud of feathered shafts sailed towards us. I looked to a corpse to my right and picked up a round shield, noticing a coat of arms bearing a fox, and tucked myself beneath its bulk. The next sound was a cacophony of thudding and screaming as the arrows either bounced off stone, embedded themselves in dark oaken shields or found their mark in the flesh of the men beside me.

It was my first time on the field. Beforehand, in my boyish naiveté, I had been most ardent for the thrill of battle. We had all heard the stories told around campfires on overnight hunting expeditions and had longed for the beauty of the fight. Described as an art, war was, and we wanted to be the artists.

Our trainers had always taught us that in the field of battle, an errant mind could cost a life but I could not resist. It was something I had never considered before but these men, the ones who hadn't even survived the first hail of arrows, where was their glory? It is a strange thing; the thought of other people dying. It never seems quite as real as when you witness it with your very own eyes.

I looked up at the sunset, casting a red and orange tinge across the rows of steel armour and pikes, glinting colourfully as if they were festooned with jewels. I wondered whether this was the last sunset I would ever see – and whether wondering was a mark of cowardice. Those thoughts themselves seemed to condemn me.

As I stood in this stasis I was still aware of the battle raging around me. Before me stood a man; an axe between his shoulder blades. A young soldier lay slumped, blood bubbling from his mouth and colouring the snow a brilliant red. I stumbled away from the corpse whose eyes stared into a realm no living person should see. I looked to my left and caught a glance of a leather-clad man pushing a woman to the ground and slitting her throat. A young boy was knocked to the dirt by a shield and trampled beneath a fleeing warhorse; everywhere these atrocities. I knew now that this was war. There was no glory, there was no pride; for how could someone feel pride for this? I could not kill for anyone, not a man, nor a woman, nor God.

And so, I ran. I was not ready to die for someone else. I was not ready to die for glory. I broke the line, a gap in our shield wall taking my place, a weakness in our army. My vision blurred and I no longer needed to see. My legs knew what to do so my brain just sat inert. I clambered on the nearest horse, a mare, as white as a winter's frost. My heels dug into her flanks and she ran like the wind on a cold, stormy night.

Before long the cold became almost unbearable. I could feel it biting down on me like an icy wolf as cold as the grave. After I urged the mare on for miles and miles it was only a matter of time before she could not go any further. At the flats of the woods she stopped, exhausted and waited for me to climb down from her. I slid myself from her eerily cold back and landed ankle-deep in the snow that blanketed the forest floor.

I looked up at the tall pines, old like crones and wise like gods. They intimidated me now, more than ever. It felt as if they were judging me for my crimes and broken promises. These trees had stood longer than most people had lived. They had seen cowards come and cowards go. I would wager that none of the fleeing ones had dared pull back their curtains of foliage and take their chances against whatever dwelt within. I forced my fear-stricken legs to move, one after the other, step after step, into the dry, dead bracken, sharp as a young lord's tongue.

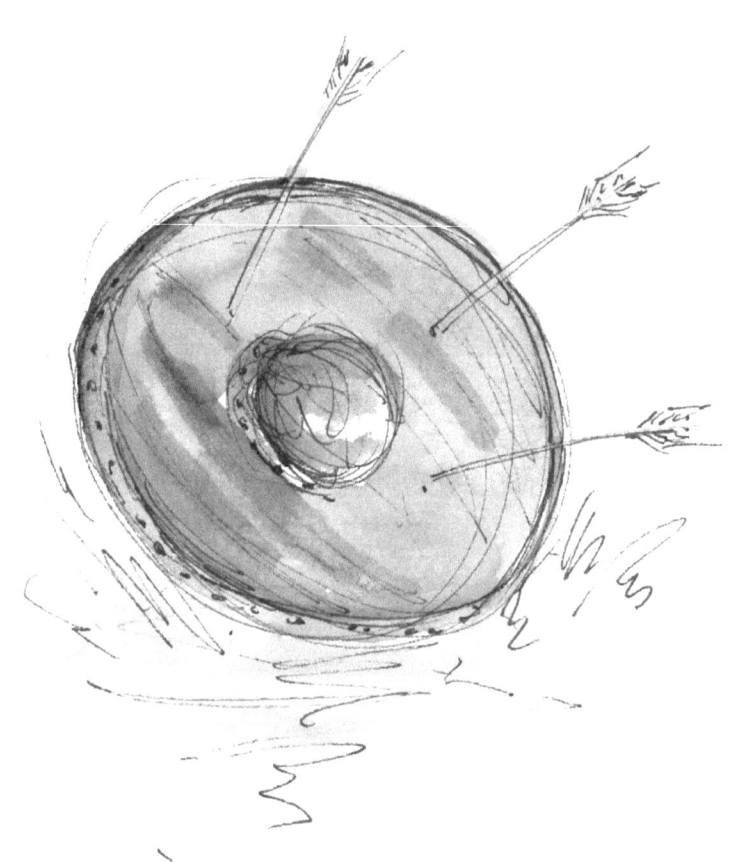

Redemption

Stumbling hastily through the undergrowth, to my surprise, I emerged into a clearing among the trees. The first thing I noticed was the warmth, or relative warmth, in comparison to the rest of the frosty wood. It was a relief, although not the sultry weather of midsummer. I found a less snow-covered area of ground, sat myself down and tried to cry. Fortunately for my remaining whisper of dignity I could not manage to shed a tear. My gaze went to the heavens, visible through the open canopy of the clearing. It was the time of evening I feared most. The time when the final valiant rays of sunlight that once so proudly beamed across the sky are sent back by the forces of darkness. Forced from the heavens, when even the raw power of the sun was made cowardly before the inevitable night; a time devoid of hope.

My thoughts wandered, a sea of ponderings regarding my mistakes, failures and inadequacies until finally I worked up enough fury with my own incompetence to stand. Leaning haphazardly against a tree, drunk with rage, I screamed to the sky, to the stars and to the last sliver of sunlight that dared show its face in the nightmarish half-darkness of twilight.

"You bastards!" I bellowed as the last rays diminished and the wood was plunged completely into a sea of darkness. "You cowardly bastards!"

What I had to do was apparent but the mere thought made me shudder with fear. I was evil, that much was obvious; but cowardly? Surely not. When I joined my brothers, I had taken an oath. If I was ever to become a man I had to piece together my broken vows and reclaim my last fragment of honour. I had to return to them, that much I knew.

I emerged from the woods less than gracefully, after several hours' trek, and I was caught immediately in the blinding light of sunrise. The woods seemed to have stolen time like a thief during the night. Dawn was here and as the day unfurled, I began my journey towards the fortress. The path, made lifeless by the continuous abuse from horse, cart and foot alike, and lightly coated in snow, stretched upwards and over a hill, hiding the rest of the countryside from my view.

Suddenly, like an apparition of black, a murder of crows took flight from the ground behind the hill, screeching like banshees as they fled from an unseen threat. For the first time since returning from the woods I heard a sound, so orderly it seemed to blend into the countryside. It was the sound of marching. Growing steadily louder as I began my ascent of the road, a symphony of pain began to dominate. Screams and moans of the injured filled the crisp morning air. As I reached the top of the hill my fears became reality. It was my army, my brothers, the ones I had left behind.

"Halt!" commanded the leader of the vanguard, a big brute of a man clad in a mismatch of mail, leather and steel plate. He clambered off his grey stallion and his hand went to the great sword on his back while with his other hand he lifted the closed helm that obscured his identity. He dropped his headpiece to the ground and my blood ran cold; it was the battle commander, Qothor the Blackguard.

Qothor was looking frighteningly cheerful.

"Dirhael! Fancy meeting you here. We were just on our way to find you and flay your craven hide," Qothor growled. His voice sounded like the scraping of steel on steel; like a novice sharpening his blade on a whetstone.

My stomach turned; Qothor was as merciless as brigands came and he had a vendetta against me specifically.

"No words, Dirhael? You truly are craven, just like your father. I knew you would flee from this battle, in fact I was counting on it; you see, how else would I be granted permission to kill you?" Qothor leered, leaning forward so that I could smell the sour stink of wine on his breath.

"When your father came to us, he wanted wealth and he was willing to do anything to get it. Perhaps he didn't understand that when you join a band of brigands you are expected to rob the innocent of their goods and then their lives. When you were born he was already dead and so you belonged to us. Clearly, the craven apple doesn't fall far from the craven tree." The half-giant bellowed, spewing volcanic hatred like a hot spring.

I studied the beast that stood before me, as cruel as a man could be. It was no wonder he had lost the raid; he commanded with rage in his heart, not wisdom. I had never wanted to be evil. I had never wanted to live the life of a hateful bandit but it was what I was born into.

"Have you no words, boy?" Qothor raged. "Have you lost your wits?"

I remained silent, my anger boiling but my cowardice holding me back. My cowardice? I could no longer bear myself. I had been born into too many things that I did not want to be. A brigand. A coward. I would not stand for it. If I were to die at the hands of this bear I would go as a man, and a brave one.

"Qothor, I cannot continue to murder and plunder as if it is done without others' expense. This is not who I am, nor who I want to be," I reasoned, shakily.

"It is past that, Dirhael, this is no longer about your leaving of the battle; it is about your lack of loyalty," he said, his voice guttural and churlish.

"How can I remain loyal to a cause I do not believe in? To a cause I despise? I want to be free of this burden, but Qothor, only your mercy can grant my wish. One day, we may meet on the field of war and then we can fight this battle, but I implore you, spare my life this once." I pleaded, entreating any human part of him left.

As Qothor hefted his greatsword in preparation to strike me down, my lips parted.

"Is it better," I questioned him, "to be born brave, or to overcome your cowardly nature through great adversity?"

Qothor stared at me, his eyes like smouldering coals. He lowered his greatsword and glanced briefly at the trees beside us, then returned his gaze to me, now standing tall and defiant before him. For a fleeting moment, I thought that I had swayed his iron will, but my feeble hopes were soon dissolved. Never before in my life had I seen evil such as I saw in his face that day and never have I seen such malevolence since. He raised his blade once more but instead of falling to my knees in terror, I was surprised to find myself still standing. I stood there, ready for his cold steel to bite down on me when the wooden shaft of an arrow sprouted from his neck.

Qothor stood for a second, his eyes wide in fear as his hand went to the arrow that had pierced his throat. He coughed and his warm blood spattered onto my tunic, then he fell to his knees, choking, and died before me.

I was so shocked by this turn of events that I didn't notice the war horns blowing in the distance, nor the army that raced down the hill. I gazed about as if I were in a dream. I saw Qothor's men raise their shields and the mystery army's cavalry charge through them as if they were toy soldiers. I saw a coat of arms, a russet-coloured fox running across a green field; these men were the militia of the fortress that Qothor failed to sack. They swept through the brigands as if they were dead autumn leaves, pushing them against the dense forest and slaughtering them like animals. How glorious they were in their vengeance I cannot describe, but they fought like devils and before long, they had won.

I stood at the foot of the great, dark wood, amidst death and suffering, but never had I felt more alive. The militia cheered in unison, a beautiful sound that I will never forget, and a soldier rode up to me on a familiar mare as white as a winter's frost.

"I believe I have something that belongs to you, friend," he called from the top of my horse.

"We have been watching you for some time; your flight from our home, your ordeal through the woods. You must have some nerve," he said laughing as he looked up at the ancient pines that rose, like Nature's bulwark, from the earth.

"Standing at the base of them, here, they seem so tall and frightful, I would think only a fool would dare go inside. Are you a fool?" he inquired as he outstretched his arm to pull me up onto my mare's back.

I shook my head and grasped his gloved hand. He pulled me up with admirable strength and I settled myself behind the saddle.

The soldier turned back to me. "Good," he said, "because we need brave men like yourself. And don't worry, you're certainly not a coward any longer."

He spurred the mare's sides and she took off, the rest of the army following us up the road. I turned in my seat to catch a last look at the woods that had changed me, like a caterpillar in its chrysalis. They still seemed tall and dark, but whatever the soldier may have said, they were never again frightening.

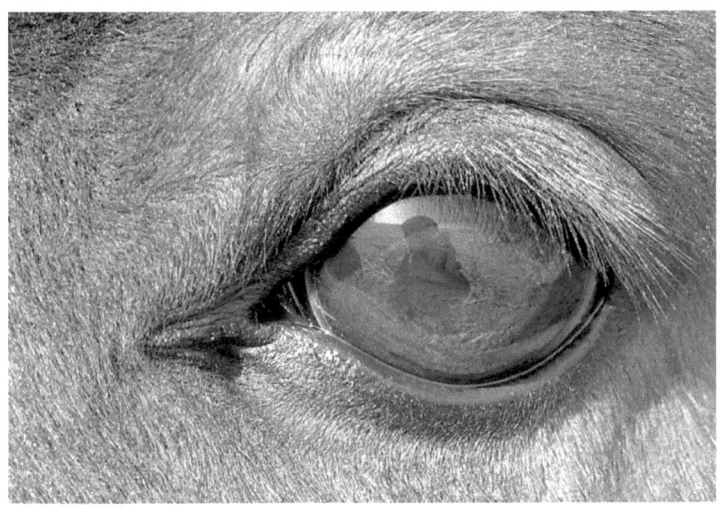

Photo of a horse's eye by Waugsberg

FAMILY TOGETHERNESS

Ray Penshorn

Digger was enduring mid-life crisis; his life seemed to be a bore.
He felt he was missing out somehow and decided to get with a whore.
Digger told his missus he'd be working away all night.
She believed every word he told her. He was her heart's delight.

They'd been married a long time and had a daughter they called Honey.
Honey was a Uni student. She loved to make easy money.
She had some friends at Uni, who were ladies of the night.
They charged big bucks for their services, and seemed to do alright.

They changed their names when on the job, where they put themselves up for sale.
They dreaded being caught red handed and winding up in jail.
Some clients changed their names as well, so rumours of them, no one could tell.
Honey decided to give it a shot. She changed her name to Sweet Darling Dot.

Redemption

She arranged to see a bloke named Pete. At a city motel, they agreed to meet.
She made herself comfy in room number eight. The door-bell rang. She said 'Come right in mate.'
When she saw who it was, it was shock and surprise. Digger was standing in front of her eyes
'Crikey!' said Digger, 'What are you doing here? Please don't tell Mama, sweet daughter dear.'

'I'll keep the secret, don't worry Dad.'
They left in a hurry feeling stupid and sad
So that is the story of Pete and Sweet Dot.
Cheating's a sin, it's much better to not.

It's a sin to tell a lie
Raymond W. Penshorn

HUMPHREY Prescott and his wife Colleen were a good-looking working-class couple in their forties. Their teenage son Peter had been missing for some time. It was a case of his having vanished without a trace. The local police had been notified but had no success in finding out where Peter was. The Missing Persons Bureau also became involved, they too with negative results. Peter's whereabouts were a total mystery.

Humphrey and Colleen were, naturally enough, upset to the utmost. They were frantic. In their grief, they decided to contact a spiritualist.

A popular TV Variety show regularly featured a well-known spiritualist named Ferdie Fortune. Ferdie claimed he could talk to the dead. The host of the show was tall dark and handsome Remington Prinshorn. The show was televised live every week in a city theatre known as The Loch.

Debonair Police Sergeant Denis Shepherdson was the officer in charge of the investigation into Peter's disappearance. He was a friend of a suave detective named Sherlock Tracy who ran his own agency called Crime Stoppers. Sherlock was in his early forties, had dark brown wavy hair with a hint of grey around the temples. He liked to wear checked sports coats. He had a black belt in Karate and was an expert violinist.

A man's man, Sherlock had helped Denis out, bringing criminals to justice on several occasions. Denis told Sherlock of his involvement with the Prescott's case, suggesting he might find some sort of clue along the way. Denis had run into dead ends. 'It's a tough one this one,' he said.

Sherlock promised he would look into it and paid a visit to the Prescotts. They discussed everything that had happened, how TV and radio news reports had cooperated and how they felt so helpless. 'Denis Shepherdson told me this was a tough one, I think I'd sooner go looking for a needle in a haystack.'

'Oh no, don't say that, please,' sobbed Colleen.

'Sorry Mrs Prescott, I'll do my very best, I promise you that.'

Denis was among the front-row audience at Remington Prinshorn's TV variety show. Sitting beside him was pretty Police Constable Glenda Cross. Both were off duty and in plain clothes. The theatre had a packed audience and cameras were on stage ready to go. There was a drum roll and Remington Prinshorn, looking his handsome best, walked onto the stage.

'Good evening,' he said as the audience burst into enthusiastic applause. Remington took a bow. 'Thank you,' he continued, 'Later on tonight, among others, we have with us, Mr Humphrey Prescott and his wife Colleen who are going to be interviewed by the well-known spiritualist, Mr Ferdie Fortune.

The audience once again gave a round of applause. Remington went on to say, 'But before we get too serious, as you are all aware, the show always begins with a song, so let's welcome to the stage, Miss Karen Lee who is going to get us all in the groove with an old favourite, 'All of Me'.'

Karen, a gorgeous blonde, stepped onto the stage wearing a pale pink one-shoulder knee-length dress with a long slit in one side. Recorded musical accompaniment began to play. Karen started to sing, making sexy movements as she did so. 'All of me, why not take all of me?'

As she continued to sing, a man named Rosco, reeking of alcohol, sitting in the front row a few seats from the police officers in plain clothes, mumbled something like, 'Yeah, know what? I just might do that, take all of her.'

Rosco stood and began to stagger toward the stage. He did not get far as he soon found himself in the vice like grip of Denis's firm hand while he flashed his police badge at him with his other.

'I suggest you remain seated.' Denis said in a tone that was not wise to be argued with.

'Yes Sir,' Rosco replied and reluctantly sat back down. Karen's song ended to loud applause and cries of 'more'.

Karen took a revealing bow. Remington approached the microphone saying, 'Thank you Karen, you were terrific as always; wasn't she ladies and gentlemen?' Another burst of applause followed with cries of more cries of 'more'. Remington eyed Karen closely. 'I can see why you want more,' he said with a grin. 'Maybe later. We'll see how we go.' Karen smiled and left the stage.

Remington introduced the flamboyant Ferdie Fortune who came onto the stage. Once again there was loud applause. After a short explanation to the audience of the Prescott's trauma, Ferdie said, 'I'll do my best to help out. Let's hope there are no more problem people here with us this evening eh Remington?'

'No more?' Remington responded with a curious expression.

'I'm referring to that chap who had his mind set on taking hold of Karen Lee during her song. Just as well that fellow sitting nearby brought him under control. You know I had a premonition something like that was going to happen.'

'Is that so? If you ever have a premonition of the winning numbers in the lottery, let me in on it. Heh,' Remington replied. 'We're all used to Rosco. He is a regular here. He's harmless enough.' Rosco was known about the place as the town drunk.

Ferdie shook his head and said, 'Winning numbers! That's what you call luck dear boy. Heh.' Remington rolled his eyes and introduced Humphrey and Colleen Prescott. At that time, Denis spoke quietly to Glenda informing her what he knew of the Prescott's woes.

The Prescotts stood on stage and were applauded. After the applause settled down, Ferdie asked several questions followed by saying, 'I hope I am wrong but I fear your Peter may have met with foul play.'

Colleen burst into tears. 'Bear with me,' Ferdie continued, 'I'll see if I can make contact. Can we have the lights dimmed please?'

The lights became dimmer. Ferdie gripped his forehead with both hands. His face had an expression that made him appear to be in agonizing pain.

'I dreaded the worst and I am so sorry to say that is what it is. Peter is no longer in this world.'

'Oh no,' screamed Colleen, 'What's happened?' She began to fiddle with a pearl necklace she was wearing.

Ferdie continued. 'He's okay he says, he's pleased to see you, and is showing some interest in your pearl necklace.'

'Is he really?' Colleen replied with a sob. 'He gave it to me for my last birthday.'

'I know you poor dear, he just told me that.'

'Where did he come to grief?' Humphrey asked.

'He was at the Snowy Mountains where he foolishly went out skiing alone when he fell into a snow covered crevice from which there was no escape.'

Humphrey shook his head in disbelief while Colleen continued to sob as the interview came to an end

After the show, police officers Denis and Glenda chatted with Remington when the TV host's' mobile phone rang. He excused himself for a moment to take the call. It was most unexpected to say the least.

It was from Peter Prescott. He was alive and well, living down in Tasmania. He had been picking apples under a false name. He had adopted the false name with the intent of avoiding tax payments. He had been watching the show and was overcome with a feeling of guilt which prompted him to let his parents know his whereabouts. He had left home when he did after having a row with Humphrey over some petty issue to do with borrowing his car and not replacing the fuel.

A brainwave came over Remington and he confided to the police whom the call was from. He asked if they would go along with his idea. They agreed as they thought it might also bring a false prophet undone. Remington insisted that they be present in the front row at the coming week's show. In the meantime, Denis contacted Sherlock Tracy and strongly suggested he be present there with them. 'I can assure you, it will be well worth your while,' he said.

Ferdie was invited back for the next show under the pretence the Prescott's wished to hear more from their departed son, Peter. Ferdie readily agreed. The Prescotts were invited for a return interview also, which they solemnly agreed to. Remington did not like to keep them in the dark but it was all for a good outcome, not to mention how the show's ratings would skyrocket. The secret went no further than Remington and the two police officers.

The week passed by and soon enough, Remington was standing on the stage presenting another show.

'Good evening everyone,' he said. 'As usual we have something very special for you later in the show but first, as we normally do, let's get the show going with a song.' The audience applauded. Remington continued to speak. 'Please put your hands together for the lovely Shannon Dale. Shannon has come all the way to be with us from Cannonvale. Yes, it's Shannon Dale from Cannonvale, heh, I'm a poet and I don't even know it.' Some of the audience gave a slight chuckle while others smiled politely.

Recorded music began to play. Beautiful Shannon walked onto the stage clad in a long silvery, body hugging, backless dress laced with glitter. She had long reddish, wavy hair that almost seemed to shine. 'Thank you, Remington, you big hunk,' she said with a broad smile, 'How do you like my strapless evening gown?'

'I like it quite a lot Shannon. I sure do,' he replied.

'I'll bet you'd like my gown-less evening strap even more, you naughty boy, tee hee.'

'I think it's time you did your song Shannon, heh,' Remington smiled. Shannon began to sing. Shannon swayed to the music as she sang and made sexy movements.

Once again, Rosco sat in the front row. A few seats along were Denis and Glenda. This time, Detective Sherlock Tracy was at their side. Rosco watched on intently. He was drooling at the mouth. During the performance, Shannon shaped her lips in a sexy pout and faced directly at Rosco. He became so carried away, he gripped the sides of his seat to stand when he heard the cold voice of Denis quietly saying, 'Don't even think about it Rosco.' Rosco slumped into his seat, cursing Denis under his breath.

Shannon sang beautifully to the end of the song. Shannon smiled, took a bow and mouthed a kiss to Rosco who was totally overcome with frustration. The audience once again gave rowdy applause. Shannon stepped back from the microphone, pulled away a long-haired reddish wig to reveal a short black-haired crew cut. To everyone's surprise, Shannon spoke to the audience in a gruff male voice, 'Thanks a lot cobbers, good night.' With that, Shannon departed the stage in a manly stride. The audience at first, were dumbfounded and agog but when they gained their senses, they soon broke into deafening applause. Rosco began to cry.

Remington returned to the microphone. 'Well, how about that? Don't it beat all?' He said. 'Wait 'til you see what we have for you next. Remember Ferdie Fortune who was here last week? Of course you do. Well, we have invited Ferdie back to dig a little deeper into what happened to the unfortunate Peter Prescott at the time of his disappearance. Also here with us are Peter's Mum and Dad, Humphrey and Colleen. Let's welcome them all here on stage.' The audience applauded.

Once again, Ferdie rambled on of what he supposedly knew of Peter's fate. Humphrey stood there biting his lip while Colleen continually burst into tears. Remington took hold of another microphone as Ferdie raved on.

'I think it's high time we invited our surprise special guest to join us,' Remington said. 'Will the person behind the curtain please come forward?'

With that, Peter Prescott walked boldly onto the stage. He wore an 'Apple Isle' T-shirt featuring a map of Tasmania, jeans and sneakers.

'Ladies and gentlemen,' said Remington, 'Allow me to introduce to you, Mr Peter Prescott.'

There was a gasp from the audience. Ferdie gaped at Peter in shock. Colleen screamed and felt a little dizzy.

'Don't worry Mum, I'm okay,' Peter said as he rushed to her outstretched arms to embrace her. 'Peter my darling.' Colleen cried as they held each other in a long hug. Humphrey, with tears in his eyes, patted Peter on his shoulder. 'Son,' he said, 'where have you been? We've been worried sick.'

While the Prescotts rejoiced, Remington pointed a microphone at Ferdie. 'What do you have to say for yourself Ferdinand Fortune? Ferdinand the bull artist would be a more fitting title, if you ask me. How are you going to worm your way out of this one?'

Ferdie spluttered his reply, 'I never ever got a really clear signal in this case. It was always blurry, very blurry.'

The audience heckled and booed Ferdie who hung his head in shame as he tried to make a quick getaway.

'Not so fast,' said Remington. 'I believe there are a couple of persons in the audience who would like to have a word with you. I dare say this could well be the sad end to your dubious career. Lord knows what kind of employment you could possibly enter into now after this ordeal.'

'Lord knows, you say,' Ferdie replied, 'That's interesting. Strangely enough, I have seriously been considering to become an evangelist and working with the Lord.

Remington shook his head and rolled his eyes. 'You've got all the answers haven't you. Get off.'

Remington announced to the audience that was the end of the show and thanked them for coming. 'Remember folks, this show is always full of surprises.' The recorded music began to play 'It's a Sin to Tell a Lie'. 'And also remember,' Remington added, 'it's a sin to tell a lie. Good evening.'

The audience began to leave. Denis, Glenda and Sherlock stood up, smiled as they watched Rosco departing, shaking his head and muttering to himself in disbelief.

'I think we might go backstage now and have a quiet word with the stars of the show,' said Denis.

'Good idea,' Sherlock agreed. 'And thanks for the tip, there goes another case I can mark off as solved.' Glenda looked at Sherlock and gave him a smile. Sherlock looked back grinning and gave her a wink.

Alabama 1954
Tylah Jackowski

CHARLIE Madison was a great guy, no doubt; talented, kind, and not afraid to stand up for what he believed in. I felt slightly abashed to say I aspired to be more like him, given the fact that I was a few years older.

When I first met him, it wasn't under the greatest of circumstances. Not at all.

The year was 1954 and I was working as a cop in a small town in Alabama. I'd seen Charlie around town many times. He was a local celebrity of sorts, with that guitar and that melodic voice. He wasn't hard on the eyes either. Everybody loved him, especially the Black folks. Charlie was sort of the poster boy for African-American civil rights in our town. He wrote songs about justice, equality and peace, and performed them in bars and at fairs. They weren't radical enough to cause a major stir, but some of the more bigoted folks really had it in for him. That's why, when they heard he had been signed to a major record label in Nashville, they decided to let him know of their displeasure, in the most heinous way.

I was on my way home late one afternoon when I heard a ruckus coming from a house.

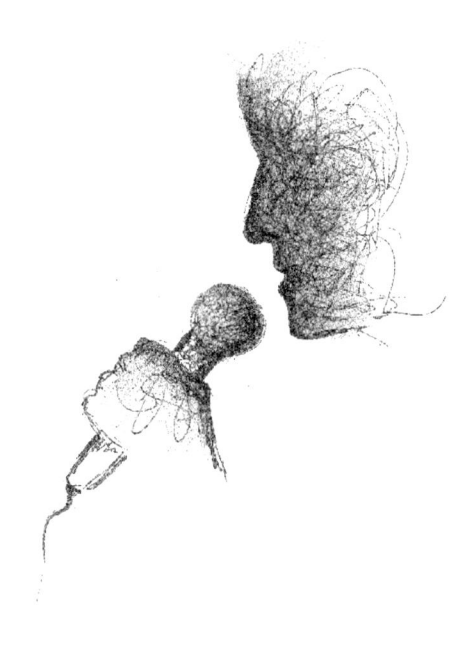

As a police officer, I decided it was my duty to investigate, make sure no one was getting hurt. I crept up the front steps and listened at the door.

'They took her away. They took her away,' a voice repeated over and over, with heavy, distressed sobs. I recognised it as Mabel's, the black woman who owned a club Charlie often played at. Then I heard another familiar voice.

'I'm gonna kill them!' It was Charlie. I'd never heard him sound so furious, or violent at all.

'Oh, please don't do anything stupid Charlie. Just call the police–'

'They are the police!' he shouted. I heard the unmistakeable sound of a fist slamming on a table. 'I have to deal with this myself.'

I froze. Charlie's words rung in my ears. The police. Oh no. They didn't. They were pretty awful to the Black folks sometimes, and they'd always talked about teaching Charlie a lesson. But I thought it was all talk. My mind raced, coming up with situation after horrible situation of what they could've done. I was so deep in thought I didn't hear steps coming towards the door.

It opened and I was face to face with Charlie. He looked terrifying, despite the fact that he'd clearly been crying too.

'What the hell are you doing here?' He looked surprised, and not at all pleased to see me. I was a cop after all, and he didn't know I wasn't involved in whatever my partners had done.

'I heard the commotion and came to investigate,' I said, trying to sound unassuming.

'Alright, well, everything's fine,' Charlie responded stiffly. He looked like he wanted to punch me.

I sighed, and looked around to check if anyone was listening in. The street was empty. 'Look, I heard what you said in there.' He just glared at me. 'What happened?' I pressed. He looked like he was going to slam the door in my face (or my face into the door.) 'Please, I can help you.'

'Why would you want to help me?' Charlie snarled. 'Aren't you with them? I assumed you were here to bargain some sort of ransom.'

I looked down sheepishly. It was true, I had done some terrible things in my past. Things I don't want to relive. Things I would never do again. But at the time, I had no choice. I needed to fit in. I didn't want to face the same fate as the Negroes and those who stood with them. I could never have had the life I'd wanted if I'd refused. I was a coward, I now realised. I couldn't go back and undo those awful things, but I could redeem myself by helping Charlie.

'I'm not with them,' I answered solemnly. 'I don't want to live like that anymore. I want to put things right. Please just trust me,' I pleaded.

His face softened a little. 'You're telling the truth. You wouldn't be begging like that otherwise.' His visage hardened once more. 'But this is strictly business. You help me, and then we're done. Got it?'

He clearly didn't think highly of me, because of my past, and I didn't blame him.

I nodded. 'So what happened?'

He explained that his friend Tracey, Mabel's niece, hadn't been seen since the previous morning. A note had been found on her bed that read: 'Write a song about her.' I listened, feeling more sickened each dreadful second.

'Those bastards,' I muttered. Charlie looked like he might collapse with grief. But there was fire in his eyes. I could tell, just from the way he said her name, how passionate he was to get her back. Tracey was more than just a friend.

I thought hard. Where would they keep her? Suddenly it came to me, as if a curtain had fallen to reveal it. 'There's this empty cabin on the outskirts of town. It was the scene of a murder a couple of years ago. Very secluded. I'd bet my badge they're keeping her there.'

My grave revelation didn't appear to bring much hope to Charlie, but he nodded and we set off, after telling Mabel where we were going in case we didn't make it back. We went on foot, quiet and invisible on the moonless night. I had my gun. Charlie was unarmed. I told him to stay behind me. I wasn't sure if anyone would be keeping watch, but it was better to be safe than sorry.

We found the cabin in no time. Urgency had made my memory sharp and I knew exactly where to go. Creeping around the back of the small building, I listened for a voice, anything to tell me Tracey was there. Both Charlie and I were holding our breath. Like a light in the dark, there was a faint sob. Charlie ran around to the front door.

'Hey, wait,' I hissed. We still didn't know if there was anyone else in there. I rushed to follow him, taking my gun out of its holster. I entered the cabin to find it dark and apparently empty. I heard hushed talking and crying coming from a room at the back. I followed it and found Charlie and Tracey, embracing. Tracey was sobbing, as heavily and distraughtly as Mabel had been.

'Shhhh,' Charlie hushed her. 'It's okay now.'

She was shackled to a bedpost of a heavy metal bedframe with a soiled mattress askew on it. She had bruises all over her body, which was barely clothed. Her eyes were sunken, and her mouth was bloody, but she was alive.

She saw me over Charlie's shoulder. 'Charlie, l–look out!' she cried, her eyes widening with terror.

'It's okay, he's with me. He helped me find you,' Charlie said gently.

'Is there a key?' I asked, gesturing to her shackles.

She shook her head. They took it. Please, they'll be back any minute. I heard them say they were going to get more—more guys,' she sobbed, breaking down into Charlie's arms. I aimed at the chain and fired. It broke and fell with a clatter.

'Let's go!' I shouted, momentarily deafened by the close-range shot. We'd definitely been heard anyway. We ran, Charlie carrying Tracey, all the way back to

Mabel's house. Mabel was still crying, and she cried even harder when she saw Tracey.

'I hate to spoil the reunion,' I said seriously, 'but we all have to leave. Now!'

'Why?' asked Charlie.

'They'll be looking for us. They won't like being beaten, especially by one of their own,' I explained, my voice heavy with dread. We all sat silently, the danger of our situation dawning on us.

'We can go to Tennessee. My producer will just think I've arrived early and brought some company,' Charlie suggested. 'We'll be safe there.'

We all agreed and packed hastily. It was lucky neither Charlie nor I had any other family. His mum had died not long after he was born, and his dad skipped town when he was eleven, he told me. Mabel had been like a surrogate mother to him ever since. I myself was never close to my parents, and I wasn't married.

The sun hadn't yet risen when we bade Alabama goodbye, but to me it felt like a new day was dawning. I'd finally found the strength to do what was right and I'd freed myself from a life of cruelty and hatred. I had redeemed myself.

After a few hours of driving we stopped to eat and stretch our legs on a hill just inside the border of Tennessee. Mabel thanked me for saving her niece's life.

'You're part of the family now,' she said, handing me a sandwich.

Tracey nodded gently – she was still fragile, but much calmer. I smiled shyly, my heart swelling with pride and happiness. As the sun rose, I sat down on the soft green grass and relaxed into the bliss. Charlie was singing. It was a melancholy song, sort of cynical, but it was gentle and sweet at the same time and it felt like home. When he finished, I asked, 'What's that one called?'

'*Daybreak in Alabama*,' he replied.

I Am Gunna Play Sun Sydney
Bernie Dowling

2017 is the 25th anniversary of the Mabo Decision
In memory of Ruby Hunter, 1955 – 2010
La Perouse, a Sydney suburb, January 26, 1992

NATALIE and I gratefully got out of the cab of my EH ute which had no air conditioning. We had the windows wound down all the way from Brisbane. The breeze rushing past the EH had been warm as in the Australian word for bloody hot. 'Warm enough for you?' is a typical comment when the weather is a scorcher. Nat and I adjusted our sunglasses and our broad-brimmed hats.

'Buddha it's hot on Australia Day,' I said, as I put my arm around Nat's thin waste.

'Survival Day,' My Cucumber corrected.

Indeed it was and we were about to become punters at the first Survival Day Concert held in Australia.

We had read about it in *Drum Media*, a Sydney street paper, which some Brisbane alternative music stores ordered from Sydney in limited quantities. The papers were free so it was thoughtful of Brisbane music stores such as Skinny's and Rocking Horse to put aside the .profit motive for these items.

The Brisbane street press itself was cut-throat at the time with *Time Off, Rave*, the more dance-music oriented *Scene* and the downright weird satire/

cultural reviews in *the Bug*. They vied for the dollars of an alternative crowd who had a huge appetite for live and recorded music but who in the main had limited financial means to fully indulge.

Nat and I liked to know what was happening in Sydney and *Drum Media* duly obliged with news of the *Survival Day* concert in honour of the holiday known by most as the more flattering Australia Day. Some Aboriginals and Islanders knew Survival Day as the even less flattering Invasion Day.

These three monikers stemmed from different views of January 26, 1788, when Captain Arthur Phillip rode a refreshing breeze through Botany Bay to set up a penal colony. A few arrogant English still call us White Australians convicts but that is just a cover for their having carelessly lost an Empire in the space of about 50 years. An irreverent rock band touchingly called Queen is doing all the anthems now. Well they were until lead singer Freddie Mercury inconveniently died, during the November just gone.

The first names to strike us in the *Drum-Media* concert ad were Archie Roach and his wife Ruby Hunter. Nat and I had seen Roach and Hunter play in Brisbane and we liked what we heard.

Ruby was one of the Stolen Generations of kids considered to have enough white pigment to be able to breed out the blackness over time. The genetic-cultural script went wonky for Ruby and she ended up on the streets where she met another homeless kid, Archie. With the help of music, they turned their lives around together.

Cross-cultural dance band Yothu Yindi was on the bill. In 1991, they had a hit with *Treaty*. A meaningful treaty between Black and White Australia was never going to happen but the song was a joyous blast of compressed air blowing away the pop rubbish from radio airwaves.

Aboriginal opera singer Maroochy Barambah, also one of the Stolen Generations, would be onstage. Opera and country are the two musical genres I do not get but Natalie was excited by the prospect of Maroochy's performance. As for country music, Aboriginals loved it, both from America and White Australia. That was until the youngsters discovered reggae and later hip hop. Then it was 'bye bye Charley Pride; see you later, Slim Dusty.'

But the winds of change had not swept across Botany Bay to La Perouse. Prominent on the newspaper poster was a photo of a performer I had never heard of: Roger Knox. Above his photo was the tag-line, the Black Elvis. Funny, I thought Presley was the Black Elvis with a paint job. Underneath the photo was a smaller appellation: The Koori King of Country. That was more like it. Kooris are Aboriginals from New South Wales. Queensland Aboriginals call themselves Murris.

At La Perouse, a crowd of thousands had gathered early. To welcome us Brisbane visitors a cooler breeze had sprung up from the northern point of Botany Bay. Feeling good.

Redemption

We looked for a comfortable spot near the stage. A tall Aboriginal man with curly black hair bumped against my left arm. 'Are you lost?' he said in a helpful voice which had an undertone of menace.

'I don't think so,' I said. 'This is the famous French restaurant, *Lapérouse*, isn't it?'

'Natalie dug her fingers into the left flesh of my waist. That was one of her signals which silently said, 'Don't start, Steele.'

The Aboriginal man smiled but you could see he made neither head nor tail of what I had said.

'Where are you from?' he asked. I told him Brisbane.

He pointed north and I saw he had a stack of leaflets in his right hand. 'That's a long way,' he said 'You must be carrying a lot of guilt.'

Natalie dug in the fingers.

'Sorry,' I said. 'Left the guilt at home. We came for the music.'

Natalie must have been somewhat satisfied with my response as she released the pressure.

The Aboriginal thought about that before he thrust two leaflets towards Natalie and me. 'Something to read between sets,' he said.

'Ta,' I said while Natalie responded with the more formal thank-you.

The man watched as we found a comfortable spot about 30 metres from the stage. I looked around. 'There are plenty of White people here; what was he having a go at me for?'

'You don't know that.'

'Did you think he was having a go at us?'

'Yair, I did,' Natalie said. 'Maybe it's your Bob Marley T-shirt.'

'I like Bob Marley.'

'Awlright,' she said. "Let's forget about it.'

I agreed and looked at the leaflet which turned out to be a folded six-page brochure.

'That's pretty cool,' I said. 'This bloke died five days ago and they have already put out a tribute to him.'

There was an empty rectangle above his name, date of birth and death. 'Looks like they could not find a photo, but,' I said.

'Edward Koiki Mabo,' Natalie read from her leaflet. She continued to read, silently, before putting the leaflet on the ground. 'He was a Torres Strait Islander. I don't think they allow pictorial representation during the mourning period.'

She picked up her leaflet and we read on in silence.

It seemed Eddie Mabo and four other claimants contested ownership of Mer Island in the Torres Strait on behalf of the Merian people. They took the action before the High Court of Australia way back in May, 1982. Success could spark other land-rights claims not just by Torres Strait Islanders but Aboriginals throughout Australia as well. The decision was to come down later that year. Poor Eddie, after 10 years of fighting the Man, he died, maybe a few short months before the outcome.

The brochure went on to have some stuff about "terra nullius" which I skipped to read his bio.

In one part it said Eddie Mabo was president of the Yumba Meta housing co-operative which bought houses throughout the Townsville area so Aboriginal and Islander people could live in any suburb they chose. This broke down the barriers of Black suburbs, Australia's unofficial apartheid.

I put the leaflet aside to think about something else. Earlier that month, on January 11, 1992, Paul Simon was the first major recording artist to play South Africa after the lifting of the cultural boycott of that apartheid nation. Nelson Mandela of the African National Congress and South African president F.W. de Klerk were in discussions about ending apartheid. The lifting of the UN ban was encouragement of fruitful discussions.

What was kind of weird about Simon rushing to play was he had been accused years before of breaking the ban, a charge he denied.

The UN ban was passed in 1980 though the British Musos' Union had a bar on touring South Africa for more than a decade before that.

In 1984, Queen broke both bans by playing a series of gigs at Sun City in South Africa. Sun City was a casino resort which held more than 6000 people in one concert venue.

Sun City was a funny one. It was in South Africa but it wasn't. The republic of Bophuthatswana was given independence as a 'homeland' for the Tswana people because South Africa looked after its minorities unlike those hypocritical western countries such as the U.S., England and Australia which bagged apartheid. At least, that was how the ruling White elite of South Africa saw it.

Another funny thing about Sun City was, because it was independent, it allowed casinos and topless dancers, both illegal in the righteous Republic of South Africa. Sun City was only a two-hour drive from the Big City of Johannesburg. Buses travelled from Jo'burg to the casino resort. The Big Smoke of Pretoria was even closer to Sun City.

Queen went to Sun City and the Big Bopper of the world's street press, London's NME, canned the band mercilessly for it. Queen's guitar genius, Brian May, mumbled something about the band not being political and playing for anyone who wanted to listen. But most of us thought they had taken the money and flown over. We rock punters can be very unkind.

Maybe Paul Simon did not read NME. The next year, he travelled to South Africa to hook up with Black African musicians such as Ladysmith Black Mambazo for his planned album, eventually a triumph called *Graceland.* None of his fellow musicians doubted that Simon's intentions were good but he had clearly infringed the boycott. His excuse that he didn't play Sun City (or anywhere else) was lamer than May's.

The next year, 1986, Steven Van Zandt, formerly of the E-Street Band, put together 50 artists for the protest anthem, *Sun City*. Van Zandt did not invite Queen or Simon but otherwise it was a group from Alternative/ Crossover Heaven.

Australian Peter Garrett of Midnight Oil was in that number as were Bob Dylan, Bonnie Raitt, jazzmen Herbie Hancock and Miles Davis, hip hop outfit Run DMC, DJ Afrika Bambaataa, Pat Benatar, Lou Reed, Peter Gabriel, metal-heads Motley Crue, Jackson Browne, Tom Petty, U2, Darlene Love, Keith Richards, reggae lad Jimmy Cliff, Pete Townshend of the Who, Bruce Springsteen, Bob Geldof, and Joey Ramone.

The chorus of *I Ain't Gonna Play Sun City* reverberated around the world. So it was kinda weird that Paul Simon was the first major artist to play Sun City, post boycott in 1992.

I felt a nudge in my side. 'Whatcha thinking about?' Natalie asked.

I looked at the leaflet in my hand. 'Nothing,' I said.

'I hope Eddie Mabo wins his case,' Natalie said. That terra nullius is the stupidest thing I ever heard.'

'I didn't read that bit. It means nothing country, doesn't it? A bit insulting.'

'It means "land belonging to no one" and it's the reason Eddie is being denied justice.'

'I thought Aboriginals and Islanders believe they are part of the land.'

'That's not a concept under British law. They are saying because Aboriginals were nomadic they don't own any particular part of Australia,' Natalie said.

'I wouldn't have thought Torres Strait Islanders would be particularly nomadic.'

'That's not the point, Steele. Terra nullius is just bullshit. Who do you think will win?'

'Nat, the authorities have been stringing it out for 10 years. I reckon they will just bumble along until all the claimants are dead.'

'I hope not.'

'So do I Nat.'

I thought about Paul Simon and the decisions he made. 'Nat, do you think we are just a pair of do-gooders?'

She spoke softly. 'No-one thinks you are a do-gooder, Steele.'

I kissed her on her cheek. 'Thanks, Nat.'

____ooo____

THE High Court of Australia, on June 3 1992, overturned the legal doctrine of terra nullius and found the island of Mer belonged to the Merian people

.

Unpinned
Courtney Smith

JAE-JIN only returned to Busan once.

His younger sister convinced their mother to return after all their long years away, her battering eyelids causing weakness in even the most determined NOs. Ji-eun would continue to whine and bat her lids with a deep pout that wrinkled her chin and furrowed her brows. Their mother continued to frown, anxiety evident on her face, but eventually relented, and within a few short months they had returned.

The familiar and strong language flooded his ears, coercing him to slip back into the dialect he managed to drop after leaving. Blunt statements and slurred vowels were not uncommon to overhear, much more so than he was used to in Chicago. His mother seemed to disagree, every harsh syllable of their mother tongue causing her to flinch involuntarily.

Collecting their suitcases, their mother herded them onto the subway to travel to their hotel in Haeundae-gu. Their mother shifted uncomfortably on her feet as they checked in, looking over her shoulder as if she was expecting someone to be there. The three of them shared a room, Ji-eun excitedly jumped up and down on the bed, the mattress squeaking in shock before Ji-eun was commanded to stop.

Jae-jin was fifteen at the time, limbs too long and hair trimmed too short. His eyes were far too bright and far too round for the face that was finally beginning to smooth out, baby fat disappearing behind soft cheekbones. His sister was eleven, hair cut into a blunt black bob and eyes as wide as his own.

They had left when he was seven, his mother dragging them onto a plane after packing their belongings. The two protested loudly, but their mother was relentless. *Everything would be better*, she told them, and Jae-jin was sure that was not directed towards either of them. Her voice shook and her hands clutched her children a little too tightly, as if they were going to be taken from her if she let go. The crumpled tickets balled in her fists were one way, PUS to ORD, and after the wheels of the plane collided with the ground, there was no going back.

The apartment they moved into was unfamiliar; too big, too spacious, and too lonely for the three of them. His mother stopped speaking in their mother tongue, just for a while, until the children got used to the strange sounds of English, and soon enough Chicago became just as much of a home as Busan was.

It wasn't the same feeling, really. In Busan, Jae-jin could talk to anyone he wanted – the other children in the park, elderly people in the streets, as well as the cats and the dogs and all of the birds. He could tear down to the beach after school, rip off his shoes and dip into the water without a care in the world.

Redemption

After moving to Chicago, all of that changed. Jae-jin struggled to talk to anyone without his vocabulary or accent butting in, and whenever he tried to talk to another his mother would herd him away as if she sensed danger. He wasn't allowed to walk to and from school anymore, his mother opting to drive him there on her way to work. In Busan, he smelled the ocean and spicy food wherever he went, and in Chicago there were car fumes and take-out foods wherever he went, but they both became familiar, like home.

They were both home, in their own little ways.

Jae-jin knew that something was out of place, even back then. It was just the three of them who travelled, and Jae-jin knew that something was terribly wrong with that. His father wasn't with them, not commanding them to move quicker or complaining about the service. His booming voice didn't accompany them on the plane, nor did he ever follow them to Chicago. Jae-jin used to wonder where he was, whether he would come to them, but he never did. That didn't bother him anymore.

Not after what his father had done.

After changing into something more fashionable, Jae-jin convinced his mother to let him travel down to the beach on his own. He retrieved his messenger bag and left the girls, waving cheerily behind his shoulder. He walked off to the beach in the route he memorised as a child, his feet following the road automatically. Jae-jin stood taller than most, his shoulders squared as he walked down the familiar, winding path. The closer he came to the beach, the louder the seagull's calls were, the sandier the road underfoot became, and the scent of the water grew stronger in his nose. He passed the parks he played in as a child, and before he knew it he stood in front of the ocean.

It was serene, despite the water being disturbed by children just out of school. The ocean was as picturesque as he remembered it, clear and sparkling in the sunlight, small waves crashing against the yellow sand. Footprints littered the beach in no pattern at all, and Jae-jin's lips tugged upwards. He pulled his Polaroid camera from his messenger bag and lined up the shot, taking a picture of the scene in front of him. He waited for it to develop, admiring the image. Jae-jin found his lips quirking further, eyes drifting upwards across the sea of people before a tonne of bricks dropped on his head. A wave of confusion hit him, before blinding hot anger.

Before they left Busan, Jae-jin remembered screaming. It was constant, harsh words exchanged at the drop of a hat, but he remembers when it was at its worst. It was not long after his sister was born, and the two were arguing. He remembers the word *child* being thrown around with malice, but he never understood what it meant. Every time his parents' arguments would blow up, he would hide underneath the desk in his room until it was all over, the slamming of a door followed by vindictive silence.

Jae-jin felt his blood turn to ice as he saw the painfully familiar face pick up the child, around the same age as his sister. The boy was dressed for the season, his cargo shorts and sandals matched perfectly with his striped polo shirt, and Jae-jin remembered that combination exactly. After all, he was the first to wear it. The man with the child was smiling sweetly, chatting animatedly with the boy like there was nothing out of place. Jae-jin, on the other hand, felt like his heart was about to jump out of his throat. His stomach was lapsing like the waves on the beach, the violent urge to puke over the sand was brawling his composure. His hands dropped to his sides like they were dead weight, the camera shaking between his fingers, and his knees soon following. Jae-jin knew he was standing in the middle of the walkway, but he couldn't bring himself to move an inch. His legs had turned to stone, and in that moment, just like Medusa would, the man turned his head.

Jae-jin knew that he would recognise his own son – after all, their faces were becoming closer and closer as the years stretched onwards. The man's face turned a ghastly, guilty white, and Jae-jin knew that his own mirrored it, down to the parted lips and hurt expression. Jae-jin couldn't turn his gaze away from the child, who had now turned to stare at him, perplexed. His heart clawed at his ribs, sawing through the bone to jump out of his chest. The man opened his mouth wider, as if he were to speak, but a feminine voice caught his attention. The three heads turned towards it, and the boy ran towards her without a second thought, shouting details about his day.

She was pretty enough, Jae-jin supposed, but her elegant beauty was only a knife to his spine. Her soft brown hair was curled and her smile was poised and perfect. Everything about her screamed textbook beauty, and Jae-jin hated every part of it. She smiled down at her child, and then to the man, before her gaze found him. Her jaw went slack for a moment, before she clenched it and forced a smile towards the young boy, who had hesitated telling his story. Jae-jin felt his eyes burning dangerously as he watched on, and without thinking, he sprinted in the other direction, as fast as he could back to the hotel.

Jae-jin locked himself in the room, the door slamming against the wooden frame, and pulled his phone out, dialling the first number frantically. After two rings his mother picked up, her voice exasperated.

'What is it, Jae? I'm busy with your sister so it better be important,' she chastised him, and Jae-jin sucked in a deep, shaky breath. His legs finally gave out, knees colliding with the floor painfully. He screwed his face up before choking out a response.

'I s-saw... I saw *him*,' he told her, and the line went silent for a moment. Jae-jin's lower lip quivered as he continued, 'He was at the beach and—and he saw me and—and I feel like—*she* was there—and the kid, and—*Mum*,' he moaned, the burning tears spilling hot down his face. His hands shook, 'I hate him. I hate what he did. I hate him so much. I wanna go home, Mum. I wanna go *home*.'

Jae-jin sucked in a selfish breath, his chest constricted painfully. His shoulders shook, shrinking him back down to a child, 'I wanna go *home*.'

They were supposed to stay in Busan for three more days, and Jae-jin knew he was selfish for asking to return, so he forced himself to see the sights with Ji-eun before the three of them returned to Chicago. He worked his way through the motions, unable to find himself enjoying anything. His heart had numbed completely, his face turning completely stoic, and eyes dead and cold. The spiciest of foods became bland, and the fresh air around them suddenly became toxic for him to breathe in.

He was grateful to be back in Chicago, surrounded by English and his schoolwork. As much as he tried to distract himself, the irredeemable three on the beach lingered in his mind.

It had been a year since he left Busan, and Jae-jin swore to himself he would never return. He couldn't go back there when he knew what awaited, lurking, mocking him just around the corner. Jae-jin immersed himself in his studies after he came back, but he knew it wouldn't be long before it all built up on him. He refused to let it show, but every time he saw a young child with their father, his blood would boil. Whenever family was mentioned from that moment on, Jae-jin would push the conversation away from himself. He knew that, one day, he would have to face it, but he never thought he'd have to do it in his own home.

Jae-jin often had lazy afternoons with his boyfriend, Grayson. The two would sit on his bed, oftentimes in silence, simply enjoying each other's company. Jae-jin would read, whether it be in Korean or English, and Grayson would tangle their legs together while he played games on Jae-jin's red DS. It was quiet, calm, but Jae-jin often found his eyes lingering on the wall beside them.

He called it his memory wall, and it was covered from top to bottom with photographs, ticket stubs, and small keepsakes. Each of them were stuck to a corkboard he installed two years ago. There were photographs of anything that had meaning to him – family, friends, places, and in doing that Jae-jin knew that there would be older photos – photos he didn't want anyone to see. Normally, those would not be an issue, but ever since he had grown closer to his inquisitive boyfriend, Jae-jin had grown paranoid of the taller boy finding out. Those pictures he would double up, placing one Polaroid on top of another, but Jae-jin was becoming increasingly aware of how obvious they were as his boyfriend continued to ask questions about each memory.

'What's this?' Grayson asked him, flicking a picture upwards. His face was far more angular than Jae-jin's, and fairer. His brown brows were furrowed beneath his neatly combed hair. It was the photo he had taken on the beach, the blue sky reflecting in the pristine water. The pin didn't allow it to move, but revealed another underneath it, hidden by the lapse of the waves. Jae-jin looked up from the novel in his lap, but his expression became disinterested after he saw what his partner was referring to. Jae-jin shrugged before turning his gaze down towards the roman letters, brain processing each one individually. Grayson unpinned the pictures and examined them carefully, hazel eyes processing every detail.

'Are these from Korea?' he asked, and Jae-jin nodded without looking, 'This one . . . it's your dad, right?'

Grayson's voice was tight, hesitant, and unsure what he was allowed to say next, and Jae-jin sighed. He dog-eared his page and snapped the book shut, tossing it onto the end of the quilt. He motioned for Grayson to move closer to him, and the boy did so without complaint. The two adjusted so that their long legs would stick out against the navy blue covers, and Grayson held the pictures towards Jae-jin. He took them and pointed as he told their stories.

'The first I took last year, at a famous beach back in Busan,' he explained, his accent revealing itself on the city name. He winced, before pointing to the other, 'I was . . . five in this picture? About that. With my father. It's the same beach,' his voice turned bitter, the inside of his mouth suddenly poisoned. It left a repulsive taste in his mouth, the three faces on the beach returning to his mind.

'You were cute,' Grayson nudged his ribs, and Jae-jin forced a smile, 'Why was it covered, if you want to say.'

Jae-jin shrugged, 'He had an affair with another woman, and it got horrible very quickly. Has a kid about Ji-eun's age – a boy. Mother was devastated, and they got divorced before we moved here. He never did anything for us, obviously more focused on *them*.'

Grayson took the pictures from Jae-jin, stilling his shaking hands, and pinned them back onto the board, 'God, that's disgusting. I'm sorry that happened to you.'

'I...' Jae-jin tried to think of the right words, but nothing delicate could come out, 'I really hate him for that. For ruining her life, and changing ours forever.'

Grayson nodded, moving closer to Jae-jin. Jae-jin rested his head on his boyfriend's shoulder, sighing deeply, 'It's a memory so I keep it up there, but I hate thinking about it.'

Silence fell over them, and Jae-jin allowed himself a glance towards Grayson. The boy was frowning at him, pale lips held in a tight line.

'How about we take a new picture?' Grayson suggested, breaking the silence, 'We can make a new memory.'

Jae-jin stared at him for a moment, making no effort to move, so Grayson did it for him. He reached over to the mahogany desk and grabbed his Polaroid camera, holding it out for him. Jae-jin took it, before frowning.

'What memory could we possibly make?' he asked, and Grayson smiled.

'Any memory we want, the world is ours.' Grayson's smile died down. 'But I was thinking more along the lines of these quiet afternoons. With just the two of us.'

'Why?'

'They make you happier than Busan does,' Grayson shrugged. 'Or something like that.'

Jae-jin lifted his head and gave Grayson a cheeky grin. 'Sounds like you just want a cute couple picture on that board.'

'Maybe I do. Maybe you do, too.'

Jae-jin bit back a grin, his eyes softening, 'I definitely do.'

The two hopped into a more comfortable position, readying smiles on their faces. Jae-jin held the camera out with his finger ready, and before Grayson could react, he pressed a quick peck onto his cheek and pressed the button. Grayson protested, but the second he saw the picture, his pout turned to a smile. Taking it, he unpinned the two pictures and replaced them with the new one. Grayson tossed the two onto the desk, and admired the new addition to the wall.

Amongst the scenery shots and family photos, the two of them were as bright as could be. Jae-jin's hair was slightly messy and Grayson's smile had grown in the second that Jae-jin took the photo. The lighting was terrible and their clothes were far too casual, but they couldn't help but smile at it.

'See? Redeemed the wall already.' Grayson nudged him, and Jae-jin smiled softly, linking their hands together.

'I love it.'

The two settled back as they were, Busan laying discarded on the desk, forgotten by the wall.

The Authors and artists

James Barrance has been writing short stories for competitions for just over a year. 'Originally, my stories were bland and had very few, if any, emotive words,' James said. 'After being in the English extension class at my school, my technique seems to have improved and my vocabulary has increased.

James entered *Write for Fun* competitions, not just in the hope of winning, but also to improve his confidence in writing.

Writing short stories is his favourite part of studying English.

Kasper Beaumont is the author of the four *Hunters of Reloria* fantasy series novels and also a short story which was published in last year's anthology. Kasper takes great delight in watching her readers become immersed in her fantasy adventures.

David Bell spent the first twenty-one years of his life in North Queensland. He worked for more than thirty years as an Administration Officer in the public service.

'For the last twenty-one years I have been an unpaid worker,' he said.

David's first venture into poetry was a sonnet that he wrote for the wedding of two work colleagues in February 1985.

'Since then I have written an assortment of verse: some, I hope, is thought-provoking, some has been in memoriam of friends, and some has been composed quickly and is intended to be humorous.'

Aaron Bowen has become passionate about entertaining readers and exploring their minds in an intellectual and psychological manner during the short period in which he has been writing,

'Due to my inexperience in the literary community, my writing style has not been established and my stories are exceedingly raw,' Aaron said.

Some of his work has been used as teaching material and text studies for younger grades at his high school.

'I am always looking forward to see where a pen and paper can take me,' he said.

Aaron won the 2017 Peter Campbell Memorial/WAG short-story contest with *A Loud Room*.

Patricia 'Pat' Cannard has had short stories and poetry published in books produced by Geebung Writers over a period of 25 years. Articles and letters-to-the editor have appeared in the *Courier Mail*, *The Australian* and the *Catholic Leader*.

Pat is the winner of a Pine Rivers Limerick competition on two occasions. She has edited a war veterans' quarterly journal for fourteen years. Pat has written stories and verse for her children, grandchildren and great-grandchildren. Originally from Wallangarra she has lived in Army married-quarters in three states before settling in Geebung and finally at Murrumba Downs. She produces the monthly newsletter at Inverpine Village.

Tyleigha Collins is a first year student of the University of Queensland. She is studying a Bachelor of Arts degree, hoping to major in extended writing and minor in drama. She is close with both her friends and family - which include pets - and dreams not of excellence, but of confidence in her writing abilities.

Margaret Dakin was born in Brisbane, and came to writing after working in various occupations, culminating in twenty years as a studio potter.

Margaret joined a writing group in 2002. Meeting with like-minded friends keeps her pushing her pen every week.

Margaret's first play, a comedy, was produced in 2007 and other full length and short plays followed. One, *Presumed Guilty* is going to the stage this year, and she is working on a drama with original music.

Margaret is the treasurer of Society of Women Writers Queensland.

Pauline Davies has passion for theatre and it inspired the Brisbane actor and director to write six plays for performance in local theatres and drama festivals, with her 2007 comedy *Hot Spots* being published by Maverick Musicals in 2016.

Having nearly completed a Bachelor of Arts Degree, majoring in English Literature/Writing and Composition, Pauline feels ready to expand into other writing genres.

She hopes this first offering of a short story to the Writers Anthology Group will be the beginning of an ongoing collaboration with other local writers.

Bernie Dowling is a Pine Rivers journalist and author. His books include fiction and non-fiction. His first novel, *Iraqi Icicle* introduced the neo-noir detective Steele Hill who returns in two stories for this anthology. Both stories are new to print though *I Am Gunna Play Sun Sydney* is in the eBook *Naughty Nineties*, available at online retailers.

Jessica Freiberg is a year 12 student who has always had a strong passion for writing.

After submitting her anthology story, she was accepted to do a creative writing course at UQ while still at high school. This course has allowed her passion for writing to really thrive and hopefully many more short stories will come from this experience.

Roz Glazebrook has been writing and publishing articles since the 1970s. Roz has had many articles published in magazines, newspapers and writers' anthologies.

Roz recently started writing for a couple of online sites, including *She* and *Weekend Notes Brisbane*.

She enjoys researching and writing about wildlife, history, bushwalking, kayaking, human interest stories, health topics, adventure and travel.

Roz lives in Brisbane and is a member of the Queensland Writers' Group and the Arana Hills Writers' Group.

Ronald Holt retired from the Queensland public sector in 2006 after more than forty years' service – the last 14 years in the Office of Fair Trading. He wrote numerous reports and departmental correspondence on a wide range of issues and is now applying those skills to his love of creative writing.

Ron has edited five anthologies in 2007, 2009, 2011 and 2013, and 2015 for the Arana Writers' Group. As well as his regular contributions to Fellowship of Australian Writers Queensland publications, AWG and WAG anthologies, Ron has had short stories published on Anzac Cove and global warming.

Tylah Jackowski is a first year university student fresh out of high school and she intends to major in writing.

Tylah is not really sure where exactly her future lies, but she knows it will have something to do with writing and bad jokes.

Jeremy Leung has always found it fun writing stories. 'It's great being the director of a vast, infinite imagination that I can put on paper and it's awesome to be able to share my thoughts with others. 'Although my passion is and always has been science, I'll be making stories whether they be on the computer or in my head.'

Maddison Lanham writes: 'Hey guys! First off, thanks so much for reading my little short story!! I hope that in some way it spoke to you, entertained you or opened your eyes to the possible hidden hurts of someone's heart.

So a little bit about me, right now I am studying Biomedical Science at Griffith University, and happily reading sappy romantic novels on the train and bus (making me miss my stop more often than not!).

David MacLaughlin began writing for a staff magazine when he came fourth from world-wide entries for a travel article. Writing took a back seat as David became active in choral and Celtic choirs and musical theatre.

After that it was time to give writing its proper priority in things cultural. As a member of Arana Writers' Group, David has contributed to the group's anthologies with articles factual, humorous, some fiction and travel tales.

Max Miller spent his first eight years living in Perth, WA, and now lives in Lawnton. He studies Economics and Computer Science at the University of Queensland, where his main goal is finding a career that won't be replaced by a robot.

His interests include technology, web development and Australian politics.

Max's vision is to contribute to creating a fairer and prosperous Australia. Visit Max's portfolio website at www.maxcmiller.com.

Virginia Miranda began writing in high school and was first published in the Brisbane State High School Year book, 1966.

Virginia is a member of Byron Writers Festival, Brisbane Writers Centre, Brisbane Writers Festival and The Society of Women Writers Qld. She is the Secretary/Treasurer of the Fellowship of Australian Writers Qld.

In 2014 Virginia self-published her first book, *Flash Fiction Volume One*, a compilation of thirty-seven stories each no more than 500 words.

Vera Murray was born in Allora, Queensland. She has been writing since her school days.

Vera is a former Pine Rivers Shire Councillor and she had edited a magazine overseas.

While running the Writer's Circle group in Pine Rivers, she edited and published three anthologies.

Her book *Move Over James Bond and Other Stories* and her first novel *Leap Year: Blood Lust* were recently published. Her latest book *Move Over plus Humorous Verses* was released in 2014.

Giang Nguyen, 16, moved to Australia from Vietnam when she was 8-years old. 'I found it was quite a difficult transition," Giang said. 'Due to this, at an early age, I learnt the importance of language and the way it can bring people together.'

She learned English by reading books from day to night and watching TV to pick up on conversational skills.

'I fell in love with literature, and to this very day, English is my favourite subject at school.'

She plans to continue studying the English language at university. In this anthology, Giang has written a story, to show a possibly bleak future 'if we do not stop our eco-damaging ways'.

Jeanette O'Hagan first spun tales in the world of Nardva at the age of nine. She enjoys writing, fiction, poetry, blogging and editing.

Jeanette is writing her *Akrad's Legacy* series—a Young Adult fantasy fiction with adventure, courtly intrigue and romantic elements.

Her recent publications include novellas: *Heart of the Mountain*, its sequel *Blood Crystal*, and short stories, *The Herbalist's Daughter* and *Lakwi's Lament*.

Jeanette lives in Brisbane with her husband and children.

Anne Olsson is a remedial therapist living and working in Pine Rivers.

She has been an enthusiastic actor on the amateur stage and, in recent years, an eager world traveller.

Anne's poetry and articles have been published in newspapers and magazines.

R. William Penshorn has travelled the world but still calls Australia home. Now retired and still touring, he spent most of his working years involved in surveying and civil engineering projects.

Ray has written several movie scripts. His interests include comic collecting, classic automobiles, rock 'n' roll, art, surfing, and, of course, writing.

His Tonka Toys collection were on display in the Queensland Museum's *Collectorama*, of 2014.

Lucy Pilgrim is an 18-year-old graduate from Pine Rivers State High School, north of Brisbane.

Lucy is studying business at QUT and working part-time in an accounting firm.

When she's not at her desk crunching numbers, she enjoys reading in a quiet space, preferably while eating chocolate.

Raelene Purtill has, in her imagination, a husband of more than 20 years, three teenage children and a suburban existence, north-west of Brisbane. In the real world, she writes.

Short stories are Raelene's preferred medium although she has produced plays and poems.

She is a member of two writing groups, Strathpine Writers Group and Vanguard Writers, a group formed following a course at the Queensland Writers' Centre. Her blog is raelenep.blogspot.com.au.

Bakthi Ross is a member of the Caboolture Writer's Link.

She started writing because of a dream and has written many children's books. Her eBooks are available at www.appspublisher.com. A mother of two children, she lives at Morayfield in Moreton Bay Region.

Courtney Smith is a Year-12 Albany Creek State High School student with a never-ending love of and passion for writing and language.

In her free time, you will find Courtney translating song lyrics, fiddling with software, or developing fictional worlds.

With a keen interest in the universe and its intricacies, she wishes to take her passions to a new level and share her thoughts with the world.

Courtney won the 2016 Peter Campbell Memorial/WAG short-story contest with *Pro Bono Publico.*

Margaret Taylor started writing as a 6-year old when she had a small poem published in the school magazine. During her junior school years she wrote a short play, which she and some of her classmates performed for the class.

Growing up, getting married, having a family and work commitments put writing on hold. After retiring, she trained as a counsellor and worked as a tutor in adult literacy. While working in this field she wrote a six-week training program for tutors to use with clients. She moved on to work as a volunteer family support worker.

Margaret has now finally retired, for the third time, and writes for the pleasure of it.

Nicholas (Nick) Thomas is a Queensland University of Technology student who enjoys nothing more than a hot cup of tea, at any hour of the day.

Nick is inspired by the rich imagery he experiences through music, film and literature. He adores the bewildering genius of Sherlock Holmes, the creation of his idol, Sir Arthur Conan Doyle and aspires to create a character of such global recognition himself. Until then, he will continue to live his life, one cup of tea at a time.

William A. (Bill) Thomas was born in Sydney and has lived for five years in Annerley, Brisbane.

He wrote his first poems and appeared in his first play in 1967. He has performed with Young Twelfth Night Company, Brisbane Arts Theatre, and Access Arts.

Bill has been semi-retired for many years and volunteers with gardening at St Vincent's Hospital and the Royal Society for Prevention of Cruelty to Animals.

Mocco Wollert was born in Cologne, Germany. She migrated to Australia in 1958. She writes in English and German.

Mocco has been widely published in literary anthologies, newspapers (*Sydney Morning Herald*) magazines (*The Bulletin*) and literary journals (*Redoubt*). Her work has mostly been poetry, short stories and articles.

Mocco moved to Queensland in 1972 and in 1980 founded the Queensland Branch of The Society of Women Writers, of which she is an active member.

Mocco has three published poetry books.

She lives in Keperra, Brisbane.

Jenny Woolsey writes stories and blogs.

Jenny is a primary teacher and youth worker, and a strong advocate for people living with facial differences, mental illness and disabilities.

In 2017 she was the keynote speaker at Queensland's Down Syndrome Association's Education Conference.

Jenny's writing is influenced by her life. She was born with a rare craniofacial syndrome, has anxiety and depression, and a visual impairment. Her three children have disabilities. Jenny's heart is for children and teens who struggle to cope with the hardships in their lives.

Jenny's published novels are *Ride High Pineapple*, *Brockwell the Brave*, and *Land of Britannica*.

The Artists

Chelsea Lomandra is a young emerging artist who won her first prize in an art competition at 5-years old. She has been making art almost every day since.

She works across a wide range of artistic pursuits from painting, drawing and sculpting to curating, exhibiting and teaching.

For the past two years she has been sharing her passion for art with adults and children by running collaborative art classes at festivals across South East Queensland.

This anthology is the second book she has illustrated.

Ken Armstrong, our cover designer and artist, has designed and rendered the previous six covers for the Arts Alliance or WAG anthologies. The foundation president of the Arts Alliance Pine Rivers, he lives in the Pine Rivers district of Moreton Bay Region.

Printed by Libri Plureos GmbH in Hamburg, Germany